SHIPLEY
(SMUGGLERS)

SHIPLEY (SMUGGLERS)

CHARLES ANCHOR

To order additional copies of this book, contact:
Xlibris
1-800-455-039
www.Xlibris.com.au
Orders@Xlibris.com.au
763639

To Christine, who gave me the space to write it, and to the two Zee's who make my heart soar like an eagle.

INTRODUCTION

Storm (noun): A violent disturbance of the atmosphere with strong winds and usually rain, thunder, lightning, or snow; a heavy discharge of missiles or blows; a tumultuous reaction; an uproar or controversy; a vehement outburst of a specified feeling or reaction.

These descriptions, gleaned from the dictionary, describe storms as bad omens. I see the tempest differently: lightning burns the air and creates nitrogen that assists plant growth; water fills dams to feed stock; torrential rains sweep clean like a new broom through gutters and creeks; and swollen rivers dump fertile soil for new places to be farmed.

Whether it's another person's rage or stormy weather or an outburst or an attack, the end of every storm brings a new beginning. For myself, I have come to see the storm for what it is, even welcome it. Every violent disturbance, every tumultuous reaction, every discharge of heavy blows, all the vehement outbursts of specific feelings or reactions lead me to a new plane. The storms in my life have given me a new dimension and shaped me into the person I have become.

Storms are an integral part of nature, but they tend to disturb the peace that most of us strive to find. Amid the turmoil, I must look within to find tranquillity.

Jerry Shipley

PROLOGUE

The shorter man lunged at me, punches flying. I ducked just enough to miss his fist shooting past my cheek. His wild punch missed by the width of a pubic hair. I readied myself for a counter. Energy sucked from the soles of my feet condensed into my response. My copybook strike caught the bottom of a chin, lifting its owner off the ground. The uppercut knocked the stuffing out of the stranger interrupting my day. His friend must have been stupid. He thought it was a lucky punch and he could finish what his unconscious mate didn't. Buzz, wrong!

The first assailant picked himself up and ran at me with a knife, gripping it as a sword. He brought the weapon up at my face from waist height. The twisted expression carved on his face showed the attacker's intention to cause an ugly wound. Visions of a gash from a large hunting knife forced me to get out of the road fast. It was not that difficult; he was slow for a young punk.

Moving forward and a quick step to the side gave me ample time and space. I launched a well-weighted hook, catching him smack dab on his right ear. His head and my fist moving towards each other at speed did the job without much effort.

The blade flew out of the mugger's hand and hit the fence behind us. I stood over the thugs lying stretched out on the ground in front of me. My heart was working overtime, pumping adrenaline through my body. Woken abruptly from my sleepy state, I paused, having no idea of what had just happened.

Less than half hour before the event, I had jumped out of bed and straight into my work clothes, flicked droplets of water on my face, and bolted out of the house. The water didn't have the desired effect, and I stayed in a dreamy trance. Automatic pilot had me dashing for the train, rubbing my eyes and feeling disgruntled over missing breakfast. Hunger was one thing, but I was desperate to get on the train and catch up with lost sleep. If I didn't get at least a short nap, I felt I'd be struggling to get through the rest of the day.

Without warning, two men ambushed me, stepping from a shop doorway to block my path. One threatened my life if I did not go with him into a nearby lane. He looked familiar, maybe a memory from a comic strip. His mate was taller, more solid, and when that guy flashed a knife, I saw no other way. It was a sleepy decision. If I were alert, I would've run. I didn't.

Seconds later, we stepped out of the alley into a car park; the cartoon character shoved me in the back. The force of his push caused me to stumble into a corrugated iron fence. I threw my hands in front of me to block my fall. It worked, so using the barrier, I pushed back, dropped low, and swept a kick across his shins. Legless, he hit the concrete heavily, resonating like a bag of soggy cow dung.

The other man came at me with arms flailing similar to an anemone. Windmill punching made his fighting style frantic and unpredictable as much as it was unsuccessful. My victory spin ended with me jumping on to the prostrate goon. Keeping my knee rammed against his chest and his shirt bunched into my fist immobilised him.

I rendered my voice in a clear, calm, threatening tone. 'Did you bring me here to rob me? Or did someone send you guys to beat me up? Or are you just a couple of mental cases?'

His eyes were glassy, and I recognised the fear in them. They signalled he knew what I was asking and was at the same time trying to plead ignorance. It only took two solid slaps across his face before he buckled.

'It was Garrett. He's pissed off about what you did to him at the river three weeks ago. He told us you go past here to work this time every day, and he gave us fifty bucks to'—he paused to let out a sigh— 'to, you know, rough you up and that.'

'Tell him it worked. You roughed up my day all right. And tell the coward he should fight his own battles.' I left them lying in the car park, and I jogged towards the train station. *God, what an awful way to begin a Monday morning. Life shouldn't be like this.*

I sat despondent in the carriage for fifteen stations to Strathfield. I moped all day, digging a sewerage inspection pit for Rhino's Plumbing and Draining Company. At two thirty, a day of sulking prompted me to make drastic changes in my life.

It wasn't him; it was me. I had a big dose of the cranks. I told the foreman to stick his job where the sun didn't shine. Instead of going home to my shitty digs in a rented room, I hitch-hiked directly to the south coast. Wearing grubby work clothes, I picked up my severance pay from the main office. My journey began from there.

Dirty clothing, a few dollars in the bank, and luck were all I needed to begin another lifestyle. For the next eighteen months of living in Wollongong, I returned to an obsession I left behind years before on the central coast. Surfing.

PART I

THE DING EXPERIENCE

CHAPTER 1

As I remember back, it was around sunup near the end of January. I stood on the beach at a prearranged place, waiting for Johnny to show up with the LSD. Two days earlier, my favourite English rock band landed in the country. The media hype came thick and fast, advertising their show in Sydney.

Excitement around town bordered on palpable. I looked forward to the show, which I thought would be a highlight in my young life. I figured the acid would add gloss and be a bonus to the historical event.

Johnny Rosecroft wandered over to the beach soon after I got there. He brought my order of three tablets called purple haze. The little purple pill stole its name from the title of a popular song. Jimi Hendrix helped market the drug without even knowing.

I wriggled my toes in the sand and watched a man throwing a ball to tire his dog. A hundred yards away, on the low tide mark, another man jogged, trying to tire himself. On a typical summer morning, Johnny and I sat on the sea wall, sharing a reefer. Small, perfectly shaped right-handers ran off the pipe in front of the pump house.

We began reminiscing over surfing sessions we'd had here in times gone by. The swell was building, but the waves refused to grow big enough to ride. A strip of cloud diffused the waking sun between ocean and sky. It coaxed a giant blob of gold to smear its hue across our view. On the horizon, beautiful colour changes appeared. The sun breached the cloud bank, creating concentrations of bright silver light. Its effect made the little waves in front of us sparkle as diamonds. While the cannabis smoke infused into our brains, nature's spectacle heralded another great day.

Several months had already passed since last I'd seen Johnny Rosecroft. I knew he'd been away. He was one of the many from our city to flit off somewhere. Back in what we liked to call the early days, surfers were trailblazers, always searching for new waves. A bunch of hard-core pioneers studied and followed coastal maps, hoping to discover virgin breaks. Nowadays, there are not too many good surfable places left unfound anywhere in the world.

Johnny's new travel tale differed from other passionate watermen. New surf spots were not on his agenda; he took no board and had no intention to use one. A matter of days before, we caught up again; he'd returned from the west coast. He had been there for the past few months, working as a deckhand on a fishing boat.

Listening to his seafaring experiences roused me to want to try it myself.

'I wouldn't mind having a go at crayfishing,' I let out. 'How did you get to hear about it?' My excitement had the better of me, and I kept prying.

When I asked when the next fishing season started, I saw him wince. The look in his eyes suggested I was crazy. Even when he highlighted the unsavoury aspects of the job description, it failed to sway my resolve.

'All right, seeing as you sound keen,' he said, 'go see these blokes.' He passed me two addresses of potential employers. The names and numbers were scrawled on the back of an empty cigarette packet.

Johnny had a lot to say about what he termed the worst job in the universe. But fishing was something I loved to do, and the nasty stuff he described didn't faze me. The incredible amount of money he earned in such a short time had me hooked.

Bringing home a big wad of cash allowed him to buy new toys, starting with a custom-made surfboard and a sound system with an accompanying stack of vinyl. In a conceited voice, he explained that he had plenty left in the kitty to organise a holiday.

'Next Monday, I leave for the Hawaiian Islands for as long as my American visa lasts,' he boasted with a sparkle in his eye.

We talked for ages, but when the swell didn't get to a surfable size, I thanked Johnny for the fishing contacts and left the beach around lunchtime.

The following day, there were four of us standing on the footpath outside the Sydney Showground. I shook crushed purple haze in a bottle of lemon squash and passed it around. Alternate swigs were shared democratically; it was a beautiful thing! Just then, a station wagon pulled up next to us, and three guys got out. One took a ladder off the racks and placed it against the high brick wall surrounding the grounds. The taller man climbed to the top of the wall and cut three strands of barbed wire. He threw the snippers down to a bloke near the car before disappearing over the top of the wall and into the grounds. Three seconds later, two of his mates followed him. We stood gobsmacked until one of the strangers roused us from our stupor.

'Well, are you coming?' He smiled.

I helped Megan up the ladder, followed her over, and James and Sandy came after us. The first half hour or so we spent searching for access to the stage. It would have been easier without negotiating the eccentric mental changes already beginning to occur.

A bunch of fans were settled in a stockyard surrounded by heavy posts and rail fencing. We found a good spot and sat in with them, baking in the summer sun for more than an hour before the crowd murmur grew to crescendo.

'Heere wee gooo!'

I threw the top rail off the yarding, but the second rail got stuck on one side. Forced by the surging crowd, I jumped the remaining rail and got pushed towards the stage. My friends got left inside the corral. Colourful fans emerged from the boundaries and out of the cattle pens. They bounded like gazelles across open ground towards the makeshift stage.

Three white mercs brought our idols to the rear of the platform. It was set up on the oval to face the main grandstand. There were streams of people crossing the grass to get the best front-of-house positions. From the corner of my eye, I saw a cop grab a girl by the hair. He stiff-armed another as she ran *criminally* out of bounds. A rugby player would be sent off the field for that kind of behaviour. The bully wearing the uniform had the law on his side. The girl tried to get closer to the megastars but got clobbered by the cop. Dazed by an arm across her throat, she sucked it up and staggered back to the perimeter.

Right in front of the platform, I discovered the perfect position. Dead centre and six feet behind the barrier, I stopped and looked around for my friends. There were too many people. I couldn't pick out any of them. I was alone amongst 47,000 other jubilant fans.

The band came on stage, *ripping it up*. My teenage fantasies began to evince in front of my eyes. From the opening song to the very end of the show, I was totally transfixed. It was amazing! Carried by youthful exuberance with a dash of chemicals, I found myself amid the throng in a clearing. Everyone near me was dancing just a few steps away, and the performers were smiling down on us.

The live sound of all their familiar songs was outta this world. A mixture of summer heat, LSD, and thousands of writhing bodies took me to another plane. I was whirling my shirt around my head, and people were ducking and weaving to avoid it as they smiled back at me.

In a complete time warp, I forgot how I got home and forgot what happened over the next couple of weeks. But two things kept running through my head. The fantastic rock concert held honours as one of the top three music events of my life. The other thing I simply couldn't shake was a fervent desire to go fishing on the west coast.

The middle of October had already passed. It had been four months since I had taken out a loan to buy my car. A bank's money made possible only because my brother had graciously gone guarantor for me. My new ride was a second-hand Victorian police car, the perfect vehicle to go surfing in. It was a panel van or *sin bin,* as they were affectionately called in those days. It had one-way glass windows on the back and sides for privacy. A wall-to-wall mattress covered the back floor.

During the week, I would sleep in the van at the beach and drive to work from there. If the surf happened to be especially good, I would not go home. Instead I'd return to the beach in the afternoon surf till dark, buy dinner out, and crash in the van. There I would lie, dreaming of another great surf session the next morning.

On weekends, I could be anywhere within 300 miles, seeking uncrowded, perfect barrels. The van enabled me to work full-time and still have the advantage of spending plenty of time in the water. But it was not enough to satisfy my sporting obsession. I was so tired from surfing before and after work; it wasn't fair on my boss or me.

When I offered my resignation, he asked, 'If it's a question of money, I'd be happy to give you a raise.'

I knew he wouldn't understand but told him the truth anyway. 'No, Pete, it's just that I miss surfing. I'm sorry, but I need a change of pace.'

I'd never forget the look he gave me. His head tilted to one side, and he gazed at me as if I were a six-legged frog in a glass bottle. I drove away, feeling quite callow, until I got to the top of the mountain with a view of the coastline.

From that aspect, I could see out over several small islands. At least three of the eight local point breaks were visible. It was a beautiful sunny day in the middle of the working week. In the distance, I could make out lines of waves running around the points in perfect symmetry.

The uncomfortable feelings left me. I pushed Santana into the eight-track player and turned up the volume, driving happily humming along to the mellifluous tones of one of the greatest guitar players ever.

The next item on my agenda was to hitch-hike across the country and go fishing. Before that, I needed to attend to a delicate situation. I asked my brother if I could leave my van on blocks in his driveway under a tarpaulin. He didn't mind the driveway being used. His problem was me skipping out on the loan he had risked his name on. I assured him I was paid up five months in advance and that he should not worry about trivialities. I couldn't say my response made him happy, but being young and optimistic, I didn't really care.

My car was a possession I did not want to sell, but I needed money to fund my trip. I had a decent vinyl collection, record player, and TV, all replaceable. They went for a giveaway price to some acquaintances. As I was arranging my affairs, my friend Dwayne asked why I wanted to go so soon.

'Well, the season starts in mid November, and I have to be there beforehand to make sure I can find a job on a boat.'

'Cool,' he said. 'I'll go with you.'

Those were the days before good, practical luggage was available. Hence, my 'kit' consisted of an ex-army duffel bag, a sleeping bag, and a Globite suitcase full of books. Dwayne was a bit more organised than me. He had a snazzy backpack and an embroidered shoulder bag. He wasn't stupid enough to carry a heap of heavy books across the country.

CHAPTER 2

A couple of mates dropped Dwayne and me just outside Camden, on the Hume Highway. The semitrailers used the highway to form an ant trail back and forth between Sydney and Melbourne. It proved as good a place as any to begin our new adventure. Within a flash, a truckie picked us up. There was no room in the truck cabin for our baggage, so we threw the bags into an empty tallow container, which made them stink for weeks.

Since that first trip from Sydney to Perth, I have hitch hiked, bussed, trekked, and driven every possible route there was across the country, even done a crossing on the now-defunct William Troubridge Car Ferry from Port Lincoln to Adelaide. But that first journey, travelling day and night, took just over three and a half days. We covered 2,500 miles, and I was sure that had to be some kind of record.

The trip averaged almost thirty miles an hour non-stop long before expressways or motorways and definitely long before tollways. There were 300 miles of dirt road, potholed with bull dust holes and strips of sharp and tyre-biting rocks, running all the way from Ceduna to Eucla. There were no bypasses around towns, and we were *hitch-hiking*. We should have been awarded the Golden Thumb Emmy for that effort.

The kind-hearted Henry, a gold miner returning home, picked us up near Kimba. He drove us about 1,380 miles before dropping us at Guildford railway station. That suburb used to be on the outskirts of the city of Perth. My first trip to Perth predated a stamp released years later, declaring that the total population of Western Australia had at long last reached the one million mark. Australia's largest state had an area of 2,529,875 square kilometres. So the scant but beautiful city of Perth looked to us like a big, beautiful, *small* town. We, on the other hand, looked like we had just stepped out of Dr Who's TARDIS.

Australia's cultural fashion was morphing into psychedelia. From the black stovepipe pants and white tees of the 1960s emerged colourful clothing. The state of West Australia hovered in limbo before the Age of Aquarius blossomed like a rainbow around the world. I wore my much-loved brown leather homemade moccasins, badly stitched but colourful. I spent several hours smashing my Levi jeans on rocks at the beach until they looked faded and fashionable.

Nowadays you could buy them already smashed and faded. Go figure! Going a step further, I had carefully sewn brightly coloured rainbows, stars, and mushrooms embroidered motifs on to them. The Indian print shirts alive with complex patterns never left my back.

A girlfriend gave me some rosary beads. I removed the crucifix and used the chain as a necklace. Both my ears were pierced—one with a strip of braided leather, the other with a gold ring. My sunglasses were imported from the States, uniquely shaped, small and round, complete with blue glass lens. Hippies almost always wore beards if they could grow them. Mine looked as if it were carefully manicured, but in truth, I never shaved. Lucky me!

The surf and sun had bleached my hair gold; the colour matched thin sideburns, reaching out and holding a beard around the bottom of my horsey face. And *I* was the more normal-looking of our duo.

Dwayne's ice-blue eyes peered out from under a straight blonde mane reaching halfway down his back. He was shorter than me by half a head and was sturdily built. He wore sunglasses with round silver rims inside silver squares, and the lenses themselves were rose coloured. A bright-beaded vest covered a faded gold paisley shirt that topped buckskin trousers. The pants displayed cosmic runes written in gold felt-tipped pen. He wore a bushy thick light-brown beard like one of Tolkien's dwarves. Puzzle rings were big then, and we both sported exceptionally good-quality ones. I wished I still had mine.

I thought that our weird apparel shocked the west Aussies and they didn't know how to react to us. The local lads stood aloof and looked as if they were about to give us a kicking. I reckoned they must have had culture shock; they just kept their distance and gawked.

The girls, though! Wow! There were two girls to every boy, just like a song said about California. They were eager to talk to us and were so friendly. They treated us extremely well, and it made us feel like rock stars. We got free drinks from barmaids, free groceries from checkout chicks, and free meals from waitresses. We were given a place to crash, cigarettes, and other things, offers from city girls, beach girls, girls in the park, girls on the trains, and girls on the buses. For a short time, it was real nice, but we couldn't dally much more than a week. We were on a mission. If we didn't find a working boat within the next couple of weeks, we would miss the season.

Johnny Rosecroft's furnished addresses and contacts came in handy. We found our way to a starting point at Fishermen's Harbour. Walking over a rail line skirting the north side of the port, we saw men coiling ropes. Some were busy constructing craypots. Other men carried slings, paint cans, bait boxes, and marine equipment. There were fishing boats being converted from prawn trawlers to cray boats to make ready for the new season. They swayed slightly as dinghies motored past. Small trucks dispatched provisions, and men hurried briskly about, dripping with sweat under the hot morning sun.

We stood in front of the marina by a massive tin shed. It opened to the north with large dusty showroom windows. Inside, there was nothing much to show except a small office at the rear of a wide room.

'Jesus! Have a look at this,' I heard someone shout out.

A short dark-eyed man, heavily tanned, with thick, curly black hair appeared. He stepped out from the glass door of the empty showroom, wearing a pair of green-and-white striped shorts, no shoes, and a half-opened, white-collared shirt. A mass of thick chest hair poked out over the top of his buttons.

'What in God's name are you blokes supposed to be? And what the fuck are you doing in my yard? Hey, hey, guys! Come and have a look at what just walked in.' He unashamedly summoned three men who were working around the side of the shed to come and see the sideshow—us!

'Holy Jesus.'

'Mother of God.'

The younger man didn't say a word; he just gawked at us.

'Do you know where I can find the owner of this fine establishment?' I addressed all four of the men, but I was pretty sure I knew who the boss was. He was pretty sure I knew too.

'Why, me.' The little man giggled.

'We came to see you about a job on a fishing boat,' I said, gingerly wishing I'd done a little more preparation before walking smack bang into a job interview.

His eyes scanned us like a microprocessor, glinting over the top of a wide grin, taking in every detail of our hippy fashion, enjoying the visual experience. We were probably the most curious things he'd seen since he left his country of birth, maybe Calabria or Sicily, definitely somewhere European.

I warmed to his personality immediately. He was down to earth although very *in-your-face*. He called things how he saw them no matter the consequences. Something about him told me there and then that he would give us a break. His impolite and uncouth brashness gave me the confidence to speak to him on a similar level. To this day, it remains the oddest and easiest walk-up start I've ever had.

Having said that, we never discussed what our rates of pay would be; there was not a word about the hours of work or the details of a job description. It was a very one-sided interview—all his side, of course!

Dwayne appeared nervous as one of the workers eyed him up and down as if he were looking to carve a young steer. My friend flared his nostrils and tipped his head. He glared at the man suspiciously over the top of his unusual sunglasses. He tightened his lips and clenched his fists.

'Okay, you dickheads, *tornate al lavoro*, and hurry the fuck up.' This was spewed out of the little man's mouth like an exotic folk song: urgent, humorous, and slightly melodic.

The three men immediately returned to their work, disappearing around the side of the big shed. I didn't know if that was the exact wording, but it was the first time I had ever heard the dings' language. In times of political correctness and all its governances, I was unsure whether the word *ding* was derogatory, but it came from the new Australians. They called each other that name, seemed proud of the title, and were comfortable with speaking a language that was neither Aussie nor Italian but a combination of both fused together.

Later I learned that the dings' language was an instrument used for conversation and only particular groups understood it. This *tongue* was not only English and Italian, but a mixture of their local dialects as well. It proved to be a convenient tool to make it impossible for outsiders to horn in on their conversations. Years later, I heard the dings referring to an island in the Houtman Abrolhos chain. It was affectionately named Ding Dong Dell.

Giuseppe possessed the dubious nickname of Cuda. He was given the notorious title after catching a three-foot-long barracuda. In front of a shocked crowd, he began eating it, avoiding its razor-sharp teeth and chewing its head off while it writhed in his hands. Cuda proved good to his word and gave us work, lots of work, heaps of work. Yeah, we had jobs! Scraping the bottom of a sixty-five-foot, twenty-eight-ton wooden-hulled boat called the *Tulip*. I hated that job!

It took nearly a week before we had the marginally more tolerable task of applying antifouling. After that, we painted the entire vessel from the top of the forecastle to the bottom of the keel. Ever since I was a kid, I enjoyed everything about fishing. As a professional, I got to learn new skills, such as coiling ropes and tying intricate knots. Then came splicing ropes and weaving cane pots.

To become familiar with sea terms, there was usually a quirky little story to which was attached a formula that made things easy to learn and impossible to forget. For example, *green*, *right*, and *starboard* all had more letters than *red*, *left*, and *port*. In order to tie a bowline, I had to make a six-shape loop and, then using the end of the rope, chase the rabbit up out of the hole around the tree and back down the hole.

It worked every time, and brought a smile to my face whenever I tied a knot. Some of the mechanical workings on this odd-looking vessel were different than most other cray boats. I learned by experience that the *Tulip* was possibly the worst-set-up crayfishing boat one could ever work on.

As the deadline for the start of the season fast approached, we got busier and busier. There were no defined hours, so we worked day and night till the boat was ready. As far as wages were concerned, I was unfamiliar with the share-catch system. My friend Dwayne had now been retitled *Geronimo*, and my good self bestowed with the illustrious nickname of *Jesus Christ*.

We were offered a one-tenth percentage of whatever we caught for the season. Divided thus, the boat takes 20 per cent, the owner and the skippers share 15 per cent, and the experienced winch man and the engineer get the same as the skipper. It wouldn't take a maths genius to realise that that only left 20 per cent, and you guessed it, that was what Geronimo and I shared because we were in training and untested.

Judging by estimates I'd earlier scanned from my friend Johnny's work diary, I figured 10 per cent was okay. We had a good chance to earn big bucks if we found the right grounds. If not, we could chalk it up to experience. Fortunately for us all, our food and accommodation were taken care of even before we set sail. We had little money while we slaved on the slips, getting the boat prepared, but there were consolations. When I needed to buy anything, I asked Giuseppe. Either he would sling us some cash or take us out to his favourite Italian restaurant.

Cuda loved to show us off as his own little amusement troupe. In entrepreneur style, he'd tell his *compadres* about the hippies he'd found. We became a colourful resource he brought into the fold to work on his boats. I didn't mind too much because he always gave us glowing reports of how quick we learned the job and how we 'worked harder than all the other arseholes down at the marina'.

Our boss proved to be a most remarkable entrepreneur. Not content owning the boatshed, pier, the Tulip and five other fishing vessels. His business tentacles held major shares in an Australian Football League team. Other irons in the fire he kept close to his chest. But people talked. I learned later he had shares in restaurants, news agencies, scallop boats, freezer trucks, and more than a substantial holding in fish-processing factories.

Evidently, Italians had had thousands of years to develop their social skills. So our Ding experience socially was as developed as it could get. Fortunately for Australian people, they brought some of their social graces and fabulous cuisines to our shores. When we dined, we would front up in our work clothes, reeking of blood, sweat, and paint. There was always a hint of fish and saltwater smell about us. But the restaurant people remained courteous. They never blinked an eye at our shabby appearance. Although Cuda amused himself at our expense, we were treated with all respect by the wait staff and served the tasty exotic food paid for by our host.

CHAPTER 3

Not too many days before the season kicked off, a man calling himself the purser showed up. Bringing clipboard paper and biro, he took special orders for food and asked what brand of cigarettes we smoked and what our preferences for wine, beer, or spirits were. At the time, I mostly smoked cigars, and I wasn't fussy about which type. I smoked pot occasionally, but it was hard to find in that state at the time. I wasn't much of a wine drinker but liked a tipple—good Scotch or maybe a few beers. When the caterer's truck pulled up with our stores, I couldn't believe it. I collected my personal order of twenty cartons of port-tipped panatellas. In a separate package, I took charge of three pints of Johnnie Walker Black Label Scotch whisky.

The hatches underneath each of the bunks were chock-a-block with exotic canned food: caviar, anchovies, lychees, and cirio, a zesty tomato concentrate that took the taste of a meal to new heights. The chain locker was draped with an assortment of exotic pressed meats and cheeses, *prosciutto*, salami, mortadella, *capicola*, and polony, most of which I'd never heard of.

Australia's budding European food culture was blooming inside this old wooden fishing tub. The food brought on board that day would make any eastern state's deli look like a sandwich truck. We loaded twenty cases of beer and three ten-gallon jerrycans of red wine into a cool room through the aft hatch. After the liquid refreshments came wooden boxes of bacon, T-bone steaks, lamb roasts, and beef roasts. These items were followed by cartons of bread, butter, and frozen vegetables. Boxes of other culinary delights came after that. The frozen stores hardly made any impact on the space in one of the gigantic freezers, but it was enough for us to survive on for months.

Then the hull scraping and antifouling job lost its first place as the crappiest job ever. It gave way to the pot baiting. With only days to go before we sailed, truckloads of bagged cow hocks and boxed salmon heads arrived. We stacked it all into the freezers alongside the food. The vilest, foulest-smelling things on the planet were our key to attracting quantities of good prey.

On Thursday morning, Geronimo and I sat on the skid board. Our new task entailed pushing wire through the cow legs and the fish eyes. The wire then got fastened strategically into the 185 craypots. Geronimo and I laughed and cracked jokes so we wouldn't cry. We scowled at the two other crew members that had stationed themselves a safe distance away. In the shade of the big shed, they sat in relative comfort, pretending to coil ropes.

The pots on our boat turned out not to be the ones we had learned to weave from cane. The *Tulip* ended up getting some steel-frame pots covered in wire netting. Fastened inside on the bottom of each pot were lumps of iron, which were pieces of railway line actually. The weight acted as ballast to keep the snare upright on the bottom of the sea. To stop saltwater from rusting the frames, zinc blocks had to be fastened to the inside struts.

All in all, a pot weighed in at around eighty pounds, or thirty to thirty-five kilos. That was the dry weight. When bait baskets filled with smelly fish heads and two or three cow hocks were wired inside, they got heavier. Soaked overnight at the bottom of the ocean, the pots were more likely to weigh a hundred pounds or more.

Out of all the 185 pots we had on board, I got to know the 4 that weighed the least. I nicknamed them the 'kids'. The seven pots that I estimated came in at over fifty kilos got titled the 'bullies'. The heaviest and most awkward pot had a larger-than-normal piece of railway line for ballast. It had little bits of wire sticking out; these tended to stick into your arm and draw blood. I nicknamed it Tom. By sheer coincidence, that was also the name of the lazy fat bastard cook cum engineer.

At last, the season began; I remember vividly it was a Thursday. We were supposed to leave port early that morning, but it didn't happen. The skipper, Gerome, (Big Guzzy), had to wait for his mistress to fly down from Broome, and she was late.

Thursday morning was brilliant. It presented us with a calm sea and a gentle westerly breeze simply perfect for us to test our seafaring legs. We couldn't leave. Lana, (Luscious Lana) didn't arrive until late afternoon, so we would have to wait for tomorrow. No, sorry. Not tomorrow! That couldn't happen. It was considered irreligious and very bad luck to sail on a Friday. *Old Ding proverb!* So we waited until Saturday.

Let me say, Thursday and Friday proved to be absolutely beautiful summer days, but Saturday got up angry. The sky was blood red. The sea foamed around the breakwater like a rabid dog. As the *Tulip*'s old Gardner marine engine chugged out of the safe little harbour, it was like sailing into a washing machine on heavy cycle.

I didn't know it then, but I was about to find out that a strong easterly wind had a nasty reputation with fishermen. Strong easterly gusts made life difficult when trying to make your way north, setting pots, or pulling pots. It brought the summer heat off the land at thirty-plus degrees Celsius, pushed against the incoming swells and the natural currents, and screwed the boat every which way. After several hours of getting blasted from the starboard side, when we thought things couldn't get worse, the swell lifted.

Mighty swells, ushered along by the roaring forties all the way from the bottom of Africa's Cape of Good Hope, seemed to me like they were angry after travelling so far. They came at us from the port side, giving the old wooden boat a thorough thrashing. They banged us in a most uncomfortable manner into an opposing offshore forty-knot wind.

The deck area in front of the wheelhouse looked like a spider's nightmare. It was loaded to the top of the gunwales with extra ropes and floats. In case of emergency, a frail ten-foot dinghy lay tightly lashed to the top of the wheelhouse. With one good oar and a broken oar, it was totally inadequate as a lifeboat for our crew. There was no outboard motor anywhere to be found.

The other thing to be considered, a life preserver, was a square orange plastic box. Sticking out like dogs balls, it shared the wheelhouse roof with the dinghy and the radio mast. The life jackets were thrown haphazardly into the head and buried under a ton of spare floats and ropes. The spare gear filled the room from floor to ceiling, making the toilet irrelevant.

Most of the time, we could see land about five or so miles to the east. But as night fell, I was beginning to feel like Sam Gamgee in the land of Mordor—very unsafe! My anxiety about the weather mounted. The sea's murderous attempt to send our overloaded vessel to meet King Neptune was bad enough. On top of all that, I felt decidedly unwell.

On the aft deck, the three-storey-high stacks of pots ran from the stern to the skid board. The piles of pots finished just behind the forecastle. They were stinking to high heaven as the baits reached maturity. The rocking and rolling shook my stomach. Reeking bait bored into my nasal passages, but they were nothing compared to the effect the diesel fumes had on me.

A pipe ran out of the side of the boat just above the waterline, panting out bilge water. The filthy water was whipped up on to the deck by a wicked wind. Next to the bilge pipe, an exhaust puttering out wet smoke and diesel fumes that rose directly into my nostrils.

Going below to the cramped, low-ceilinged eight-berth cabin with four double bunks aside was nauseating. The experience left me feeling like I was wading in puddles of pus. Probably not quite that bad, but that analogy gave a pretty apt description of how I felt at the time. A small hatch opened through the floor to the left of the helm in the wheelhouse. It let you into the galley by means of a ladder. The galley consisted of a double top burner gas stove screwed to a bench six feet long and one and a half feet deep with no sink or tap water, just a cupboard under the bench and a wooden plate rack with cup hooks on the bottom.

The baked enamel cups clanked and rattled out of tune. They chorused with the dull clunk of the plates in their shackled wooden lodgings. It was not a good place to be, but I was nominated to replace the cook. The lazy fat engineer/cook was hanging over the skid board, heaving his guts up. Someone had to step up when the boss got hungry. Personally, I thought Cuda just wanted some entertainment. Geronimo could not even function as a sea slug; he was beyond seasick and heading into comatose. He crammed on to a small deck space in a pool of vomit, moaning like a shot moose.

In order to prepare the meals, my first task involved scampering over the giant stack of craypots. It was a battle to untie some of the traps covering the aft hatch. The boat was pitching and tossing like a rodeo bull against the onslaught of the elements. Sea spray mixed with dirty boat fumes drenched my every move. With considerable effort and world-famous comedic postures that had the appreciative crew in stitches, I retrieved the wooden box of T-bone steaks.

The wheelhouse was crammed like a banker's elevator at lunch hour. Luscious Lana had huge bosoms, which I didn't really mind squeezing past on my way to the galley. She stood about six feet, the same height as her boyfriend. Lana's brother Bruno, a wraith of a lad but a good worker, had somehow scammed his way on to our journey. Thinking about it now, he was probably brought along in case the hippies couldn't cut the mustard.

Giuseppe graced us with his presence, this being the first outing of the *Tulip* since he'd purchased it. With a new crew, he definitely would have wanted to see how we all performed. Michael Happaluto, (Happo), was Cuda's main man and a fine fisherman. He spoke perfect ding and knew everything there was to know about the crayfish industry.

Geronimo and the lazy fat bastard engineer/cook were lying on the outside of the wheelhouse, incapacitated from seasickness. With the steaks under my arm, I clambered over their prostrate bodies and slithered through the packed wheelhouse. A gloomy hatchway led me into the foul depths of the galley. The galley was set in an open area behind the sleeping quarters.

Below deck was a cramped area that ran on all the way up to the chain locker in the prow. A centre post formed an obstruction between the kitchen and the locker. All the blankets on the bunks were moist from salty air. The salamis, mortadellas, pressed donkey meats, and Roman cheeses hung in the chain locker. They added a sickly sweet flavour to the mouldy atmosphere.

I began to cook, and I was pretty pleased with my effort. When I brought up five plates of T-bone steaks with onion gravy, mashed potatoes, and boiled peas, that was it. The lazy fat dumb-shit prick of a cook cum engineer lost his cook title there and then.

'Well, it's not as good as Italian food, but it's a damn sight better than that other shit fatso makes' was the general consensus.

My severely tested anti-seasickness powers had by now failed me completely. I retired to the forward deck to lie down on a pile of ropes and floats. There I gnawed on a steak like a mangy dog until at last I let everything go. The old tub was now punching into head-on swells as we veered west by north-west. Waves broke over the bow, saturating me, washing me and the floats and ropes down into the front of the wheelhouse. I didn't care. I couldn't care if I was dead or washed overboard. I was sick, sick, sick.

It was a long time ago, and I don't remember exactly how long we motored through that awful indoctrination, but when we let out a sea anchor and hunkered down for the night, I had a six-pack set of abs from heaving all day. I was miserable, and I felt absolutely worn to a frazzle. Then after a shitty night below decks, we were roused again into work mode. Sunrise was still a half hour away. I quickly washed my face with seawater and a special soap liquid they called Comprox. Supposedly, the soap lathered in saltwater; it didn't work for me! After lightning-fast ablutions, I ducked back below to make coffee for everybody, making it doubly strong to offset the foul-smelling quarters of the cramped space where four of us lay tossing and turning. With spew-spattered clothing, we slumbered unshowered, farting and wheezing and sweating. For five hours, we endured horrible rocking, banging, and creaking fits of so-called sleep.

Dwayne, for he was no longer Geronimo the Brave, was relegated back to Dwayne the Conquered. Dwayne was sitting on a hatch on the afterdeck, looking green and pasty. He couldn't speak. Everyone else except for the lazy big fat so-called engineer/ex-cook with shit for brains was chatting away like a bunch of budgerigars in a hollow branch.

My cup was steaming, and I sipped slowly and looked at the most beautiful sunrise I had ever seen. We were, I was told, about twenty miles west of the mainland in about thirty fathoms. Cuda and Big Guzzy were in deep discussion about a ridge traced out on the old Furuno echo sounder.

We dropped a header float with a flag attached then laid a perfect line of pots running north to south along the inside of the ridge. Next we steamed back past the start of that line and lay another set of pots. This line inched over to where a three-fathom hump lay across the sea bottom on a slightly different angle.

After we set those pots, the *Tulip* was left with a third of its traps as we steamed off. The back deck, half stocked now, had a cleared space the size of a two-car garage. To get some relief from the stench of our precious baits, I washed the crud away with a deck hose. Dwayne and the lazy fat prick ex-cook cum engineer played no part in setting the lines. They lay on the deck like crucified figures in the open air, mouths agape like drowning fish in the sunshine.

This time we cruised for almost an hour and a half until we found some interesting ground. Finally, the last of our traps were laid in a similar order to the southern lines. Even as we set the pots, the seasickness had already invaded every vital organ in my body. The crappy feeling penetrated to the very core of my being. It was tough work even without feeling nauseous, and I had witnessed tougher men than I crumple and quit. But there was something else going on in my mind. In a weird way, I was absolutely enjoying the experience.

The sun came up quickly and painted silver ripples around us on the surface of a calmer ocean. In my motion sickness death throes the previous day, I had seen flying fish gliding over an inhospitable sea. I swear they had smiles on their faces. I loved the ocean; I had surfed in it most of my life. The smooth green swells sliding past our boat gave me a new perspective as to where these beautiful surfable things came from and how far they travelled just to give us that wonderful exhilarating ride.

My deep affection for boats went back to childhood. On an excursion, I was taken for a ride out of Bobbin Head. Steaming up Cowan Creek, I got to steer a Halverson luxury cruiser. The captain stood beside me, wearing a cap with a gold braided rim. His spotless stark-white uniform was adorned with shiny brass buttons.

Harking back into the past was a cathartic experience. As I stood staring out from the deck of the stinking fishing boat, I felt nauseous from the fumes and the rank bait. The now and the past were a parallel universe, but the saltwater underneath me was as familiar as an old overcoat.

The boat rolled gently. The open space around was filled with deep blue water reflecting it off the white sky. My vision transcended the stench of the filthy boat and fused into me a deep affinity to the ocean.

This could easily be the rest of my life, I thought.

CHAPTER 4

The full moon in late February had seen our Western Australian rock lobster catches hit rock bottom. The skipper pulled the pin, and we steamed back to Freo and called it a day. After my first fishing experience, I pocketed an obscene amount of cash and fled back east. Leaving the seasickness and bait boxes, I headed straight for the airport and jumped on the first plane out, impatient to pick up my van and surfboard, longing to immerse myself in the womb of Mother Nature again.

The first thing I took care of was to pay off my car loan. My brother didn't believe it possible to earn as much as I did in such a short time. He did everything but straight out accuse me of robbing a bank or selling drugs. I learned a long time ago not to argue with his fucked-up sense of reason. Leaving his house, I felt relieved to no longer be indebted to him.

November to April was the best time of year to get quality waves in southern Queensland. In the past, work commitments made it difficult to fully take advantage of the cyclone season. There had been times, however, when the weather bureau reported a significant low-pressure system up north. I would spin my boss some fantastic story and take a week off. The speedometer racked up a thousand-plus miles for me to get amongst some cyclone surf. This year, however, things were different.

With a healthy bank account, a brand-new board, and no debts, I took my time, free to surf my way up the New South Wales coast. It was the middle of March, and I was enjoying a week of Byron Bay's best surf breaks. Warnings of a massive cyclone speeding south 300 miles north-east above Rockhamton were all over the news. Threats to towns and shipping blared from the car radio. The news steered me, full of hope, directly to the town of Noosa Heads. The town's secrets hadn't been let out yet. It was a pretty little village with a few shops and small bunches of houses nestled around the mouth of the Noosa River.

For two nights, I slept in my van, parked near the gateway to Noosa National Park. The storm swells had not yet arrived. Every day I got to surf perfect four to five foot waves breaking right outside my back door. On day 3, I hooked up with a couple of fellow wave nuts who rented a flat on Hastings Street. They let me use their kitchen and bathroom and crash on the lounge room floor. Rent was paid by shuttling them in the van to surf spots anywhere between Alexandra Headland and Double Island Point.

When the expected cyclone eventually crossed the coast north of Rocky, it formed into a rain depression. There was no devastating wind, but it dumped rivers from the sky, drowning houses and ruining food crops. The swell rose, but except for two 'big' days, the waves didn't reach the size I had hoped for. No complaints though. I was surfing myself stupid, albeit on smaller waves.

On a particularly big day, the peak of the storm sent waves into Tea Tree Bay at twelve to fifteen feet. The bigger waves closed out the whole bay, making it difficult to get out to the line-up. I first met Marin when we jumped off the black rock together. We paddled like hell to get to the back of the incoming monsters. The two of us were the only ones in the water at the time. We sat close, discussing where the best take-off spot would be.

The first wave of the next set loomed out of the deep, and the guy took off on his kneeboard. It was massive, and the brave heart paddled into it deep on the inside. From the back of the wave, I saw a flash of the underside of his board as he executed a re-entry.

My turn. I paddled into my monster of choice from the same take-off point. I dropped to the bottom, preparing to crank a turn and line up for the tube, but something caught my eye; it was too important to finish my ride. I speared the nose of my board through the fluttering crest and flicked off over the back of the wave.

The man in front was floating face down near the black rocks. The surge was carrying him fast to destruction. Paddling as fast as I could, I reached out and grabbed him before the next breaker hit us. He lay prostrate across the front of my board as the white water seized us like the devil's hand and smashed us into the shore. We were cut to bits by the rocks, and the man in my grip was lifeless. Holding tight to the limp body, I sacrificed my board and dragged him to the sand.

For half an hour, I did everything I'd ever been shown to revive him. I turned him on his side and watched a gallon of sand-laden saltwater spew out of his mouth. There was no detectable pulse, and he was not breathing. I rolled him on his back to begin my badly learned version of resuscitation. The cardiopulmonary compressions weren't getting a response.

Time to try the mouth-to-mouth business. As my own air breathed into him, I heard a loud crack from inside his chest, followed by a stream of air hissing out of his lungs, and he started gasping. He lifted his head, coughed, and spluttered until his eyes glimmered without recognition that his life had been returned. We sat together, bleeding from a hundred small cuts. His head was turned down between his knees while he continued to hawk and spit. I placed one hand on his shoulder in a feeble attempt at comfort.

Three days after the near drowning, I got pretty sick. It might have been that I wasn't eating healthy food or maybe surfing in dirty floodwaters. For five days, I lay, barely able to move, in the back of my van, which was parked outside the Hasting Street flat. The man whose life I'd saved I now knew as Marin. Onlookers must have told him of my heroic deed. As my new best friend, he basically looked after me the entire time I was laid up. He brought food, water, Aspros, and butter menthols for me. Even while I slept, he'd sit in the front seat of the van, keeping up a one-way chat while I yo-yoed in and out of fever.

People called Marin 'Doc', and I presumed that was due to the fact that he always carried drugs. He lived in a tent in The Woods camping area at the end of Hastings Street. When he wasn't surfing, he hung around the flat because there was usually someone to smoke ganja with. He had an endless supply of top-quality pot.

After I shook off the bug, he became part of our surfing crew. Since his kneeboard got smashed to pieces, he would swim out in the break and bodysurf with a pair of navy-issue flippers. It didn't matter how big the waves were; he would take off deep inside with a heart as big as a house.

No one knew much about him except that he was sometimes seen with a couple of American guys. They didn't surf, just blew into town and out again. We all assumed they were his dealers because he never introduced them to anyone. Then one day, he and I went picking magic mushrooms. Man, we got so many gold tops. When we cooked them up and handed them around, it seemed like everyone in Noosa Heads got a brain full.

Everywhere we went over the next three days, we would run into people who were off their faces on gold top mushroom trips. Amid the magic festival atmosphere, three of us found ourselves on top of Noosa Hill after a psychedelic walk through the forest.

Jenifer and I lent ourselves to a psychotherapy session for our friend. Under the drug's influence, Marin was acting very unstable. We sat on a grassy patch in a huddle, talking softly till two in the morning, while Doc unloaded details of the nightmare of his active service in Vietnam.

He told us that as a navy pilot, he was sent smack dab into the centre of 'Horror Ville', ordered to ferry troops and ammunition over jungles in a flimsy helicopter. He flew through deadly skies laden with thick fog and hailstorms of bullets. His countless dangerous missions involved a variety of tasks, ranging from dropping leaflets and spraying herbicide to gruesome taxi services picking up dead bodies and wounded soldiers.

He was a mental case before he took any psychedelic drugs, and I completely understood why. I empathised with him during our powwow, and I watched his earlier tension fade away. During the huddled hours, he changed. The insanity morphed into a calmer trip for Marin as he unloaded his incubus into the night air. Seeing his new mood, I felt assured that he would feel even better if I left him and the girl alone on the hill.

As I fumbled and groped down the track in darkness, I recalled hearing that Jenifer was a psyche nurse. Jenifer was one of the many girls who hung around the boy's flat, but I didn't know her well. Being together in deep conversation for ten hours straight, it was obvious that she liked Marin. My distinct impression was that after I left them, the therapy would have a happy ending.

The night sky remained a tar pot all the way to the edge of the ocean. Finally, I made out the dark silver disc of the bay. The expanse of water appeared magically lit by a mysterious source in the night sky. Small nocturnal creatures rustled in the underbrush around me as I sat on the rock overlooking the jump-off point at Tea Tree bay until the sun came up.

CHAPTER 5

Capitalism doesn't really do it for me. There's never been a period in my life where I wanted to be rollicky rolling rich. It goes without saying that it's great to have money. Money is the great enabler. It is helpful to get you to places to do stuff and buy stuff. So I'm not about to tell you that I would knock back a million bucks whether a gift or a well-paid job except, of course, if the work or the gift had dubious strings attached.

In fishing, it seemed I had found my niche. I loved the sea and the adventure and the physical work to keep me fit, strong, and healthy. After I got used to the seasickness, I settled into a new working life, which gave me enough money for the freedom to live the life I loved so much. It afforded me the opportunity to go surfing all over the world for at least five months of the year.

I once believed that almost everyone in the world was basically a good person in some way. A person could be sad or happy, rich or poor, sick or hale, criminal or saint, but the intrinsic nature of mankind was generally good. That being said, I once found an exception. After seasonally trekking back and forth to Western Australia from the eastern states, I had the pattern down pat.

I arrived early November and did the walk of shame. This meant scouring the fishing harbours to find an employer with a boat wanting a deckhand. For me though, it wasn't actually a walk of shame. I would simply walk into Giuseppe's marina and ask if he knew where I could get on a working boat.

I worked the *Tulip* for two seasons out of Fremantle, followed by a season on *Cray Angel* from the southern end of the Abrolhos Islands.

The island season started in March each year. It extended for as long the catches remained profitable or until the stocks of crays crawled over the continental shelf, where it was too deep to hunt.

This year, when I walked into the yard, the first boat I saw was the *Tulip* over by the pier. The old girl sat tied to the jetty along with several other boats. My hope was that there would be a different boat waiting for me to make enough money to go surfing for the entire off season.

'Holy shit! It's you, Jesus! You've come back for more. Come in, my friend! Come in!'

The little man smiled a lot, but he even smiled when he was tearing strips off some poor bugger who'd rubbed him the wrong way. Today, though, he seemed genuinely happy to see me. He took me on a little tour of his place.

The showroom now had merchandise for sale. We walked between an assortment of fishing implements and marine paraphernalia necessary for the boating industry. Dinghies, life rafts, life jackets, pots, ropes, and anchors were all strewn haphazardly over the floor. The scene still didn't convey to me the idea of a showroom. In fact, it made it look more like a storeroom with ticket prices on some of the items.

Around the back of the ersatz showroom, there was a steel-hulled, decommissioned research vessel. All 140 feet of her was tied to the jetty next to the old faithful shit box and two of Cuda's other fishing boats. The *Aliante Oceano* was the flagship of his fleet, skippered by his brother. The other beautiful craft, *The Atlantic Wyf,* was charged to Cuda's brother-in-law.

Giuseppe was in an extremely good mood and shared a few humorous stories with me. My suspicions grew, and I began to wonder what I was getting myself in for. On his invitation, we strolled back on into his office. Cuda sat in his big megalomaniac-styled office chair and beamed across at me. He picked up the phone.

'Geldo! Listen, don't worry about getting that winch man from Sydney.' He covered the mouthpiece with his left hand and, from the side of his mouth, asked, 'Can you winch?'

'Never tried it,' I admitted.

'I've got the best winch man in Western Oz standing in front of me! Now come and get your fucking boat off of my fucking wharf, or I'll double your fucking rates,' he blurted into the phone, still smiling while vitriol dripped off every syllable. A garbled reply came out of the phone. Too late. Within a flash, the handset got slammed back on to the receiver.

'Well, Jesus,' he said, 'you're leaving at eight o'clock tonight, you lucky son of a bitch.' He laughed a big hearty laugh, like he'd just won the lottery.

'Thanks,' I uttered, trying to sound appreciative but not quite pulling it off. 'Then I better get going and take care of some stuff. Before I go, though, if you've got a sec, I'd like to talk to you about a bit of a venture.'

After he smashed the phone down, he laid his five-foot frame back in his chair. When he whipped his feet up on to the desk, his heels hardly reached across the short space. He clasped his hands together behind his head, looking for all the world like a man who had just inherited a kingdom.

'Uuuuh . . . Let me start by saying what a wonderful seafaring boat you have out there,' I proffered.

'You in the market?' he jested.

'Well, it's . . . er . . . well, you see, I have a contact in Durban, South Africa, with a product that could be quite profitable,' I said, getting straight to the point as I imagined he would like.

'What sort of product, and how profitable?' His eyes took on a greedy look akin to a Hollywood villain.

'Well, let's just say very profitable, but not entirely legal.' Now I was quite sure I shouldn't have brought it up.

'Sometimes, in business, it's not the legalities—it's the challenge.' His eyes reflected devilish wisdom as a satanic smirk crossed his lips.

I felt like I was in a conference with Lucifer the Greedy. A glint in his eyes flashed across at me. Bearing a leering, lustful look, his feet fell from the desk, and he brought his contorted face closer to mine.

'You already know we hippies smoke a bit of pot. Well, er, the best pot in the world comes from Durban in South Africa. It's called Durban poison. Good-quality ganja fetches between $200 and $300 a pound on the street here. In Africa, my contact can get tons of it for less than five bucks a pound.

'I was thinking of a sailing boat or even a fishing boat, but it would have to be a big one with converted fuel tanks or drums to go the distance. That big sucker you've got on your jetty could do it easily, and the boys over there will bring the gear out into international waters without any drama, all good and safe like.'

He didn't mention any figures to me, but I saw the wheels in his head calculating to the nth degree how many pounds his steel boat could hold, how much the fuel cost, and how much the profit would be. He was having a reverse ecclesiastical conniption, almost in rapture. It was like watching a Disney cartoon character go from Mr Walker to Mr Wheeler or from Mr Jekyll into Mr Hyde.

What the hell have I unleashed just to get a smoke and a bit of cash? I began to have second and third thoughts.

'Listen!' I said. 'I've gotta run. I'll be back around seven thirty tonight.'

After this little chat, my head was spinning on reflection of my time spent working for this company. Some things started falling into place until a picture formed in my mind. The revelation of another side of Mr Hyde became clear. Up to this time, I had only met Dr Jekyll. A twinge of trepidation ran through me, a twinge that was soon to be amplified.

CHAPTER 6

That year, on my trip to West Australia, I decided to bring my car, which made things much more comfortable. Three friends accompanied me, and we all chipped in for fuel—another bonus.

Getting a walk-up start on the same day we blew into Perth was a good and a bad thing for me. I had a new job but little time to organise my travel companions and possessions. What to do with my car was paramount. The surfboard, guitar, and incidentals would be left in trust to my buddies.

Four of us drove up to visit some people we knew in Scarborough. They had a visitor, Marin, the bloke I had met some months before in Noosa, who was staying with them. He was a returned Vietnam vet with lots of hard-earned psycho-baggage. He smoked us up big time, so by the time we got back to the *Tulip*, it felt like I was walking in three feet of snow. My vision was warped, as if I was looking through two-inch lead pipes. On top of that, it felt like I was speaking left-handed.

I drove back to the marina and parked in the yard by the side of the showroom and addressed the group in my van.

'I'm going to the office to say goodbye to Cuda. I'll meet you around back at the jetty.'

It was getting dusky outside as I pushed through the glass entry to the showroom. I made my way across the floor towards a slit of light emanating from the office door. It was coyly ajar. I walked in and got a surprise at seeing a group of well-dressed, brown-skinned men huddled around Giuseppe's desk. They were speaking in whispers. Giuseppe looked up, startled like a deer in headlights.

33

'Geronimo,' he mistakenly called me. 'My friend! What can I do for you?' His words were staccato.

I had never heard him speak in this tone before, and I stopped dead in my tracks. The huddle shuffled themselves down into anonymity, pulling up their lapels, dropping their faces into their expensive suits, and turning away.

'So sorry, Mr Coradabello. Didn't know you were busy. I just came by to say thanks for getting me the job and goodbye. Ciao. See you in a few months.' I had to this point never called him by his surname, but it fell out of my mouth as naturally as if I had used it for years.

'Sure, sure, my friend. See you in a few months. Okay.' He seemed to gather himself out of surprise as he spoke. '*Chiuse la* fuckin' *porta* on your way out, will you? And tell that prick Geldo not to bother me. Just get his fucking boat off my fucking wharf. *A dopo*!'

As it turned out, back at the jetty, Geldo was nowhere to be found. It seemed that the mysterious new owner of the *Tulip* hadn't bothered to attend the first voyage of his new money-making venture. Instead, a Czech skipper, Larko, told us he would be in charge of the vessel.

I handed Taffy my car keys and arranged to meet my three travelling companions sometime early in the new year. Before going aboard the *Tulip*, I grabbed my kit bag and suitcase full of books out of my van. Being stoned and a little anxious about leaving my three favourite things with a bunch of mates, I totally forgot my wallet. It was wrapped in a towel under the front seat of my car.

The veteran Marin moved forward and gave me a Californian man hug. Then as he shook my hand, he laid two orange barrels of LSD into my palm. 'See you, brother,' he said sentimentally.

'Peace, bro,' hailed Taffy, waving my car keys at me.

'Kill the pig, mate!' cried Gazza as he came towards me to copy the soldier's hug.

In those days, if a boat happened to get exceptionally large catches, most boat owners would roast a pig on the spit and tap a keg or buy a few cases of beer for celebration, hence the expression.

So we chugged out of the small fishing harbour again, and it was not on a Saturday, but the weather was fantastic. The sun had dropped its red swords below the ocean, and the first stars were beginning to glow brighter in a crystal navy firmament. Larko was on the wheel, and Mighty Mouse strutted around the deck in a T-shirt and shorts with his chest out and arms stiffened in the hope that it would make his muscles look bigger. It didn't!

Then there was Rocardo, a Portuguese gnome with short-man syndrome, one of the worst cases I'd ever witnessed. Besides these blokes and myself, there was a kid, maybe sixteen or seventeen, who was recently paroled from juvenile detention to the boat owner's auspice. He was dumb as dog shit, lanky, with home-cropped hair and skinny arms sporting badly drawn gaol tattoos. He was cursed with the most irritating voice known to man. His tone fluted through his nostrils, making it sound like fingernails scraping down a chalkboard. Every comment he ever muttered always, always carried complaint or criticism. Everything and anything came out with a whingeing, iron-scraping timbre to his voice.

On that voyage, I found the Czech skipper to bear the closest resemblance above the level of knuckle-dragger to anyone belonging to the human race. Larko was a decent fellow with a lot of boating experience and many riveting tales to tell. He knew quite a bit about all sorts of boats, from canoes to cruise ships. Although he had some experience with wet lining and trawling, he admitted to me that he had never before worked a cray boat.

The owner—the mystery man, it seemed—had lost his crayfishing licence for a few years for nefarious undertakings, alleged crimes involving what I would have considered to be hanging offences. With the *Tulip*, he was getting back into the game, making his re-entry to the lucrative fishing industry. No pots had yet been pulled, but there was anticipation amongst all those who should know that this season was set to produce some bumper yields.

The *Tulip* was ready and raring to go fishing. All the gear had been prepared before Geldo, often called the Rook, signed the sale papers. However, there were nasty stories about the Rook all over the fisherman's grapevine, information our crew had no idea about at the time we signed on. He was a big-time criminal.

At one time or another, he had attracted allegations of piracy, major fraud, attempted murder, kidnap, and rape. All were serious hanging offences, but somehow he was able to squirm out from under them. His expensive lawyers struck bargains and arranged conditions so that most charges went away. In other cases, witnesses mysteriously declined to testify, resulting in those charges being waived by the courts.

The most serious offence for which he was actually convicted was for arson. Some said he did time in the big house, but the jury was still out on how much Geldo actually paid to get off. What he hadn't expected, however, was that the West State Fisheries Department would step in after his court case. They took his licence off him for no less than three years.

The penalty cost Geldo hundreds of thousands, possibly millions in lost income. The WSFD acted because the Rook had burnt down a fellow fisherman's fishing boat, taking 120 licenced pots out of the state's crayfish quota. So it was no fluke that the crew had been pulled together from a bunch of out-of-towners.

Anyway, there we were—the new crew of the *Tulip*. A Czech novice was the skipper. The stacker was an angry, often-violent Napoleon Bonaparte lookalike. Skinning the pots was an egotistical halfwit and pathological liar from Port Moresby. A low-intelligence, baby-minded criminal held the position as a needless extra. And moi, the naive hippy who thought all people were good-hearted, was the winch man.

The Rook lived on a lonely stretch of rugged beach in a desert with its edge touching the Indian Ocean. Next to his place, separated by a derelict forty-foot fishing boat on a jinker, stood his brother's house.

Gossip had it that daily, between them, the brothers schemed and plotted how they would carry out their next set of evil plans (I say this pretty much tongue-in-cheek, as I never personally met the brother). Brother Lannis worked the *Black Queen,* moored inside a reef a mile north of the *Tulip*. Through binoculars, I thought he looked bigger than Geldo, maybe a bit older too. The Kraggasti brother's infamy was mostly based on scuttlebutt and the Rook's bragging. It rang true when I witnessed the nasty acts he committed over the time I worked on his boat—acts including the severe beating he gave his skinny ward in front of the shocked crew.

We found a small rocky islet two miles south-west of Geldo's shack. Protected from the southerly wind, we dropped anchor in about thirty feet of clear water over a sand bottom. This spot was to be our home for the next two or three months. Minutes after arriving, I was already thinking of excuses to leave this very *unfine* company.

Two weeks after we began working from this anchorage, the owner came on board. The Rook took over from the temporary skipper. Larko's last day was spent directing the boat owner to our fishing grounds. Back at anchor, Rocardo quit for some mysterious reason and joined Larko when he went back to shore with Geldo in the dinghy. That was the last I ever saw of either of them.

Our daily regime then started around 3 a.m., when Geldo's aluminium fourteen-footer would motor out from his desert shack and thud into the hull of the *Tulip*. Each morning, he would bring his own food for the day, along with a grumpy greeting. Then he'd begin ordering us around like we were scurvy dogs on his pirate ship. We would weigh anchor and chug out to the lines. Work finished when all the pots were pulled and the catch processed and stacked in the freezer.

From mid November, the *white season* began; crayfish migrated into shallow water to spawn and shed their outer carapace, showing off a brand-new whitish shell. Having done as nature ordered, they then started their return journey out into deeper water, and the fishing boats gave chase, until the water went beyond eighty fathoms, which was about fifty miles from our little rocky islet.

Early in the season, our working days finished quicker because the pot ropes were much shorter and we didn't have to travel so far. Working hours were extended by the time we got close to the continental shelf. Our coils of rope, roughly measuring 175 fathoms, stood 2 feet high off the deck.

In the deeper water, a lot of fishermen joined two pots separated by two-fathom bridles. This method saved time and obviously used a lot less rope. The downside was, it was more difficult to get a good bottom placement. It would also take a lot more skill to wrangle the cumbersome towers of rope without knitting them into a bunch of macramé.

Experience and skill in resetting the traps was essential in raising the number of crayfish a boat will catch. But we were also granted an enormous amount of luck that season. Every day, we were pulling up massive hauls of crayfish. The work was extremely physical, winching up miles of rope and skinning and baiting the pots. Then with hundreds of crays to process, we were often still working at midnight.

Geldo never anchored out overnight, which meant hours of cruising back and forth to the fishing grounds. Sometimes we took turns on the wheel to get a break from processing hundreds of crayfish. I didn't blame Geldo for not wanting to sleep below decks, but the long-haul driving took its toll. The atmosphere was tense with perturbation amongst the crew. Everyone was cranky from too much work and not enough sleep. Every day was the same; after a short but deep sleep, we'd be up again at 3 a.m. to do it all again.

For some reason, I kept tallies of the number of processed boxes going into the freezer. I developed a nerdy habit of recording the day's catch inside the back cover of one of my books. Back then, I scrawled some details with a tired hand inside a copy of Dalton Trumbo's *Johnny Got His Gun*. It was for a twelve-day period with a catch totalling nearly 75,000 pounds of crayfish.

At $1.10 per pound, my share for the cash price should have been $12,500. But we were working a freezer boat and processing our catch directly for export. The export price at the time was around $3.40 per pound and usually collected a month or so after the season finished. At the bottom of the page was scrawled 'Thank you and goodnight!' Apparently, I must have been happy about those tallies. Little did I know though, the following couple of weeks were set to be even more lucrative.

For a fortnight, we were killing the pig, pulling up between fifty and ninety 110-pound bags every day. Our record was 98 bags in a single day. It was a period of sleep-deprived torture to earn almost $1,800 in a 15-hour shift. Though I said I was not *that* into money, but I enjoyed doing the maths on that day. As tired as I was, my dreams were jam-packed with surfing all over the world with a brand-new quiver of surfboards, and enough money to support me for the rest of next year.

Then several days before Christmas, the swell got huge. Very few boats were able to leave from the neighbouring ports and anchorages. Their setlines of pots lay unprotected in the rough seas. Our boat didn't have any trouble getting to the gear because we were already anchored offshore with deep water all around us.

Normally, cray boats were set up for the winch man to throw a grappling hook over the floats to wrestle them on board. He'd then run the rope through the tipper, over the skid board and around the winch. On the *Tulip,* however, with an extra man-kid, I had to wait until the scrawny pup handed me the rope. The only thing I had to grapple with was his annoying voice and constant complaining.

An important fact about seeing the floats come on board was getting to know which line of pots you were pulling. It provided an inkling of which set caught the most crays, which was essential information even for a winch man, especially me, the kid who hoped to become a skipper one day and maybe even have my own boat. Because I didn't always get to check the floats, I never really knew what gear was coming up. But I did recognise a lot of our ropes—the lengths they were joined, the different colours, and the types of knots.

On today's outing, we were working in about twenty fathoms. This meant the rope to each trap had to be at least twice that length to compensate for the tide's tendency to pull them under the surface. So with an average of 40-plus fathoms of rope times 185 pots, it was exhausting work.

I was fit and strong and could winch pots till the cows came home. Funny thing was, I was beginning to feel that the cows were already in bed! Although I was busy spinning ropes through my hands for hours on end, it occurred to me that some of the ropes looked unfamiliar. When I finally realised that a rope *definitely* wasn't ours, I pulled the foreign pot away from the skinner's hands, checked the floats, and yelled to the skipper.

'Hey, stop! Geldo, these aren't our pots.'

I couldn't be sure how many other fishermen's pots we'd pulled that day, but I was definite about this one. Geldo's response knocked me for six. He pulled back the throttle and the *Tulip* ploughed to a halt. He stormed out of the wheelhouse with an angry look on his face, and for a moment, I thought he was going to attack me.

I braced myself when he drilled an evil glint into my eyes before brushing me aside. Then he grabbed the pot rope, hauled the floats towards him, tied them in knots, and threw them overboard. The trap followed the knotted floats and ropes and sank without a trace. I was horrified at his callous disregard for his fellow fishermen.

'That's it, Geldo. I quit!' I screamed at him, and I would think he wasn't used to being screamed at.

He turned his large frame to face me; the menace in his eyes was alarming. He took a step towards me, fists clenched. I stiffened into a pose, ready to defend his blows, but he paused, grunted, and stormed back into the wheelhouse. The angry boat owner took us back to our moorings without another word, jumped in his dinghy, and disappeared to his home in the desert.

The Rook didn't come back the next day or the day after that. Mighty Mouse, Skinny, and I assumed he was out recruiting another winch man. Left at anchor two miles from shore, the crew had been at the ready for work each morning, but there was no skipper to take us out. When the owner didn't show, I caught up on some reading of my prized collection of books.

One sunny morning, when Mighty Mouse saw me, book in hand, reclining on a pile of ropes. He sidled up and looked over my shoulder.

'What'cha reading, Jesus?' he asked, skewing his head to look at the open pages in my lap.

'Frank Yerby's *Judas, My Brother*. It's unreal. Yerby does great research. It's set in the time of—' came my excited reply, but he broke me off.

'What else have you got to read in that suitcase of yours?'

Great, I thought. *Here's my chance to introduce him to some of the wonderful authors, philosophers, and hippy gurus I'm into at this time.*

We went below to my bunk, where I opened the case as if it were full of gold. I watched proudly as he flipped through the titles from some of the magical writers. Timothy Leary's *Politics of Ecstasy*, Carlos Castaneda's *Teachings of Don Juan*, Aldous Huxley, Khalil Gibran, John Steinbeck, Voltaire, and Tuesday Lobsang Rampa—all the really good stuff. There was even a copy of Padmasambhava's *Tibetan Book of the Dead*, which to this day I never did finish.

'What the fuck is this shit? Haven't you got any Westerns or *Playboy*s or porn or even some fucking comics?'

Now I knew for sure he was not a normal red-blooded Aussie.

CHAPTER 7

Mighty Mouse turned his back to me with a look of absolute disgust written all over his dial. But I wasn't one to give up that easily on the opportunity to offer enlightenment to a fellow human being. If only he could see that the mind was a bigger entity than he had ever imagined.

'Did you know that the Greek word for *person* is *persona* and that *persona* translates as "a gathering of consciousness"?'

'What are you talking about?' Now the disgust dripped off his tongue.

'You can't see unless you look.'

'See fucking what?' he accosted.

'See your own mind,' I offered gently. Man, I was a fucking prophet.

My book-learned mantras were taking effect. Well, at least he hadn't walked off yet. Did it trigger a curiosity for deeper understanding of life and the search for awareness of self? Probably not! He was born cognizant but threw the proverbial baby out with the bathwater.

I believed I was Johnny-on-the-spot to switch his light back on, but naivety was the sister of ignorance and a cousin of arrogance belonging to the family of youth, and I was a youth guided by the relations who brought along a touch of impatience. It was going to be too much work. Maybe I'd get back to a deeper discussion later. For now, it was time to enjoy the day.

I climbed on to the top of the wheelhouse. 'I'm going ashore. Do you want to come?'

'Not in that thing' came his caustic reply as he pointed to the roof where the little tin tender was tied.

'Well then, if you're not interested in coming ashore, can you at least give me a hand to get it down off the roof and into the water?'

Earlier that day, I packed sandwiches and filled a large plastic bottle with lemon cordial. I didn't leave then because the sea was a bit rough. But by lunchtime, the swell had evened out, and the wind blew light from the north-east. Two sets of hands made it easy to launch the dinghy. I jumped down on to the seat and took up the odd pair of oars, ready for Mighty Mouse to cast me off. It surprised me when the skinner climbed over the bulwark and leapt on to the seat at the stern.

'Oookay, so you decided to come after all,' I stated with a degree of apprehension.

Not expecting him to tag along, I had already dropped one of the tabs of acid Marin gave me. The beautiful sunny day, I was sure, would be a fantastic time to explore the shore under a psychedelic magnifying eye. Rowing with odd-length oars was a difficult enough task, but trying to get my new offsider to sit still was a downright handicap. It didn't take him long to spot the food box, and in minutes, he decided he was thirsty.

'Is that lemon squash? Give us a drink, will yah? What's in the bag? Is that something to eat?' He stood up, trying to get past me as I rowed.

'Wait till we get to shore, mate. Please sit down. You are rocking the boat. It's hard enough to make headway with these shitty oars, and you're not helping.'

Without trying to sound bossy, I thought it was a reasonable request given that whenever he tried to move about, the tinny took water over the stern and we were still a mile from shore.

'Who died and made you the fucking captain, mate? I just wanted a fucking drink, and you're turning it into a fucking mutiny.'

It impressed me that he even knew the word *mutiny*, even if he didn't get the context right. With the lysergic acid diethylamide beginning to operate my cortex, it would be almost impossible for him to upset me, and I began to look at him in a different light. He was young like me, fresh-faced, and the health of his youth filled his aura with greens and pale blues. When he looked at me, I couldn't see the indifference in his stare anymore.

In my bent consciousness, I believed he actually liked me, even looked up to me. Maybe it was remiss of me, but I asked him if he wanted to take a trip. It took a power of explaining, but once he understood the type of trip I meant, he jumped at the chance with both hands.

Shipping the oars back through the rowlocks, I unfolded a plastic envelope and showed him the tiny orange barrel.

'A quarter of a tab should give you a good taste for your first acid trip,' I explained as I began to cut it with my fingernail.

'How much did you take?' he countered.

I faltered. 'Well, I've had these before.'

'Fuck off! How much did you have?'

'One tab.'

'Well, give me the same as you, yah fuckin' hippy poofter.'

He wouldn't make salesman of the year, but what the hell. With that kind of attitude, he convinced me he needed his mind expanded more than ever.

'Yeah, okay. Here, take it.'

The little tablet was pecked from my open hand and swallowed like a seagull's chip in a rude, crude, unadulterated instant.

We reached the sandy shore, and Mighty Mouse jumped on to dry land and ran up the beach into his own private world. I pulled the boat out and whacked the anchor into a thicket of brambles above the high tide mark. My new tripping buddy had disappeared into the sand dunes. I stripped off my shirt and dived into the clear shallows to cool off from rowing miles with odd-length oars.

The sun's warm rays dried the seawater into biscuit crumbs on my back. The sand swirled in patterns like the skin of a living creature under my feet, stark against the brown grass hills on the other side of the dunes. I was Lewis Carol, Sherlock Holmes, Robinson Crusoe, and Dr Leary marooned on a deserted island. My legs felt light, giving me the sensation of hovering, and I meandered like liquid over the dunes.

The dugite was a beautiful creature when you looked closely without fear of snakes, even highly poisonous ones. The one basking on the sand in front of me was nowhere near fully grown. It lay on the warm sand, smiling, comfortable in the midday sun. I stood a few feet away, admiring its spectacular scale patterns. Without warning, its back suddenly shattered. Mighty Mouse came from behind and brought a heavy stick down with a force accompanied by a thunderous scream.

'Dugite, they are the most deadly snakes in the world!' he bellowed. 'Kill the fucker quick! Kill it!'

Of course, it was already well on its way to snake heaven, almost cut in half by the heavy and needless blow.

'That's just not cool, man,' My response understated his frantic behaviour.

I turned to look into his face. He was terrified; the acid had brought the baby and the bathwater back to his gathering consciousness and left him helpless and in despair. The drug took charge, twisting his mind into defensively violent actions. I began waxing guru.

'It's okay,' I spoke softly and calmly. 'Everything is okay.' His violent act didn't rile me; it enlightened me.

I couldn't help myself. I kept lapsing into swami mode. If I had been straight, I probably would have punched him and left him on the shore, but now everything was going to be all right; everything was calm. The poor little snake kept writhing, trying to figure out how to join itself together, trying to live even in its agony. Grabbing the tree branch from the skinner's hand, I whacked the dugite across the head to kill it outright and relieve it from its pain.

We walked together in silence over the dunes till we came upon a run-down fisherman's hut. Lying by the side of the hut was an oar that was a perfect match for one of the oars we had on our dinghy. My jacked-up thoughts kept me in a holding pattern of pious fervour. The angel, the protector, the one who looked over us saw what we needed and put it in our way. The oar was a sign. It was up to us to become aware and act on the opportunity.

We are not stealing the oar. It is given to us. I suppose I was ranting about something like that when Mighty Mouse slumped to the ground and began crying out.

'Now I understand—it's us. We are the ones,' he sobbed while not making one bit of sense.

'Don't cry, man. You just made a giant breakthrough into working out what our life is all about.'

I had no idea why I said what I said or what the fuck I was talking about, but the weird thing was, he appeared to understand me. He got up and pushed a saintly smile across his face before skipping off down the beach like some fucking fairy boy.

Hunger and LSD didn't go hand in hand, so neither of us wanted to eat anything. Thirst was different. The gallon of lemon cordial went so fast we nearly drowned on the stuff. We had about a mile and a half of rowing back to the *Tulip*, and I sagely suggested we get a move on 'before the light of day no longer supported us'.

With two matching oars, the tinny moved straighter and faster out over the incoming tide. The effects of the acid were still quite strong, so feeling like superman, I was happy to do all the rowing. On previous LSD trips I imagined, I had been where my trip buddy was now. He would be experiencing the deeper recesses of his conscious mind. I was happy for him. I smiled at the decky, watching him trying to tackle the mental bathwater he was swimming in.

Earlier that day, when we set out for land, Australia was a massive target. All we had to do was head east, and there was no way we could miss landing on shore. But on the return leg, we were heading back out into the ocean, and the *Tulip* was only a tiny speck on the horizon. On top of that, the incoming tide was pulling us north with such force that without a little help from the northeaster wind, we might well have ended up at the Abrolhos Islands.

Mighty Mouse sat in the rear, facing out to sea, while I rowed, my back to the *Tulip*. I relied on his good sense to steer us in the right direction. I explained that we would have to aim ten degrees south to offset the drag of the tide. My mistake was to trust that my explanation would penetrate what was left of the skinner's brain matter. When I checked to see our position, we had strayed well north of where we should be if we had any chance of getting back to the boat.

Previously, having to row into shore with odd oars was affecting me like kryptonite. I asked Mighty Mouse to take over and give me a break for a while. We swapped seats, and I directed him to head south against the tide. The short south swell had the tide behind it. The sea hit us head-on. Though the waves were small, they managed to splash over the bow, sloshing around our feet. I ripped the top off our lemon cordial bottle and used it to bail out the water.

Mighty Mouse began laughing a mad laugh, a hysterical laugh, a fearful laugh. Losing concentration, he completely missed the water with the oars and fell back heavily into the front of the boat. His head bled a little when it cracked against the metal seat. His hysteria kept up so that he could no longer row. We swapped places again, and I urged him to bail while I took to the oars. This time, I didn't trust his warped navigational sense and made sure to check regularly to see that we stayed on the right course.

The skinner continued bailing the water out of the dinghy before he threw the bottle out with the water by mistake. There was still a good distance to go, and without a bailer, we were going to be in trouble.

I reached over and pulled his cap off. 'Use this to bail, and don't fuckin' lose it, or we're stuffed, okay?' I instructed with panic in my voice.

The laughing fit left him, and the seriousness of our situation loomed back into his reality. He hat-bailed all the way back to the anchorage.

Skinny threw us a line when we banged alongside the freezer boat. He was livid that we went ashore without him. Every second, word from his nerve-jangling voice bore an expletive. He cussed and swore and carried on like an imbecile until I began to wish I had another LSD tab to shove down his throat.

Mighty Mouse, on the other hand, looked serene. He quietly watched on as the young goblin continued raving at us.

I wondered, *Did the acid trip change him? Would it change the skinny kid? Does it change anybody? Am I changed because of it? Is that what it's supposed to do, or should we take it just for kicks? Or shouldn't we take it at all? Hell, I don't know. I'm just a kid myself.*

I dived overboard and swam around with the hundreds of fish beneath the *Tulip* to clear my head a bit. After tying the dinghy back on top of the wheelhouse, I bathed in briny water and Comprox on the front deck before settling down with a good book. In the background, I could hear Mighty Mouse lighting the flame of the skinny kid's consciousness with his new-found wisdom from his first-ever LSD trip.

CHAPTER 8

For hours on end, we kept ourselves amused, catching fish over the stern while waiting for Geldo to return. Below the keel was weeks of crayfish heads and guts thrown over the side from the processing of our factory boat. The herring and garfish attracted to the free food were swimming below us in the thousands. We held a competition using multiple hooks on each line to see how many fish we could catch with a single cast. Even though we weren't earning money, it was lots of fun raking hundreds of fish in to fill the bait boxes.

Early on the day before Christmas, we heard the drone of the Rook's dinghy coming towards us, and we gathered on the port side to meet him. Geldo slammed into the side of the *Tulip* with his little boat and, to our horror, threw something on to the deck.

'This'll be great bait,' he rasped.

We stood there, gobsmacked. The bastard had shot a baby New Zealand fur seal through the head and brought it out for us to cut up and put in the pots. There was no way I was going to be a part of Geldo's total disregard for the protection of these rare creatures. I went below and packed my bag and my suitcase full of books, came up, and told him to take me to shore. There was a murmur from Skinny and Mighty Mouse, which got me thinking that my reaction might be dangerous, but I was too angry to do much about it.

When the pirate took me directly to shore, he curtly pointed towards a desolate sandy track and said, 'Get the fuck off my property.'

I wanted to tell him it wasn't his property because he was only a squatter, but I thought he might kill me. So making sure to keep my voice as calm as it could be, I asked, 'What about my pay?'

'Get it from the factory in Fremantle,' he snorted, spat, turned away, and swaggered off towards his house.

Two hours later, a factory truck picked me up on its daily run up the sand track, collecting bags of crays. Between the little port of Sealer and the factory was a spattering of fisherman shacks. Outside each squat was a mini shed that accommodated the daily catches. There were no bags of fish outside Geldo's, just me with my kit and my suitcase. It was only sixty miles to the town, but it took us forever. The driver stopped umpteen times to load sacks of cackling live sea cockroaches bound for the factory.

Abilio, the truck driver, used to own a cray boat. After his fourth child arrived, his wife didn't want him away at sea any more. She imagined that doing the bag run would provide a good income and more time ashore, time he could spend with her and the kids. He complained that it did neither, but he appreciated my help slinging bags on to the back of his truck. An extra pair of hands helped reduce his estimated arrival time at the factory. We got there just on sunset.

In a fairly underwhelming appreciation for my work, Abilio gave me a warm bottle of Coke. He conjured it out from under the driver's seat. I chugged it straight down, as it was the only liquid I'd put through my kidneys since early that morning. There was a half-mile trudge down to a strip of beach under the floodlit pier. I meandered sadly towards the moth-attracting luminescence bombarding the darkness. I was broke as a whore's hymen with no food and no fixed address.

Generally, at this time of year, the jetty would be swarming with tourists. They'd be casting their lines to catch some of the myriad herring attracted to the lights on the pier. Oddly enough, probably because it was Christmas Eve, everyone must have been with their families or celebrating somewhere else. As the night ripened, I could see party lights and hear the revellers, but I was too depressed to go find someone to party with. I unrolled my sleeping bag on the beach and lay down, looking up into the magical depths of the Milky Way in 3D Technicolor brilliance. It was the worst Christmas ever, but to this day, I have never regretted it for a second.

Come morning, it was easy to hitchhike down to Freo. Lots of holidaymakers were leaving early, wanting to get back to their homes before the highway went into the gridlock that would no doubt follow in the afternoon. Because I was on the road before a sparrow fart, I got a ride almost immediately all the way to Mosman Park. A free train ride later to Freo, I made a beeline for Cuda's place and arrived a couple of hours well after lunchtime, absolutely ravenous.

Cuda was busy dressing down one of his yard workers in true abusive fashion. It was Hank the Krout. Hank saw me first, and his look of recognition caused Cuda to turn around.

'Hey, Jesus, you must be telepathic. I was just thinking about you. Why are you here? Aren't you supposed to be working for the Rook?'

'I quit! He was too much of an arsehole to work for. Now I need to figure out how to get my money out of him without threatening him with a gun.'

'Ooh, mate, I wouldn't do that to that joker. He'd rip yer head off and spit down yer neck.'

'Don't worry. I was speaking metaphorically,' I quipped. 'All the same, he owes me thirty grand, and I think it's gonna be difficult to get it.'

A big cheesy smile crossed the little man's lips. He stepped towards me, reached up, laid his hand on my shoulder, and in a quiet voice, said, 'I can help you out with *your* little problem matey, but I want you to help me out with a problem of my own.'

It appeared like he'd completely forgotten about Hank until he looked back around my shoulder.

'Are you still the fuck here? Get back to work, ya lazy fuckin' waste of money.' The familiar half-joking half evil tone spilt melodically from his lips.

I smiled sympathetically at Hank, and he returned a fractured smirk, shrugged his shoulders, and toddled off. He was barely out of earshot when Cuda began explaining our 'You scratch my back and I'll scratch yours' proposal. I didn't like it, but if he could get my money from Geldo the pirate, I supposed it would be worth it. Plus, there was an offer of some big bucks and a bit of hooch for the hippy in me.

There had been a week of preparation for what I would do for Cuda, but it only took him two days to get my money from the pirate. Well, he gave me twenty-two grand out of thirty. It was a giant rip off even without factoring in my calculations of the share bonus we should collect from the exported crays. I had diligently kept a record of every pound of fresh crayfish we caught and knew what I had earned as the winch man. Unfortunately, Geldo's figures differed from mine in his favour, and the outstanding balance of $8,000 was non-negotiable.

It crossed my mind that Cuda might have put a levy on it. In those days, the cash I held in my hand was enough to buy a family home. I'd earned it in a very short time, so I chalked the loss up to experience and tried to forget about the missing $8,000.

With nowhere else to go, I waited for my next job. With Cuda's approval, I slept seven nights in the captain's cabin on the deserted research vessel tied to his dock. It was still dark outside when I got a wake-up shake from Roberto, a driver I'd never met before. He introduced himself politely and took me over to the river.

The flashy-looking speedboat tied to the wharf tacitly gloated a large expense account. Its sleek lines and polished wooden deck covered a 357 Hemi V8 engine. Chrome controls glinted speckles of light on to the plush leather seats surrounding the back deck.

Jumping on board with the driver, I was surprised to see Happo waiting in the boat. I untied the mooring line, and the little machine motored slowly out of the river mouth before zipping across the open water towards Rottnest Island.

Anchored just inside the island, Happo and I transferred to an ocean-going sloop. My shipmate spoke Italian to Roberto, who grinned as he steered the speedboat back towards the mouth of the Swan River and, without so much as a ciao, faded into the predawn haze.

PART II

AFRICAN ODYSSEY

CHAPTER 9

Weighing anchor, we set out from the lee of the island in the early hours of morning. The skipper got under way by motor, as there was absolutely no wind to propel our fifty-foot yacht north through the fishing grounds. Already there were dozens of navigation lights flickering like moving towns ahead and astern. When the sunrise woke the wind, we hefted the sails to gain every inch of energy.

By eleven o'clock that morning, the Doctor was in the house. A howling southerly wind affectionately called the Fremantle Doctor stormed up behind our boat, propelling us to maximum speed. For the next ten to fifteen hours, nature's turbines set the pace as we scooted along into the night. And the next three days were pretty much the same, but although we were making excellent time, the crew was exhausted.

Except for the skipper, we were greenhorns when it came to working on sailboats. Although fit and strong, I was not used to the type of skill required to make one of these contraptions run properly, especially in strong wind conditions. Unlike this yacht, fishing boats didn't heel over at top speed. With sailboats, there was a lot more hands on deck work to keep her fair while under way. On most working boats, craypots and ropes were mostly always towards the stern, but on this thing, we had guy wires, shrouds, and ropes (or more correctly, lines) going in all directions.

It took a while to become accustomed to sailing and settle into our respective labours. At mid-morning on day 4, we changed course and headed west-north-west. With a following wind and calmer seas, our tasks got easier. We ventured further away from land and hooked up with the south-east trade winds, and they painted us into the seascape as a tiny speck in the vast Indian Ocean.

After a solid week, we had travelled a thousand miles west, and the wind kept everyone busy, but we were no longer running out of puff on the winches. I was scaling the mast like a spider monkey and running the decks, fitter and stronger and loving every inch of the experience.

The *Crumpet* had been renamed for our journey; in a previous incarnation, it was called *Sea Dragon*, so I was told, but the architect for this mission wanted a cuddly, endearing name for her. The renaming did little for the confidence of my Italian counterparts, as they were superstitious about a boat's name being changed.

Then as an added insult, Happo complained, 'They had to go and use a Pommie pikelet for a name.'

It had been over a year since I'd worked with the other deckhand on a fishing boat. He was a curly-haired brown-skinned individual originally from southern Italy. He was born Michael (with a list of middle names) Happaluto, but most people called him Happo or Harpo. He was fit and lean like me and only a year or two older. We had become good friends. He knew the fishing game well but, like me, had no experience on sailboats.

Antonio Belario was our main man on the vessel; he was the navigator, the skipper or captain, and the man responsible for our safe return. The other dings nicknamed him Bella Boy or Boy Beautiful. It was not only because he looked a lot like a young Elvis Presley; it was more the way he ponced around. He would flick his fringe back like he was on a catwalk and always walk with a straight back like he had a stick jammed up his backside. It struck me as curious that he enjoyed a girly sort of nickname. I thought he was either naive, egotistical, or just too unimaginative to realise it wasn't that much of a compliment.

Bella Boy was in charge, but our new friend, the quiet one, seemed to me to be the real master and commander. He carried the nickname Riddler. Riddler was introduced to me as Ernesto Igmas; he was the short, dark-skinned European type with a muscular build, blonde wavy close-cropped hair, and green eyes. They pierced rather than viewed when he looked at you. He had a frustrating quirk to his conversation in that he always answered a question with a question in an abnormal way.

His guarded manner made it difficult to converse with him. If the talk got personal, he would switch to ding or change the subject completely, closing the book on who he was or what he was on about. He overacted the mystery-man image to an A-class wanker level, which also made him painful to be around. Even after being in his company at close quarters for weeks, the most recognizable thing about him was that he was an arrogant arsehole.

On reflection about this adventure, I began to hypothesise about his name: Ernesto Igmas. At a reach, even his name suggested an enigma—hence the obvious nickname, I suppose. Ernie's only saving grace was that he didn't talk much, at least not to me. His overrated ego and arrogance niggled me for a while, but living in close quarters with fishermen, I was used to tolerating bossy know-it-alls, and there were occasions when I almost got a smile from him with one of my daily wisecracks. By the sound of his foreign accent and apparent fluency in Italian, I presumed he was from that country, but not even Happo could say for sure if he was.

'Have you seen nothing?' I joked, offering my hands to the wide blue expanse.

'Yeah, for the last eight days, I've been looking at exactly that—nothing,' replied Happo.

Since we'd sailed out of sight of land many days before, the Indian had hosted an uneventful journey. All the hype of blustering winds and humongous swells we'd been expecting had so far eluded us. The consistent rolling of our yacht and the same blueness of the never-ending ocean had a hypnotising effect on the four of us as we slowly picked our way over thousands of miles of empty blue ocean.

We were all guilty of daydreaming, and for myself, I was a little stir-crazy. At first, I kept imagining I could see things in the water: floating logs, containers, dead things, and jumping sea creatures, especially on the helm at night. They might have been real, but the vastness and the loneliness of this sea contorted my senses.

It was a slow trip, and I was becoming bored with the sameness of everything we had done and seen since we left the mooring. Naively I was hanging out for a bit of bluster so we could work out on the rigging. Daily I grew antsier, knowing that we were still nowhere near the halfway mark of this epic journey.

Most things I'd done in my young working life and the places I'd been felt like an adventure, and even when I looked back on it, a lot of it seemed surreal. On the first half of this voyage, I began to feel at the time a bit ho-hum about the whole odyssey. What was it about youth that made us want more and more excitement and yearn adrenaline even when we were daring fate by just being where we were? Like in this case, I was over a thousand miles from the nearest land on a relatively small, ill-equipped vessel, and I was here thinking, *Boring!* Then in answer to my arrogance, things changed.

Up to this point, the wind had been friendly and useful, and the south equatorial current helped push our craft towards East Africa at a good pace. Happo and I were sitting on the forward deck, chatting mundanely about nothing in particular. It was nice in the sunshine, and copping the occasional spray whipped up by the bow waves kept us cool and alert.

Then out of nowhere came the call. It was Antonio who first saw the squall. It was coming at us from the south off the port beam. It was no more than ten miles wide but was dark and threatening, like looking down the throat of a giant coal mine. The sea under the clouds appeared disturbed, maniacal. Marbled white lines of foam contrasted against the darkened ocean as the front came straight towards us at astounding speed.

As he turned on the engine, Bella Boy squealed orders in our direction, alerting us to jump to work just at the exact moment the squall slammed into us. There was barely time to reef a sail before the boat was thrown over, and the starboard gunwale was pushed inches below the surface until the skipper turned her out. The kite popped like a gunshot; Happo and I raced forward to drag the sail back on deck as the *Crumpet* skidded and shuddered ahead of the whipping wind before she regained her poise.

Then the rain hit, fairly pummelling us, whacking our heads and backs, and bouncing up off the deck like stinging insects into our turned-down faces. The temperature dropped by five degrees from the balmy, sunny day minutes before. We worked the sheets feverishly on command to keep the yacht from responding to the masterful storm. Wind whistled through the shrouds like a black cockatoo on speed and pushed us west by north-west with help from the hefting sea. It was difficult to move about on the flooded deck with the driving rain pelting us from every angle.

There were no harnesses on board, so it was 'hang on tight' at all times or be swept over the railing. It was ironic that only moments before, I had been wishing for a bit of excitement, but this was just plain scary and much more than I wanted conjured up. The yacht thrust forward, pitched, skewed, and heeled at the whim of each ferocious gust, but she kept her point ahead and her bum in front of the storm.

The gale continued to blast us for the next three and a half hours. As the swells lifted, the pitch of the boat resembled a big dipper ride at Luna Park, only more terrifying, as we came down the back of the wind-whipped waves. The pointy end pierced the surface like a spear. Seawater swept over the entire length of the boat with such force that the whole craft shuddered under the impact before poking her head up to speed ahead into the next onslaught. The mast shook, and the shrouds rattled louder than the noise of the motor.

Bella Boy was screaming directions inaudible against the cacophony of the storm. By then it didn't matter really because we had reefed the sails and scrambled to the safety of the cabin to huddle down, hanging on for dear life.

Then as quickly as it had hit upon us, the maelstrom passed over, leaving behind a magical serenity with a gentle tailwind. Bella Boy ordered Happo to take the helm as he went forward to check the mast and sort through what was left of the spinnaker. Amazingly, everything was intact except for a repairable tear and a popped eyelet. He yelled at me to bring the spare sail and stow it in the forward hatch, and I imagined him requesting the torn one to be mended, but he spoke in ding.

I stood facing him with my hands spread out in a bemused gesture. 'None capeesh, *el capitano*.'

He scowled at me as he dragged the damaged sail over the cabin roof.

The *Crumpet* had been pushed along comfortably at a reasonable rate for weeks when that storm hit us. Watching the back of the weather moving off to torture something else, I changed my mind about wishing for a bit of bluster. As it happened, it was the only significant bit of rough seafaring we encountered on the westward run.

Nearly a fortnight after the bit of rough, as the sun began a slow dive into the ocean in front of us, Bella Boy alerted us that the *Crumpet* was nearing our pickup destination.

'Keep your eyes peeled,' he hailed.

The tension mounted, and we strained our eyes and ears in the growing darkness until we found ourselves plunged into a night without moonlight. From my lookout position, I could hear Ernesto talking to the skipper in a muffled foreign language. The navigator spoke in English, assuring him we were exactly where we should be to rendezvous with the cargo boat.

I couldn't hear Ernie's response, but the skipper reacted by looking directly at me. I'd already picked up whom they were talking about, but Bella Boy made it even more obvious when he switched back to speaking Italian.

The breeze was light; the swell, over three metres, was dark and glassy. The *Crumpet* glided over the humps and dropped sharply into the troughs, which made it difficult to maintain our footing. I ballet-danced up to the bow and wrapped both arms around the railing.

Immediately I caught sight of a faint light off to the north-west. I performed a Rudolf Nureyev grand jeté back to the cockpit, aided by the pitch of the yacht, and pointed in the direction of the light. For several anxious minutes, I was beginning to doubt if my discovery was real as the light seemed to have disappeared.

Then after what felt like an eternity, Bella Boy whispered to Ernie and pointed to a faint green blur emanating out of the darkness. He reached down and switched off our nav lights. We furled the sails and started the motor. Antonio altered course to intercept the vessel, which meant we had to go side-on to the swell, making our ride even more uncomfortable.

Our brief was, if we spotted a vessel around the rendezvous point, to maintain silence until we verified its identity. In making sure this was the boat we were supposed to meet, the less anyone else saw of us, the better. Radio contact was to be made only as a last-ditch effort. The four of us were transfixed on the light, watching it grow brighter and straining to discern its identity.

Suddenly, a loud crackling came over our radio, and an oddly distinctive accent boomed through the speaker near the helm.

'Is zat you, *Crimpet*? Kem bick. Over.'

'Narwhal!' was the only reply from our skipper.

'Yah, it'z *Narwhal*, um, garn ti heed inti za swell and stind by. You reed me? Over.'

'How many you got on board?' asked our skipper and then added, 'Is Pepper with you?'

'Ve gat six, and Pepper's ganna throw you the rope, akay? Over.'

None of us could believe our eyes when we got closer. We were quite taken aback to see the boat by the glow of its nav lights and a yellowish floodlight shining off the back of its forecastle. The *Narwhal* was a rusting, filthy piece of floating junk, and here they were more than 200 miles from land. I wouldn't have ventured into a swimming pool on board that thing. My pulse was racing at this point, and I was pretty certain these guys were not your strait-laced churchgoers who threw money in the honesty box on Sunday mornings.

The crew of the *Narwhal* looked and smelled to me, if I may be believed, like pirates from the seventeenth century except for the fact that they didn't wear wide belts with big buckles and swords. They wore three-quarter pants and striped tees, and I swear one of them had on a Wee Willy Winkie cap, just like Captain Hook's first mate, Smee. They were a grubby-looking lot, and even standing off their beam twenty yards out, wafts of a shitty smell blew over us from across their deck.

It was gloom time; the sun had well and truly stopped sending messages from below the horizon, and my senses were on high alert. I strained to survey each of the crew members of the *Narwhal*. It was impossible to detect facial expressions, of course, as four of them were as black as coal and looked to me like shadows with clothes on.

Mainly, I was concerned that they might be carrying weapons. I was pretty sure they couldn't be carrying guns on their persons, as their clothing was too skimpy. I couldn't see on to the deck, as our sailboat was below the *Narwhal*'s bulwarks, so I hopped up on the cabin roof and clambered a little way up the mast. As the wheelhouse light spilt across their aft deck, I snapped a look at the cargo we had come for.

Masses of oilskin parcels littered the deck, maybe forty or fifty in all, not even tied down. The bags were just lying on the deck, moving about with each shift of the swells passing under the rusty hulk.

'Ve gat pilleys to lift 'em across, okey?' An electronic voice broke out of the *Narwhal*'s loudspeaker.

Before Bella Boy answered, a short Caucasian man stepped out from the wheelhouse. He had on cream-coloured shorts and a mohair jumper that was speckled—whether with design or grease and dirt, I could not be sure. He spoke with an accent slightly garbled from where I stood, but he sounded like he was rebuking the skipper of the *Narwhal*. The rest of his crew went silent and feigned looking busy.

'You gotta your'a hatch'a ready, Iggy?'

He addressed our enigmatic crew member as if our skipper wasn't even there, dealing only with Ernesto. When I turned to look for Iggy's response, I was taken aback to see our oddball friend holding a pistol in his hand and making no attempt to hide it. Ernie responded to Speckled Jumper in a foreign language, and for the duration of the operation, I didn't understand one spoken word. My job was to stay on the wheel and hold the *Crumpet* steady alongside and keep the motor puttering away quietly until the cargo was transferred.

Remarkably, even amidst the rocking and the rolling, it took just an hour to shift hundreds of kilos from vessel to vessel. Of course, our load was not stashed or secured until each parcel was checked. To get it into its secret hold took a lot more time and effort, but at least we were not next to the stinking *Narwhal*.

Maybe it's time to admit it, but as the others went below to stash the precious cargo, it became apparent that the stench from the crew of the *Narwhal* had rubbed off from the cargo itself. In closed quarters below deck, the smell was overpowering. Nothing we had on board would conceal the odour. If authorities came across us, we would be in deep trouble.

I assumed the skipper on the *Narwhal* had left the packages loose on his deck so they could be easily jettisoned if they were to be boarded by the law. On our boat, they were being lodged inside the infrastructure of the yacht. What I hadn't been privy to was that some panels in the hull had been previously engineered and installed with plastic airtight containers. It was amazing to me that several days into our return journey, after the panels were sealed, I could not detect any odour.

I had never intended to be involved in the smuggling operation, yet it was me who gave the plan to the boss. I was the one who had lined up the contacts out of Africa, done the introductions, and got the intel on locations to transfer the cargo. It was my intention to bow out of the pickup and the delivery mission. But the Cuda told me I owed him, so here I was.

Of course, I wanted a cut of the money and a bit of blow, but that would be enough for a stupid young hamburger hippy like me. Got to say, looking back, I was a pretty green kid with not much more than a sneaking suspicion about the real business of the people I worked for.

The boss had insisted I go with the *Crumpet* to mediate with my South African friends. After the pickup from the *Narwhal*, I started to get a different picture of why I was there, and I became very jittery, if not a little paranoid. Ernesto and Bella Boy had purposefully kept me away from the transfer. What was that about? It crossed my mind that I might have reached my use-by date and become an inappropriate witness with a share of the loot that could be better used elsewhere.

My fifth, sixth, and seventh senses kept alarming me to Ernie's slight glances, remembering that he had been in possession of a concealed weapon for the past weeks. What else was he capable of? Also, none of my contacts were on the rusty tub when we exchanged cargo. One was supposed to be!

For the next week, I was a cat on a hot tin roof, more jumpy than a young colt on cracker night. I was going crazy wondering what I would do if a death threat got real. I slept little and light and kept a hammer under my pillow. I always made sure the fish knife with the ten-inch blade was in the sheath over the hatch. I had also taped a long screwdriver under the lip of the forward hatch cover, just in case!

All my time was spent in fluctuating degrees of anxiety, fairly shitting myself and developing more and more paranoia by the hour. Instinct mixed with the threatening feelings urged me to behave as normal. It didn't stop me continually forming scenarios in my mind and trying to figure out how I would react to each one of them if it came to a life-or-death struggle.

CHAPTER 10

Often my thoughts would turn back to a time when I lived and worked with my brother. My brother, 'the Streak', was heavily committed to martial arts. *Obsessed* is probably a better term. As far back as I can remember, he trained at every opportunity, and baby brother, moi, was the one he tried out his new skills on for homework.

I would come home to my little corner of the Streak's house, where we lived with his wife and two kids. My room was in a corner of a closed-in veranda consisting of one single bed, one wardrobe, and a small bedside table. The rest of the floor space was covered in judo mats. Apart from paying my brother rent, I was also expected to make myself available for him to attack me with the latest moves he'd picked up at karate, aikido, or judo lessons.

The Pink Panther movie hadn't been released, where Inspector Clouseau came home to be surprised and attacked by his chauffeur, Kato. That was a funny film, but my life was a horror movie. Not a day went by where I got away unscathed either physically or mentally. I hated it so much. I was ambushed, punched, kicked, thrown, and grappled whether I wanted to be or not.

Sometimes I would fight with everything I had to try to get the better of him. He was six years my senior, bigger, stronger, and extremely well versed in the eastern fighting arts as well as his boxing training. I came close to a win a few times, but not when I lost my temper. I discovered my best successes were in defence if I calmed myself and remembered to follow his instructions on how to stop or deflect his blows. When I got the occasional hit on him, I knew I hurt him, and I would really try to, but it meant he would fight back even harder. So I practised more defensive strategies.

Hence, my shitty life boarding at my brother's place gave me the confidence to keep calm, think defence under pressure, and execute a counter-attack.

In my early teens, scrapes used to follow me around, presenting me with opportunities to practise some of my big brother's hard-learned lessons. Closing time at the pub where I grew up, in a rough and tough neighbourhood, produced a lot of angry guys tanked full of booze suddenly feeling an urge to become superheroes.

Contrary to what some people thought, the culture of the street fighter didn't just pop up out of a tree stump. The rockers and the surfies came later than the bodgies and their widgie girlfriends, but they carried on in a similar way, scuffling about in the streets.

Then the popgun phenomenon of England's skinheads spread to Australia in the sixties and seventies. Only God knew how or why, but it did. They got into their own shit-for-brains acts, but the common denominator was to beat up some poor bugger walking home from somewhere, usually at night. And if they were unfortunate enough to be alone, it was even more likely to happen.

What seemed the quickest and easiest way to start a rumble was to object to someone looking at you the wrong way, almost always starting with some low-intelligence diatribe. Stupidly, I would throw back a counter that usually contained knuckle-dragger language so they wouldn't miss the point. Then I'd wait for the king-hit or sucker punch to come at me, whether from the front or from behind, as I would attempt to walk away. I was used to an ambush, and my brother's hard love always paid off for me.

Apart from the unfriendly street prowlers, there was a danger of evil creatures in unexpected places. Living over an hour's bus ride from the sea was consternation in itself without the other shit I had to put up with at the Streak's house. Fortunately, it was less than a mile to the river. At least there I could swim and dive out of trees like a water baby. But one day there was an incident.

My girlfriend at the time, Myra, obliged my invitation to go for a swim. The river was really just a creek, but everyone misnamed it. After a million years, the creek had cut a gorge through the escarpment and chucked a boomerang-shaped turn, leaving a crushed sandstone beach and a wide pool for us to enjoy. Although a favourite for locals, it presented some difficulty when scaling down the cliff face to the beach.

Locals referred to the swimming hole as the Spot. The Spot catered mainly to older teenagers and young adults. It had all the hallmarks of a natural fun park. We dived or swung on a rope out of a tree on the other side of a hundred-yard-wide pool with a basking rock in the middle. In flood times, the water squeezed between bundles of rocks and came out the other side as a jet stream. It was a perfect place to see how long one could swim against the rapids before being swept downstream.

Myra was full of youth. Agile and athletic, she had no trouble descending the hundred-foot cliff down to the Spot. Climbing to the bottom, I reached up to guide her down the last step. A look of horror was reflected in her eyes as she stared over my shoulder. I spun around. Ten feet away, a man emerged from the tree line, burning eyes straight at us with a menacing look on his face. Next to him were two younger men wearing leering looks.

A rock overhang blocked any view from the top of the cliff above us, and a stand of casuarinas below concealed the climb-down point from the river.

The older man stepped forward. He eyed Myra up and down before a gruff voice belched from his crooked mouth. 'Yeah, brung us a present, did yah, young fella?'

As naive as I was, I understood our situation was grave. Starting from my stomach, a niggling feeling fast turned to dread.

'Let us past please,' I squeaked.

Without warning, the man lunged at me. His punch hit my cheek as I was moving to the side. It was hard. It knocked me backwards a step and almost to the ground. Any more of those hammer-like blows would see me out. He kept coming at me, but this time, I knew what to expect.

The ground under our feet tilted towards the river. He was coming down; I was facing up. With a step to the side and a frantic grab at his clothing, I used his own momentum, and all it took was a little force to send him spinning into the thicket of the oak needles.

Blood streamed from a cut above his eye; sticks and leaves were hanging off the fresh wound. Before I could move back to Myra, a second man grabbed me from behind. He felt strong enough to hold a bull out to piss, and I couldn't wait to be free from the embrace. My atemi-waza karate was not properly learned, and what had sunk in was rusty, but it was enough to dispatch the farm boy from my back. *Fumikomi* was a stomp kick to the instep of an opponent, and my fumikomi was a beauty. The monkey on my back howled as he let go and grabbed his ankle.

Fortunately, the branch that hit me across the head from behind was rotten; it smashed into hundreds of pieces, spraying splinters and dust into the air. I reeled, shocked and blurred from the impact, and turned groggily to face my assailant. I noted the third man holding Myra with her arms behind her back.

Mr Evil closed on me, waving the blood and sticks from the bleeding side of his face. He let go a straight jab aimed at the middle of my head. It was coming in fast and hard, and I wanted no part of it. This time, I ducked uphill. His air punch put him slightly off balance as I swung a powerful sidekick, connecting with his ribs. The force of the blow sent him sprawling through the thicket again and whacked him head first into a tree.

'Fuck this!' he let out. 'This guy knows kung fu shit. Let 'em go.'

The third man held on too long to Myra. I ran at him, and he let go and raised his hands in the air, mouth open and eyes bulging like a goitre sufferer. That day at the river was a life changer for me. It was the first time I fully appreciated the benefits of my brother's warped sense of guidance. That man, Garrett, became obsessed with payback, even paying people to hurt me.

The downside of the event was, Myra never got over the attack. Her paranoia grew so bad that she would not venture out of the family home. All attempts to console her were to no avail, and our relationship ended. The unhappy time gave me no reason to stay in that town any longer. The two thugs' attempted assault three weeks later helped to firm my decision. The upside, if you can call it that, of the maniac's actions was that it forced me to leave that life behind and search for a more peaceful one.

But the path of a man's life can be fickle. No matter how much I tried to follow a way of peace, a black cloud threatening violence seemed to hover above me.

CHAPTER 11

Meanwhile, on the deck of the *Crumpet*, the tension was thick as a bucket of freeze-dried molasses. Even Happo, who I had worked with and thought of as a friend, seemed distant. He spoke more in his first language with the others. Bella Boy hardly spoke to me at all. Most of my meals I ate alone, whereas before the cargo was loaded, we all ate and drank together in the galley or around the helm. Most times, we would have a wine or a few beers, light up a cigar or a smoke, and tell a few jokes or stories before going about our chores. I sensed something bad was about to happen and that something bad was going to happen to me.

Eight days after the pickup, I opened my eyes after dropping my guard and falling into a deep sleep. The long nights of being overcautious had caught up with me, and waking up this morning felt like I was coming out of a coma. No one else was in the cabin. I grabbed my hammer and crept to the front hatch, lifted the cover slightly, and peered out. The three men were standing right above my head; they were speaking in hushed tones, their feet pointed towards the bow. I was behind them.

I could only see the lower half of their bodies from the slit in the hatch. The sight of the pistol in Ernie's hand sent a laser beam of panic through my body, causing a shudder. My mind went into overdrive, convinced it was going to be a life-or-death battle, a battle I was determined not to lose. There was no way these mongrels were going to kill me without a fight.

At this point, fear became my friend; it helped formulate my decision to defend myself to the last breath in my body. I was not a trained soldier, I'd never before experienced deadly violence, and up until then, I had never been in a position to consider how I would respond to such a threat. For God's sake, I was trying my best to be a flower child, you know? Peace, love, and all that shit. But I was a love child no more; now I was just plain angry. It was an anger that allayed my fears because I knew how far I would go if my enemies wanted to take my life.

Ernesto spoke in a foreign language in a whisper as I closed the lid. Then I heard foot patters on the deck coming back to the rear entry. I raced over to my bunk and hurriedly bunched up some blankets to make it look like I was still asleep. Beside the doorway on the starboard side was an alcove. I tucked into it and waited, hammer ready.

Happo didn't see me as he peered through the door; he didn't descend the steps. I watched him checking my bunk from across the gloomy cabin before he turned and went out to join the others. I could hear the low tone of his voice addressing one of the men. When the hatchway darkened again, I watched Ernie creep down into the cabin towards my pile of blankets. To my shock and horror, he raised his pistol and fired three shots into the place where my body would have been.

All my training came back to me. I was calm now; I launched myself from the alcove and smashed down with the hammer, catching Ernie's wrist and knocking the gun to the floor. The Riddler's forearm shattered on impact, but he didn't scream. He grabbed at his wrist and pivoted around just in time to receive the side of the hammer's head whack into his chest. It knocked him backwards against my bunk, and his head hit the wooden surround with a crack. He fell to the floor, completely unconscious.

Beside the galley table, we kept a basket with an assortment of cleaning rags and string and bits of rope. I pulled it down and emptied the contents on the floor. I snatched two pieces of stout, short rope and tied Ernie's legs and arms tight, not caring about the shattered arm. Stuff him. He wanted to murder me. I had no love for him.

On deck, it was unnaturally quiet. With the drama unfolding, I had not noticed until that exact moment that the yacht was drifting, not sailing. Without sails up and the motor shut down, everything was still except for a gentle rock from the relatively smooth ocean.

I was enraged, but although I knew I did not want to kill anyone, I sure did feel like putting some hurt on the other two accomplices. Reaching down over Ernie's prostrate body, I picked up the gun and cautiously crept out of the hatch to peer out.

Bella Boy was standing over Happo as he sat by the main mast on the cabin roof. Happo was crying, literally sobbing woefully, with his head buried in his hands. The skipper was trying to console him in a hushed whisper. The scene took me completely by surprise. I was ready to bash the shit out of these guys, but seeing them so upset took me aback.

'All right, arseholes, get up and move to the bow. Now!' I ordered as I showed them the business end of the pistol.

Another surprise: Happo beamed at me.

'Holy suffering sheep shit, man! How the—Wow! Oh man.' Although he rambled, I got the distinct impression he was relieved to see me. Maybe he was my friend. Maybe he had no option but to go along with the prick down below. They moved as ordered and stood by the pulpit on the bow.

Bella Boy looked stunned and a little scared but gave no clue as to how he felt about me instead of Ernie coming out of the cabin alive. But I was determined I was going to find out.

'You rotten mongrels.' I was livid. 'You've got plenty of explaining to do. Start talking. You first, Pretty Boy!'

I had to hand it to the poncey skipper; he asked me where Ernie was and why I was carrying a gun. He pretended to be in a different universe. My dander was off the Richter by now, so I lunged forward and planted a hefty left jab to his diaphragm. He gasped as all his air got punched out. Taken completely by surprise, he dropped to his knees, and when I kicked him with my bare foot in the bum, he fell sideways to the deck.

'You're weak as piss, Belario,' I hissed his name through my teeth.

I couldn't use his nickname; maybe I didn't want him to think I was being endearing. I scoffed his name like it was poison in my mouth.

'You haven't even got the balls to fess up. Now come on, tell me. What's your plan after you kill me? Arsehole!' I sneered.

Happo spoke, stammering, 'Man, this shit is crazy. That Iggy was a loony tune. He told me to go down and see if the Aussie bastard was still sleeping, said he was gonna renegotiate your cut of the cargo. He pulled out that pistol, man, but I didn't think he was going to shoot you. Well, maybe I did, but I was scared, man. I didn't know what to think. Then when you came on deck—oh boy! I was scared, dude, but I'm glad you're here. We heard shots, and man, I was shitting bricks!'

I let him ramble, trying to figure if he was being straight with me. The inflection in his voice made me believe him for the most part, but I was too scared and angry, and up to this point, my trust levels were shot to bits.

With my attention focused on Happo's confession, I missed seeing Bella Boy ply the screwdriver from the side of the hatch. He jumped up suddenly and rammed the tool towards my stomach. Stupid idiot. I easily fended the thrust with my left arm and, with my right, punched him with the heel of the pistol, straight into the middle of his face. He went down to the deck like a sack of whale meat, blood streaming from a broken nose. The screwdriver flew out of his hand, spun on the deck a few turns, and plopped over the side.

'Well, at least I know whose side you're on, you prick.' My voice dripped with disgust, but inside I was regretting what might have to happened if we were to get back to my homeland.

He was the skipper. He was a vital part of our ability to navigate and handle this innocent-looking yacht full of not-so-innocent cargo to safety. Like it or not, we needed him, and like it or not, I was not about to dispose of him like they were about to do to me.

There were some things I proved to myself that day. I was not a killer. I didn't like being that angry, but I learned what lengths I would go to if I had to defend myself.

It was a stupid question, but I asked anyway, 'Can I trust you, Happo?'

He was crying again. He showed a whole new side of himself. From the very first time I'd met this guy, he gave me the impression that he was confidence incarnate. I'd never seen him back away from an argument, and fisherman argued a lot and argued hot. He usually showed a big ego. He never shied away from hard work and was a great talker. He would come out with some of the wittiest pickup lines I'd ever heard when it came to chatting up girls. His sobbing was not put on, and I knew in my gut he was still my friend, so even before his obvious answer, I was okay with him.

'What are we going to do with these two then?' I spoke softly.

Happo stopped sobbing and looked up into my eyes with a quizzical tilt of his head.

'We heard shooting! We thought when you came out that . . . ?' His voice trailed off, and I explained to him that Ernie was alive and tied up below.

'Oh crap, dude. That guy is big trouble. You're gonna have to get rid of him, man!' Happo's voice was frantic.

I sensed the pressure Igmas must have put on Happaluto to get us to this position and just how afraid he was of him.

'Okay, first things first,' I started. 'Get some rope from there.' I pointed to the forward hatch then added, 'Let's get these two tied more securely.'

Unfortunately, Ernesto was in pretty bad shape. After we'd tied Bella Boy to the pulpit, we dragged the Riddler to the deck. He was still out cold. The rope wound around his broken wrist had trapped the blood, grotesquely inflaming his arm; it looked terrible. The lump on the back of his head had swollen, and blood from a small crack in the top matted his hair to look like a swollen chook's bum, but at least the bleeding had stopped. We laid him out on the cabin roof with his legs tied, and I released the bonds on his arms.

'Bring up the medical kit, Happo.'

He reluctantly made his way below to retrieve it, cursing Ernie as he went.

As best I could, I tended the prisoners' wounds and secured them both above decks. I kept the pistol in my belt, although it occurred to me to throw it overboard. All things considered, it might be a small advantage as a bluff—only a bluff. I was not sure I would be able to fire it at a person if it came down to the wire.

It wasn't that difficult to treat Ernie while he lay like a corpse. His broken arm was splinted, wrapped, then rebound above the fracture, and tied back tight against his body. To ensure he wouldn't fall overboard, I tied rope around his waist and strapped him to the mast. Antonio was secured about ten feet away from his fellow prisoner, but both were in plain sight of the helm.

We reset the mainsail and the jib and tacked against a strong east-south-east wind that helped to keep us creeping in the direction of home. It couldn't have been much more than half an hour before the Riddler regained consciousness. I gave both prisoners a drink of water. Ernie looked surprised before he took a sip, but the skipper gulped his down.

Stepping down into the cabin, I looked at a chart with Bella Boy's calculations written in fine pencil lines. To me, it might as well have been written in Greek, so I plucked it from the tabletop and scrambled up on deck to recheck the bonds on the prisoners. After checking the compass, I tapped Happo's shoulder to see if he could make head or tail of the chart. He glanced over it for a second but didn't seem interested in trying to make sense of it.

The sun kept blasting away at us, so I plonked a hat on each of the prisoners' heads to stop their brains from melting. My mind was spinning, trying to come up with a plan, a plan that would hopefully keep us all alive. The situation was ridiculous, like camping inside a bottle of funnel web spiders. There was no way we could keep these prisoners out here in the sun for the next couple of weeks, and there was nowhere we could lock them up without their bonds. Worse than that, Ernie looked dreadful; he needed professional medical attention as soon as possible.

A little after three o'clock that afternoon, the wind dropped to very slight. We goosenecked the sails to keep some speed, and fortunately, there was a following sea, which helped the sea log dial on the dashboard register four and a bit knots. Happo stayed on the helm, and I was in the galley, making sandwiches. I kept a close eye on my friend, the wheelman, ensuring he was not communicating with the prisoners.

I noted that Happo looked everywhere but at the two men tied to the boat. His eyes were red. He kept rubbing them, trying to keep focused, and he looked freaked out. More worrying to me was the fact that he didn't stop mumbling to himself. I'd never seen him act this way before, but these were pretty desperate circumstances; I kept hoping he could pull himself out of his downward spiral.

'Here, mate, get this into you.' I smiled as I handed him a corned-beef-and-tomato-sauce toasted sandwich and a mug of hot coffee. I was trying to sound confident, and I thought I pulled it off. He looked at me again like a child did when he was in trouble with his angry father.

'Come on, mate, you know we're going to get through this. Everything's going to work out all right,' I offered.

Stepping up on to the outer deck, I hand-fed the skipper before going over to the Riddler. Igmas was awake now, but he looked shaken up. His eyes were glazed. I didn't know if it was from pain or concussion or both. I broke a piece of the sandwich and put it to his mouth, but he spat it away without saying anything. I indicated a drink by holding his mug in the air. His look was icy, almost threatening. He held my gaze for a few seconds then nodded his head.

When I brought the mug to his mouth, he sipped slowly and drank almost half before turning his head aside like a spoiled brat. A smile crossed my lips when I thought about this horrible man who had just shot three bullets into me without a second thought, and here I was, feeding the devil and treating his wounds. All I could think of between the two of us in this relationship was that it was going to end badly for one of us. I had no idea which one.

In my daydream, I turned my head towards Bella Boy. He was staring hard and viciously straight at me. As our eyes met, he quickly shifted his gaze downward. We both knew where we stood in this adventure, but at least I knew for certain he was never going to get on board with Happo and me.

He was a countryman of Happo's. I wondered, was ethnicity thicker than friendship? Could the skipper sway my workmate? From Happo's point of view, he had a lot to lose by me staying alive. His boss, his family, and all his connections and his lifestyle could be thrown away like dirty dishwater if I was allowed to live.

I had to force myself to keep focus and to realise that I was alone in this dilemma. Happo was a pawn, useful but very low on the trust board. As hard as I tried, I could not think of a way I would be able to keep all three contained for the entire journey home. We were sailing into the first night since the attempted murder.

Would the bonds hold? Would my friend stab me in the back, either figuratively or physically? It crossed my mind to tie Happo up as well so I could sleep, but if I did that, it would be impossible for me to singlehandedly get us home. The bad plan alarm bell was ringing in my ears like a big dose of tinnitus. Without Happo's help, I would have no chance of surviving this situation. I grimaced as I thought about such simple acts as how to manage their toilet functions. They would have to be untied for that. What would I do?

A little while before sunset that first evening, I got an answer. Ernie signalled to Happo and spoke in Italian. I shouted at the wheelman.

'What did he say, Happo?'

'He needs to take a shit.'

I took the wheel from my decky mate and nodded in the Riddler's direction.

'Okay, Happo, go untie his legs first, then untie him from the mast. Untie his good arm, but do not trust him.' Slipping into my best cowboy pose, I pointed to the pistol in my belt. 'Tell him no funny business or he gets it.' I bluffed adequately, I thought.

'How's he gonna get his pants off?' Happo implied by his question that he didn't want to do it.

I grinned back at him. 'Decky's job mate. You're it. Do it before you release him from the mast. It'll be easier.'

Happo gestured as only a Mediterranean man could. He conveyed everything he didn't want to do in one simple statuesque pose. I sent back a serious grin.

The yacht was sailing along nicely; it was not rough at all, but the setting sun brought a stiff tailwind and hefted us forward in a surging motion. The cut of the hull gave us a comfortable rocking motion from side to side. The twosome stumbled awkwardly to the port bow, where the pulpit cut back and fastened to the deck. We used this spot most times instead of the head for our business, as it was slightly obscured from the helm with a rail to hang on to, so it was natural that Happo moved the prisoner there.

Igma's trousers were left in a crumpled heap near the mast on the other side. He winced with pain as Happo turned him around with his back to the sea. Grabbing at the cowling with his free hand, he squatted awkwardly. Happo held his shoulder by the scruff of his shirt. My gaze shifted to the skipper lashed at the bow then to the top of the rigging for only a moment when I heard a yell. It was Happo!

'Ah fungulo tu bastardo!' He kicked the Riddler in the face so viciously that Ernie shot backwards into the ocean.

I couldn't see properly from where I was. I stood up and looked over the transom to port, and I caught a glimpse of the Riddler's green shirt sinking below the dark-blue water.

'Happo, what in fucks name . . . What are you doing?' My screams choked with disbelief as I spun the wheel.

The *Crumpet* responded with a short-angled turn. The mainsail swung across the deck, and there was a shudder until we completed the tack and the yacht came out in a slow amble.

'Throw that life buoy over.'

Happo stood there as if frozen. I swung the wheel and instinctively lowered my head away from the shadow of the boom as it swung over my head. My needless distraction caused the vessel to list slightly as I was caught fumbling the pistol from the waistband of my shorts. Recovering the boat's track and my composure, I aimed the gun at him. Screaming at Happo had no effect.

'Happo! Shit, Happo!' It was useless. I stuffed the gun back in my belt.

Ernie had well and truly disappeared. We searched until well after dark, but there was absolutely no trace of him. I didn't realise people could sink that fast, and I fully expected him to pop up any moment. I instinctively checked around the hull to see if he had caught hold of a trailing rope, which was stupid because I'd already seen him sinking behind us.

As I walked past Antonio, his eyes were big as saucers. For a few moments, he fought to loosen his ropes in a panic, but he settled down when he realised how fast he was tied. It was peculiar how the mind worked even in serious scenes like this. I restrained a smile as I imagined Bella Boy would never, ever ask us when he wanted to go to the toilet.

Happo had transformed from a snivelling coward to a maniacal psychopath. He taunted Bella Boy, pointing and yelling at the spot in the ocean that had just swallowed his ally.

'You are going next, you fucking backstabbing *bastardo*!' He turned to stare down at Bella Boy.

I came from behind, wrapped my arms around him, and pulled him away from of the hapless prisoner.

'Stop it. Stop it, Happo! Look at me.' I felt his tension soften, so I dropped my arms, and he turned and looked straight into my face. He was calm again.

'We need him, mate. You hear me? We need him to take us home,' I pleaded with him until he nodded dejectedly.

It was well after ten o'clock. I had the spotlight searching, hoping but knowing all along it was useless. Happo and I had only a vague notion of our bearings when Ernie went over, but Happo didn't want to find him. He was not even looking, and I knew it.

Being the better sailor, Belario would have had more of a clue where to search, but I couldn't risk letting him take charge. He was nowhere near the instrument panel when Igmas was kicked overboard, and he was scared out of his wits. So I made the decision that he would be no help in a productive search and left him like a fly in a web at the front of the yacht.

I was sick to my stomach. How long was long enough for a search to save a man's life, a man who only a few hours before had tried to kill me? He had a broken arm and a serious head trauma and possible broken ribs. If we found him, he would have to be kept prisoner until we arrived back in Australia. Then this same person would probably try to kill me again. The whole thing was screwing with my head.

Finally, I wrote on the chart 'Stopped searching at 20:22 hours' on the date with a position I only made from guesswork. With a heaviness closing around my heart, I turned the compass to 190 degrees again and locked in the sails. I stayed on watch at the helm until the sun broke through the morning mist in front of us. It was a shrouded golden orb, and the sea was deep green, giving an appearance of a religious experience akin to looking into the ceiling of a beautiful cathedral.

All night I'd played with my terror and my guilt and my anger. Sleep was something I hadn't given the slightest thought to. As the sun climbed above the nesting clouds on the horizon, it started to heat the deck, and for the first time in many hours, I thought about my other two shipmates.

Yeah! Shipmates. That's a funny term for this *pair,* I mused. *This situation is outta control.* My eyes filled with tears, but only one squeezed out to run down my cheek. *Should never have got into this little venture. Never will again. Oh shit.* The shape on the bow moving and letting out a soft moan interrupted my thoughts.

'All right, Antonio,' I shouted. 'I'll get you some food and let you off the leash as soon as Happo comes up, okay?'

He stared at me coldly. He looked awful. Though usually an Adonis, a photo model, now his hair flopped over his brow, making his two black eyes look like railway tunnels. His face was caked with salt and blood, and his nose was swollen. I could see he had slept in such discomfort his face was contorted, making him look as if he'd aged twenty years.

I called down to the decky below to put the coffee on for the skipper and me. He stomped up the ladder out on to the back deck and pissed over the stern, enabling the following wind to blow droplets on to the transom; some of them hit him on the legs.

'Oh, for crying out loud, man. Go round the side. You're going to get piss on me,' I squawked my protest.

He grunted and moved over to starboard to finish shaking the last drops off.

'Are you up to taking the wheel, mate? I'll get breakfast if you like.'

'Whatever, man. I don't give a stuff.' His voice trailed off in a forlorn whisper.

I was happy to know that our food would be made with a clean pair of hands instead of Happo's piss-soaked maulers. The coffee came up in a few minutes, and Happo slurped noisily at his mug.

I pulled Bella Boy up by his ropes and waited for him to get feeling back in his legs before jumping him over to the mast. He sat straight down on the cabin roof, letting out a loud *oomph*. The sting had gone out of his eyes, and I determined he had mellowed considerably.

'*Aspetta un momento*! Will you? My legs have gone asleep.'

His mug of coffee was leaning against a bollard on the forward deck. I released his hand ties, but his feet I left bound together. He took the mug and wrapped his hands around it as if he was cold. A few moments later, he had sipped the last of the dregs.

'You need to take a piss?' I asked.

There was a pregnant pause as he looked sternly into my eyes until finally he said, 'Yes, but keep him away from me.' Still clutching the mug, he pointed with the top of his head towards Happo on the wheel.

It was already a hot day. I allowed him to untie his legs and take his pants off. He looked at me with a terrified face. I didn't feel good about being happy to see him squirm, but I smiled and glibly assured him he'd be safe.

'You can hold your own on this one, skipper,' I chided.

After he finished, I left his legs untied and shuffled him back to the cabin roof. Tying his hands behind his back and lashing the ends to the mast, I left his pants on the deck, went below, and fished out a pair of shorts and assisted him to dress.

'Watch him, Happo. Don't touch him,' I ordered as I went below again to prepare the food.

I imagined Happo had got back his sanity, but even so I kept a watchful eye on him as I cooked a mess of scrambled eggs, bacon, beans, and rounds of toast. The galley was well equipped, and it didn't take long before we all had enough to stave off the tummy rumbles. Of course, I had to hand-feed the prisoner; I wasn't letting the murderer anywhere near him. Even if Happo didn't physically abuse him, Bella Boy might well have choked on his food with fright.

It was a long day and even longer night for me. I got absolutely no sleep. Happo, on the other hand, never left his bunk from sundown till dawn. Bella Boy had to endure his above-deck stateroom exposed to the elements on a hard surface. To make matters worse, he was tied to the mast. The current state of affairs made it uncomfortable for at least two of us. While Happo slumbered in relative luxury, I tried to console myself with the fact that at least Antonio had a blanket and a pillow. He was a twisted lump, tied up like a Sunday roast on the deck in front of me.

Here was a man with a broken face, staring bleakly out over the ocean. It was a poignant experience. This man who was supposed to be in charge of our vessel had now been turned into my prisoner. I had never been in such a powerful position as this before, and it was making me sick to my stomach that I couldn't come up with a better way to treat him. The only conciliatory approach to the situation left me no option but to change the status quo.

CHAPTER 12

Our second day after Igmas disappeared brought even warmer weather. Before the sun poked its head out of the water, the air around us felt like it was coming out of an oven. We ate a hot breakfast, bacon and eggs, but the rest of the day was crackers and cheese with anchovies and canned tomatoes. The food was not very appetising, but I'd lost interest in eating and really only made food for Belario's benefit. Conflicted, I tried to reason out the best way to handle the other two people on this boat without any of us ending up following Igmas into the drink. I couldn't think straight, too tired, being without sleep for the last forty-something hours.

Earlier on, I'd hatched a plan that might allow me to get a few more hours' kip without losing another life, especially mine. But I knew it might be half-baked given my present state of mind. Everything I could think up had a reliance on Happo staying onside. The dichotomy was to trust him, but I didn't want to tell him what I was going to do. It was going to be risky.

There were a bunch of tools under the bunk near the alcove. I pulled the door off the chain locker and ripped the timber lids from under the mattress on Ernie's bunk. Then I grabbed a handful of nails and screws and threw them into a coffee mug. Out on deck, I untied Bella Boy's legs and waist rope and led him down into the cabin. The mast was stepped through the centre of the cabin between the forward bunks. It proved to be the best place to tether the hapless skipper. At a pinch, Bella Boy could stretch out in much more comfort than where he'd previously been strapped to the mast above decks.

The new position didn't stop him complaining loudly. He started back into his story of innocence, the one he had devised in a different universe. When that didn't work, he used the argument that he was the only one who could get us back to Australia.

'I would have to untie him,' Belario moaned. 'I would have to trust him.'

That sure was not going to happen, not on my watch, but I didn't bother telling him that. Instead, I heaped two pillows around his back and gave him another drink of water before I responded to his incessant protests by frivolously pushing a rag into his mouth. He spat it out with an indignant grunt, but my action had the desired effect. He spoke not another word.

I left him smouldering while I made toasted sandwiches from frozen bread, lined them with corned beef, and topped it off with tomato sauce. I brewed another big pot of coffee and dug out a bag of peanuts in shells from the back of the pantry. I divided the fine cuisine between us with a little extra for the other deck hand.

When I brought him his meal, Happo asked, 'What's that racket going on down there? Why are you busting up the galley?'

It was going to be another long night, so I attempted to explain to my trusty shipmate how it was going to go down. He was on the defensive.

'Look, man! Don't worry, I'm not gonna throw that ding tosser overboard. It was just that other piece of shit. He was the one that was going to knock you off, man! I did us both a favour.'

It shocked me to hear my friend unapologetically talk about the foul deed he'd committed. He had obviously thought it over and came to the conclusion that he did it to protect me. Maybe he did, and maybe for me it worked out more convenient, but I did not ask him to. It was the last thing I expected to happen to the Riddler. With great restraint, I didn't argue with him; the murder was still so fresh in my mind I couldn't talk about it.

'Listen to me, Happo. I'm doing this to save all of us. This is the only way it is going to work, either you are with me or not, your choice, but remember, there is nowhere else to go. Let's just get through this, all right?' It was difficult to speak without showing my rage. I tried to cover it well but couldn't. My hands shaking and my voice half an octave above where it should have been made it obvious that I'd failed.

When he sensed my changing mood, he cast his eyes to the deck and nodded. 'Yeah, man, yer right. I'll take the wheel till three thirty in the morning or whatever. Go get some sleep, man.' He sounded sad; if a whipped dog could talk, it would sound like him.

After feeding the prisoner, taking him on deck for ablutions, and retying him inside the cabin, I got back to work. The slatted door of the yacht couldn't keep a kitten out, so I nailed my timber slabs over the doorway, locking both of us inside. What the skipper didn't realise was that I had slipped a sleeping pill into his food and drink. He was out like a light. As a precaution, in case Bella Boy got free, I set up a string line with coffee cups hanging off it between my bunk and his. It was an old cowboy trick I learned from John Wayne movies. I dug the gun down deep under my mattress but kept a hammer under my pillow and went fast to sleep.

The first thing I noticed when I roused at three and stuck my head through the gap over the top of the makeshift partition was that the long-bladed knife was not in its sheath. Happo sat dreamily behind the helm and eyed my face with indifference as if on the verge of sleep.

'You look like you need a break.'

'Yeah, man, I sure do. I just about drifted off a couple o' times. What are you going to do with skip?'

I was dismantling the barricade when I answered; he didn't like what I said.

'Fuck it, man! Why don't you believe me? I'm not gonna do anything to him. Why do I have to sleep up top?'

My response was reflected in the way I passed him his mattress. I'd had a good sleep, but I was in no mood to argue. I pushed the bulky foam block on to his lap and told him to find a comfortable spot. When he laid the mattress down behind me, I firmly asked him to move away. He gave a feeble protest as he moved up on to the roof of the cabin by the mast. The grumbling didn't stop until he settled down with a pillow and one blanket.

When he got himself comfortable, I strode over to him and, making sure the safety catch was on, raised the gun to his head and asked quietly, 'Where's the knife, Happo?'

He tried to bluff, but I saw by the look on his face he knew he'd been busted. I stiffened my arm, emphasising the barrel of the gun pointed directly at him.

'Okay! Okay! he shouted at me.

I knew he was scared. I didn't want him to be, but I was fed up and didn't want any more shit to go down. He pointed up at the mast. There was a bag made out of tarpaulin usually kept for fishing line and other odds and ends. For handy access, I'd hung it there weeks ago just under the gooseneck. I reached into the bag and retrieved the yellow-handled weapon, sheathed it, and stuck it into my belt along with the pistol.

'Get some sleep, my friend. You're back on at sunrise.'

'Friends now, are we? You just threatened to shoot me! Fuck you, man!'

'What was the knife for, arsehole?' I parried.

No answer. I let it be and went back to my watch, grappling with the unfolding tensions between the three of us, trying to figure a healthy way out of it.

As we inched our way back to Oz, the dream run we had on the way over couldn't have been more different. Fortunately, we did not get a repeat of the vicious squall that attacked us on the westward leg, but we were copping a hard-driving southeaster, which made it necessary to tack long and hard, forcing us more northwards than I would have liked.

The sea pushed in on the *Crumpet* from three different directions, which made moving around the deck uncomfortable. Happo and I found it difficult, as the yacht heeled over for miles before we'd tack and slope the other way. In these kinds of conditions, the *Crumpet* was not really a one-man operation. She was configured to require both Happo and my sets of hands, at least for a couple of hours at a time.

Bella Boy was no longer part of the equation. The sleeping tablets were running low, so I substituted the bulk of his medication with claret from the two 5-gallon jerrycans we had on board. He remained below deck, tied to the step in a catatonic don't-give-a-shit state. I didn't want to untie him, as I knew I couldn't trust what he'd do, but I was becoming more concerned about Happo. He started back on his mumbling-to-himself caper again and got progressively worse as the rough ride and broken sleep took its toll on our minds and bodies. Conversations waned to mere one or two words, and I sensed a growing animosity between us.

Sleeping arrangements had to change. Not only was it unsafe to have Happo's bed on deck; it was wet and uncomfortable. In a dangerous revamp, I let Happo sleep below while Antonio and I stayed by the wheel. I kept the prisoner's hands tied and a rope around his middle that was attached to the boat. The gun was tucked into my belt, and I made sure the knife was well out of reach. Instead of covering the hatch with boards, I tied ropes across the exit. This made it possible for me to look into the cabin in case Happo had smart alec ideas.

A change of shift meant Happo would take the wheel, and we'd revert to the old system of tying Bella Boy below. This way, I could sleep for a couple of hours. However, I didn't bother screwing the boards over the hatch again. I used the ropes to block the entry. My paranoia forced me to make sure to check Happo in case he was carrying anything that could be used as a weapon. He was livid about this intrusion, but he didn't protest aloud. He just glared at me as I patted him down, and then he went off mumbling to himself. These precautions did not make me happy, but it was too risky to leave them out.

After three days of trial by weather, we were exhausted. Interrupted short naps instead of sound sleep added to our crankiness. We didn't know what part of the Australian coast we would see first. Both of us were terribly underprepared to sail, let alone navigate our way back. It was proceed due east with fingers crossed.

It was impossible to rely on the only person on the yacht with a decent knowledge of navigation, so we pressed on, hoping the weather would settle soon. Happo's mental state was getting worse. He mumbled incessantly and would no longer make eye contact. I lost him as an ally, but what worried me more was that some of his ranting reminded me of his actions before he murdered Ernie. I sensed that either the skipper or I was in danger of attack, but I could not have predicted the insanity of Happo's actions.

It was six o'clock in the evening when I shook Happo awake and quietly ordered him to take the wheel. He looked at me strangely. I knew something was really wrong, but we had jobs to do, and it was his turn. I brought the prisoner below deck and took a long look at the deckhand. He appeared haggard and miserable. His eyes were glazed with dark rings under them.

I poured a measure of claret in a mug and offered it up to him, but as much as he loved claret, he didn't acknowledge me. I could live with the silence, but I was concerned about his state of mind, and I felt helpless to do anything about it. All I could do was rope off the hatch, stay below, and wrestle myself to sleep.

It was the witching hour. The boat turned recklessly and jolted me awake. I'd slept through my shift by almost two hours. Bella Boy was staring hard at me as I switched on the light. Fear reflected in his dark eyes. He didn't speak.

'What's going on, Happo?' I literally screamed at the empty helm as I desperately attempted to untie the ropes across the doorway.

Emerging from the lit cabin, my eyes took a while to adjust to the absolute moonless night. My torch battery was low, and with the gun in my right hand, I stumbled and fell into the hutch next to the wheel.

'Happo! Happo! For crying out loud man, where are you?' I was frantic.

He was nowhere to be found. I loosed the main, and the boat flopped to a rocking and rolling drift. Fortunately, the wind had died down a bit, but it was still strong enough to make moving around the deck in the dark very trying. Paranoia had me acting crazy. I thought he might be hiding over the side until I moved away from the entrance to the cabin so he could attack Antonio. Of course, there was no sign of him there.

I zig-zagged my way towards the bow, checking every hidey-hole I could think of. Nothing. I shone the feeble torch beam all the way up to the top of the mast. Again nothing. The front hatch was tightly secured where I'd screwed it permanently shut.

For an hour, I kept calling out over the dark water around every side of the *Crumpet*, my mind racing. Did he fall overboard on purpose or commit suicide? How long had it been since he went over? I had overslept, but the erratic movement of the boat woke me. Was that when he went over, or did the *Crumpet* actually sail smoothly by itself for a length of time? Where were we? It was dark, and there was no starlight; everything was totally blacked out. Was the darkness part of Happo's plan to leave us? I went below and told Antonio the bad news. His response took me aback.

'Good riddance to the wop bastardo!'

'Well, my friend, there's just you and me left here now. How about you suggest something constructive instead of being a shithead?' I retorted.

'I ain't your fucking friend, and he was a murdering bastardo. He wouldn't have lasted five *minutos* when we get back, just like you won't either.'

'You're not seeing the big picture here.' I was beginning to get angry with him again. 'I have no idea where we are and no clue how we will be able to sail home if we don't start working together.'

He looked at me with a supercilious grin; I was sure he was enjoying my discomfort. He disgusted me. I wanted to spit on him, but with forced restraint, I just gave him my best evil stare and yelled into his stupid face, 'Get constructive, or you can join your compadres. I've had enough of this whole shit-for-brains escapade.'

The boat flopped and banged, riding side on to the swell. I didn't tighten the main sheet or start the engine. It was difficult to motivate myself to keep going on; my soul was hurting. Happo was a friend, and because of someone's fucked-up sense of greed, he'd lost his life in his prime. It was like being in a trance as I moved to the front of the yacht and sat with my legs dangling over the bow, my head on my forearms resting on the pulpit, thinking.

One of my schemes would be to simply sail with the wind as far east as I could, jettison the contraband, and stay on the radio till someone picked me up. The problem with that was what to do with the skipper.

Exhaustion and mental stress were not the best way to formulate options if one wanted them to succeed. At that time, I convinced myself that I didn't have anything left in me to figure out a positive solution.

Bella Boy was obviously out of control. If I untied him, it would be only a matter of time before I joined Ernie. A worse fate would be when we arrived home and the skipper told the bosses his version of the story. There was no way this man would come onside. I flashed on the gun in my belt and a crazy thought crossed my mind. If I shot him, it would solve a host of problems. Fortunately, I recognised madness immediately and perished the thought.

I grimaced at my own stupidity and went on searching for solutions. *Easier said than done,* I thought. When you watch people getting shot on television and they deserve it, you cheer for the good guys. In real life, I could not murder Antonio even though he would probably kill me if he got half a chance. My dilemma was how to keep us both alive until we reached land. My hours on the helm had me thinking of a few alternative plans, but most of them were half-baked, and none of them included murder.

One thing in my favour was the fact that the bosses did not know my real name. I used to turn up every season and ask for work on the cray boats. I'd collect thousands of dollars in cash at the end of each season and put my moniker in the pay-book: a scribbled J. Christos. Incredibly, no one ever asked me for proof of identity for the money. Most of the men I worked with called me either Geronimo or Jesus Christ. Nobody except for Cuda seemed quite sure which hippy was which. They knew I lived in the eastern states but didn't have a clue what state. If we made it back to Australia, I could lose Bella Boy somewhere up north and simply disappear into the landscape.

With a bit of luck, the skipper might get caught for drug smuggling. If that happened, I was pretty sure he wouldn't talk to the police, especially about a murder and a loss of life. The bones of a plan started to form in my exhausted mind, and there was still time to etch out the details before my shipmate and I came to blows. Broken sleep on the bow gave me sore arms and no solutions.

Daylight brought a day hotter than any other since we began the voyage, and the sea was calm and glassy. The weather had opened a wide clear space all the way to the horizon, making perfect conditions to look for a man in the water. I wanted to search for Happo but had no idea where or when he left the yacht. My pathetic plan involved a half-hearted circle covering about twenty miles. All the while I scanned the sea through binoculars, I was forced to listen to Belario cursing for wasting his time. Happo was gone forever. With a heavy heart, I accepted his fate and resolved to move on. I was mad at Happo for leaving but would always remember him as a good friend.

CHAPTER 13

A couple of days went by without a word between Bella Boy and me. The weather stayed fair, and I spotted a school of tuna. I resurrected a braided nylon trawl line from the tackle box and, in less than ten minutes of trawling, hauled in a fish weighing in excess of thirty-kilos. When I gutted it and threw the scraps into the water, the school came within inches of our boat. Some of the fish swimming by were twice the size of the one I brought on board. I was sure Bella Boy enjoyed the fresh meal as much as me, but he didn't remark on it. He didn't even offer a thank you or a *grazie*. Ungrateful bastard. The tuna steaks were probably the fondest memories of the entire homeward journey, but I didn't have long to savour the moment.

A couple of weeks before April began, the *Crumpet*'s position was far enough north to be affected by the last month of the monsoon season. We had to have been a long way from where I thought we were when we encountered the rains. Swirling clouds from the south-east changed their hue from light-grey wispy steam to menacing dark sacks. As far as I could see on the southern horizon, the sky was a deep, dark, blue-grey full of pregnant clouds. When the clouds broke, it didn't rain; it dumped water like an upturned pail. The bursting clouds saturated the· sails and flooded across the deck. I managed to collect bucketfuls and pour into our freshwater tanks, which were desperately low. With the sails flapping during the rainstorm, we didn't go forward much; we just bobbed around under the torrential downpour. Water poured down through the hatch into the cabin and ran in under the bilge boards.

I knew how to activate the bilge pumps with a flick of the switch. But what I didn't register at the time was that monsoon rain was generally associated with heat rising up off the land and sucking the cooler ocean air into its place. Had I been more experienced, I might have realised we were in tropical waters and guessed we were getting closer to land. I might have been a lot more careful to look out for dangerous reefs. I was preoccupied with filling the freshwater tank and feeling pleased with myself for thinking of it. The rain started to ease off, and the hissing noise of the hosing rain quieted for the first time in three hours. Then I heard it!

The sound of breaking surf had always been a comfort to me. I had often pondered the fact that I could not happily live inland away from the sound of the sea; it was in my DNA. However, the roar I could hear now was extremely disturbing. It was close, and it was very loud. The booming breakers were only a couple of hundred yards from us, and I could see the spray shooting off the back of them.

In a mild panic, I raced to the helm, punched the starter switch, and pushed the throttle forward. In my haste, I'd given the stick too much fuel, and the motor did not respond. The jib and the main were flogging. I pulled the main sheet taut and swung the wheel to force the *Crumpet* to swing into the offshore wind. She responded and crept slowly away from the boat-eating rocks. The few seconds it took to get underway had pulled us to within forty or fifty yards of the danger.

Finally, the engine burbled into life. I loosed the main sheet, and we motored back out to sea. When I got to where I thought was a safe distance, I untied Antonio and demanded he grab the wheel and get us safely to land. Neither of us had any idea where we were. Any charts on board would only be helpful if we could see familiar landmarks. We had to proceed, relying on the echo sounder and a sharp eye.

Antonio began cursing me for almost getting him killed, but fortunately, most of his cursing was in his first language, so it had the same effect as water on a duck's back, which was no effect at all. From our new vantage, we could not see a break in the reef, so Bella Boy headed south. While he drove, I stood by the mast on the cabin roof, keeping a watchful eye on him as well as the reef.

The skipper was not his normal smug self. He'd been tied up and on sleeping pills and claret for a number of days. His black eyes had turned from purple to a yellowish brown, and his nose could have doubled for a thug in a *Phantom* comic. I sensed he was out of his depth on this mission, but he was doing a far better job than I could.

Half an hour after our near disaster, we saw a large black rock protruding from the submerged reef, and to the south end of it, the water was calm. Bella Boy aimed for the channel, and we motored through without incident. The rain was keeping us wet without the severity of its earlier pounding. After a couple of miles inside the reef, we motored into a giant glassy pool with no wind at all. The jib was flapping and useless. Keeping tension on one of the sheets to make sure it wrapped tight, I fixed the problem with a couple of extra winds on the furler. With the sheets wrapped around the sail and the furling line cleated, it wasn't going anywhere.

The sun was sinking fast behind us. In front of us in the distance, I could see a haze normally associated with heat rising from dry land.

'This reef must be a long way out,' I yelled to the skipper.

His response was curt and abusive, and I yelled abuse back at the miserable bastard. Our tolerance for each other had turned to shit. Our situation was dire. We should have been working together to get this yacht to shore, but we were far from that scene. We were smuggling a cargo that could land us in gaol for the rest of our lives, and the arsehole on the wheel persisted in carrying on like a wanker.

I couldn't wait to hit land. I'd be off before he could say Jack Robinson. At that point, I couldn't care less about this whole stupid undertaking, and my mind was set to abandon it the first chance I got. Then the fickle finger of fate stuck its pointy nail into my box of plans.

Our yacht, loaded to the gills with contraband, was heading east under motor at around eight and a half knots. The sea was a postcard of calm glassy water, not even a ripple, when the *Crumpet* hit something. I discovered later that it was a sunken ship, or more accurately the steel superstructure of a sunken ship. The submerged spire became a scalpel and gouged a trench through the hull alongside the *Crumpet*'s keel from bow to stern, gutting it like a fish. It literally slashed the expensive craft into jagged halves. The ballast in the keel pulled down at a critical angle until the whole bottom snapped off and sank.

I jumped to the starboard side as the other half stayed together only by a thin skin of the cabin roof. The weight and buoyancy of the loaded side panels stretched apart and threatened to rip the vessel completely in two. As the engine sank to the bottom, the mast toppled to port with a gigantic crash, leaving me on one side and Bella Boy opposite.

Miraculously, the airtight panels holding the illegal cargo kept the halves afloat. The pulpit was still intact on the bow and helped to keep the sections from separating completely. I saw Bella Boy grab the side rail as the mast came down on him. It didn't look like it hit him fair and square, but it had enough force to push him under the water. I dived in and swam over to where he went down. He was only a foot or two below the water line, but he couldn't move as his arm was tangled in a sheet up to his shoulder.

The pistol fell out of my belt as I dived in, but I still had the knife. It came out of the sheath and was sharp enough to cut the rope with a few quick thrusts. I grabbed the skipper and pulled him up to air, where he clung to the floating mast, gasping.

In a spluttering voice, he continued pricking it out, so I thought, Fuck *this, mate. You are on your fucking own, you thankless bastard!*

Losing all patience, I swam to the other half of the floating wreck, determined to get away from him as far and as fast as I could.

We sat on our respective sections of flotsam, looking like spoiled brats who didn't get enough cake at a birthday party. I certainly didn't give a thought to how we were going to get to shore or where the shore was for that matter. For the hour or so that passed by, I had lost the plot. The rain had stopped completely, but the sun would only give us another half hour of light at most.

We weren't moving. We were anchored to something. I dived under and saw how the mast had snagged on a huge conning tower of what looked like a big old battleship. Coming up, I deduced that the tide was running out, and I decided that we were better off anchored until it turned back towards Australia. I made several dives to see what I could salvage to propel us to shore. We had plenty of material from our wreck, so I cut some sailcloth and rope and brought it to *my* half. In the mood I was in, I determined not to do anything more for Belario. I was becoming the same sort of arsehole he was, only this time I was satisfied to be acting this way.

The next morning, I felt that a night clinging to a rolling piece of flotsam was one of the all-time shittiest experiences I'd ever had. It was premature thinking on my part. The new day dawned, and things went from bad to worse. Before the sun rose, the ocean was pastel pink and turning bright yellow as Sol made his entrance.

At approximately eight o'clock, I judged the temperature to be seventy degrees; it was shaping up to be a scorcher! The skipper didn't look right. He had folded himself into a piece of sail so he wouldn't fall off, but he wasn't moving. Even when the sun blasted us from its eleven o'clock position, Bella Boy remained motionless.

I had to check on him; it's who I am. I've worked with wankers in close quarters for years and always found a way to get through it.

God help me, I thought, *he might be dying. I better check.* So in the water I went again.

Physically, he seemed okay, although he appeared to be suffering mentally far more than I could have guessed. He was sobbing quietly inside his cocoon sail. I tried to talk to him, but it was as if I wasn't even there. I shook him by the shoulder and reassured him we were going to be okay. When he did not respond, not even to give me a hard time, I knew it was serious. But it was more than not hearing me; he was somewhere else in his mind. I had that sickening feeling again, like I was responsible for the poor sap's safety.

For the next hour and a half, I kept diving under the wreck trying to find anything to help us. I brought up a jar of green olives, a gallon of tomato sauce, and some string to tie the knife sheath on to my shorts.

I was also able to salvage a piece of board to make a crude paddle. The guts had fallen out of the yacht; the incision made sure of that.

We were left with no food and no water. And bugger all chances of rowing the pieces of fibreglass for who knows how many miles to shore. On top of all that, the only other human in the world with me had gone insane. What do they say? Life sucks, and then you die!

On some of my freedives, I made sure to check the snag that was the only thing keeping us in the same place. I could see that its grip was weakening and was not sure how long we would be held here. I had to come up with something soon, or we could be a couple of skeletons washed up back in Africa.

Do I believe in God? Unequivocally! What happened to us perched somewhere in the middle of a giant stretch of water had a scientific explanation, sure, but it defied belief that it happened at exactly the right moment.

I kept thinking that I would dive down and cut the snag when the tide began to come in. I had no idea if the cumbersome hulk of the riven yacht would drift with the tide, no idea if I would be able to paddle tons of jagged, broken junk the distance we needed to get to dry land. There was nothing to do but try.

I wanted to get Bella Boy on to my side of the wreck and make sure he wouldn't slide off or try to drown me. So my first job was to wrestle a piece of flat steel off the Riddler's smashed bunk. Working underwater and with great difficulty, I used the tool to loosen the metal rails holding the two pieces of our boat together.

Before shifting the skipper, I temporarily lashed the two halves of the *Crumpet* to each other to make sure they didn't separate prematurely. Next, I bashed a bigger hole through the scupper that was about a foot underwater, then threaded the rope and lapped it over the smooth shell.

When I swam over to him, the skipper looked like he was in a trance. His eyes were wide open, but the expression on his face reminded me of a wooden doll. I asked him to come over. No response. When I rolled him towards the mast, there was no resistance. I understood that he was in shock, but I was totally fed up with him. He had been a pain in the butt since he and Ernesto had attempted to murder me, and it did run through my mind to leave him and strike out on my own.

It was probably just as well that he lay there like a limp dick and let me manhandle him over to my side. He was wrapped in a part of the sail I'd cut off for him, and I heaved him up on to the top of our wreck and put a loop of rope around him. The tide was now turning, and it was getting close to zero hour. I readied to cut the snag.

So this was where the God part came into the equation. The direction of current slewed the hulk around, and she popped off the snag and started moving eastward. I unhitched the rope, loosening the port side of our wreck, and we moved even faster. Then as if on cue, an onshore wind stiffened. It was hard to believe, but it was aiding our progress, moving us as if by a giant hand.

I looked skyward and whispered, 'Thank you.'

Bella Boy didn't protest when I ripped the sail away from him and raised it over my salvaged piece of wood. It helped a little more. We were on our way. The tide, the wind, and the junky sail proved to be a lifesaver. My only wish was for Bella Boy to help me hold the canvas against the wind. After an hour, my arms and back were aching from the strain, and I had to rest. With no sail, I could feel our progress slow a little, which made me angrier towards the dummy lying next to me.

PART III

ALICE AND THE BLUE DUCK

CHAPTER 14

It was the advent of the Age of Aquarius, the blossoming of the psychedelic age of peace and love, when a young Alice Bergstrom started conducting her first business venture. Responding to the tastes of the era, her handmade crocheted flowers leapt off the shelves. Then it wasn't too long before she branched out into costume jewellery and her working hours protracted well into the nights to keep up with demand. Most of her products were based on cottage craft, so when she got an idea from a casual boyfriend from Phoenix to make berets, she produced a new line of her own versions with flair and dazzle to market them with a tasteful sales campaign.

A simple scrap of leather with two holes punched through and a stick made an excellent hair clip for long-haired girls as well as some of the new generation of boys. The hairclips sold well, but when Alice hand-carved her unique designs into them and called them bergy berets, or bee bees, for short, the sales went ballistic. The hippies loved them as much as anyone, and she posted them to customers, friends, and their families all over the United States. Pretty soon, she was forced to hire helpers to produce enough bee bees to fill orders from large department stores. The west coast hippies tried to copy her designs, but the Californians in particular never let up ordering from her workshop in New York. The business rocketed along until she had enough funds to rent a small space, turn it into a factory, and hire piece workers. She was young, talented, and very like her father in innovation and marketing.

When Alice was a small child, her father started a middleman enterprise involving shipping space and export goods. Such a simple plan in itself turned the smooth-talking, hard-working father into a virtual overnight success. Money rolled into their family business by the millions like magic. What' was more, the entrepreneurial magic seemed to have rubbed off on Alice even as a teenager.

In a completely different vein of business from her father's, she amassed for herself considerable sums of money in a few short years. But Alice was restless. A constant niggling inner voice kept fuelling her desire to visit exotic parts of the world before the biological alarm clock chimed. Thoughts of growing a family and settling down had been inflicted on her from a young age by her mother, but that only made her more determined to break out of her parents' so-called normal view of the world. Every day, she felt like a prisoner, watching her friends and family glued into the older generation's rationale.

Finally, the wanderlust overcame her, forcing her to work long, hard hours and organise an escape from New York. Her first big move slid her from costume trinkets and cottage craft into the world of fashionable jewellery. She began dealing with the New York Jewish diamond sellers.

She placed her younger brother Lazarus into a management role and created a myriad of upmarket designs for the jewellery that would take their products to a higher-end market. The plan was boosted along when she was put in touch with a savvy diamantaire and a precious metal supplier to ensure product quality. The business came together so freakishly fast that she often mused about it falling into place by divine intervention. In truth, it had nothing to do with that.

Aaron Bachman was a business associate of Alice's father. Many years before, the very wealthy Mr Bachman began buying Bergstrom shipping space. In fact, it was Aaron Bachman who had given Mr Bergstrom the first financial kick along, from which he never looked back. The bond between the two businessmen tightened, and they became regular visitors to each other's homes and solid family friends.

Mr Bachman was very impressed by Alice's business acumen. He began hatching a scheme that he believed would benefit both of their families' financial futures. In his estimation of the Bergstroms, Bachman took it upon himself to give Alice the privilege of seeing his son Joel with a view to marriage. He figured that he could tantalise her into a spousal agreement by connecting Alice to New York's elite gem and metal suppliers.

Mr Bachman's presumptions had the exact opposite effect on the young businesswoman. Bachman's attempt to coerce her into an arranged marriage pulled the trigger on Alice's shot to get the heck outta Dodge. Within a few short months of Mr Bachman's outrageous offer, she booked a flight and simply flew away from her business, her family, and her country. Her first trip was to that strange place in the world they called the Land Down Under.

Alice arrived in Sydney in time to escape a particularly bitter New York winter. She saw more of that foreign land than many Australians ever will. On a whim, reflecting the Age of Aquarius, she decided she would call herself Aster 'Bee' (for Bergstrom) Nightingale. It seemed like the hippy thing to do. After all, she thought, it did have a nicer ring to it than *rainbow* or *sunflower*.

When the southern climes of Oz started cooling near the beginning of the Australian fall, which they called autumn, she figured it was time to move on. Packing her considerable belongings into a giant knapsack, she left the city of Adelaide and hitchhiked north up the centre track.

Arriving in Darwin, Aster Bee stayed at a youth hostel just outside the city. After a good look around, she toyed with a strategy to hitch into town and look for a boat to Timor or Indonesia; she wasn't fussy as long as she was travelling. However, the first lift she got changed any plans she had of leaving Australia any time soon.

Standing beside her giant backpack in the shade of a pandanus, she looked like a fashion model on a photo shoot—tall, athletic, tanned, and scantily dressed for the heat. George could not pull up quick enough to give this girl a lift. The air brakes on his vehicle hissed as he came to a halt only twenty yards ahead of Alice. She left her pack where it lay by the road and strolled casually to the door.

The vehicle looked like something out of a comic book. It resembled a big blue bus on steroids. The big blue monster was high off the ground, with all-terrain knobbly tyres. The passenger door puffed open, exposing steps going up to the driver's compartment, which was about six feet off the road. George looked down from his driver's seat. 'How far you going?' he asked.

She looked at him hard, studying him like a bug in a bottle. After a very long pause, she responded politely, 'How far are *you* going?'

George had never before picked up a hitchhiker. He never really chose options that could be risky, so this would be a first for him. He was a trust funder from old money family. He had so far lived a sheltered life in school and university, never really leaving the study desk or the classroom. He possessed not one ounce of street smart. Picking up strangers was something other people did, not him.

George was quite literally at a loss to answer. It wasn't an easy question for him either, because he had no idea how far he *was* going. His lifetime of studies had turned him into a physicist with degrees in mechanical and chemical engineering, and he was a patented inventor.

George had his own laboratory, but he also lectured as a professor of physics at a university in Victoria. For the past year and a half, he received handsome payments for some extracurricular consultancy work. The Asia Pacific Agency for Nuclear Energy (APANE) relied on his expertise and often called on him to mentor specialist workers as well as contributing expert advice to their programmes.

Becoming overburdened with work, and after much planning, he decided to take a sabbatical. He set out to fund his own field trip and follow his two other passions, entomology and ornithology.

Through his affiliation with the university, the government had graciously granted him permits to carry two barrels of ethyl alcohol for the purpose of pickling bird skins and collecting insect specimens. He expected to find many new species and hoped to finish a thesis before the beginning of next year's first semester.

'Well, er, you see, miss, I—' He was trying to give the shortest answer he could think of, but she interrupted.

'Okay, I'll just get my pack.' She smiled up at him.

Alice always thought of herself as a good judge of character, and she deduced that George would not give her too much grief on the short journey to the city. As she got back to the vehicle, George was standing on the ground by the rear of the big blue monster.

'You can put that up here,' he said, and he pointed to the luggage hatch high up on the side of the bus.

It was only then that Aster noticed that the bus had a propeller and a rudder neatly tucked in under its rear behind the wheels.

'No way!' she exclaimed. 'This stays with me, buddy!'

'But, er, but . . .' he stammered. 'There's not a lot of room, er . . .'

Too late! Alice had heaved her pack up through the front door and was already inside the bus, dragging her huge load up the aisle. She had noticed a motorcycle tied to the roof. How it got up there surprised her almost as much as the propeller, but that was nothing compared to the interior of the vehicle.

A twin passenger seat behind the driver's compartment was semi-normal bus decor. Behind the seat was a floor-to-ceiling set of shelves crammed with glass jars, all of which wore labels, but only a few had residents: creepy, crawly things such as Alice had never seen the like before. Their tiny corpses were looking out at her through clear liquid. Next to the shelves was a table topped with a typewriter and an open box filled with notes. The chair had wheels like a regular office chair, but it was bound to the desk with an occy strap. On the far side of a bed was a bookcase jam-packed with all kinds of weird science magazines and books, books which appeared to her as something she would never ever attempt to read. The manuals and the glass jars prompted the girl to ask.

'What are you, George?'

He faltered in answer again. He wasn't normally a person who stammered, but George found this girl so disarming. Not only was her beauty distracting, but also she had an air of confidence and spoke with an accent, which George found intriguing although curiously difficult to respond to. The more he tried to compose himself, the sillier he felt. He blurted out his profession and his intention to travel into unchartered insect territory to seek out insects never before seen.

To the American, it sounded like the introduction to a *Star Trek* serial, and she smiled. The bus driver tried to tone it down and relax, and when he saw her smiling, he stopped talking and broke into laughter.

'Yeah, I know. A bit weird, eh? But I love what I do, and this is going to be a wonderful experience for me,' he blurted through a huge grin.

'No, honestly, I don't think it's weird at all,' she replied openly. 'As a matter of fact, I think it's fantastic! Well, maybe, I mean, I wouldn't go searching for bugs, but I have to say I made getaway decisions under very similar circumstances to end up where I am now.'

She pushed her heavy pack along the centre aisle, moved an esky off the seat to the floor, and sat down. By the time they got to the city centre, they had struck up an easy conversation. This led to a mutual decision to have a pre-lunch drink. After a couple of wines lasting the entire afternoon, their relationship rolled along to a dinner date. As they dined and chatted, George couldn't believe he had invited this total stranger to stay the night in his unusual accommodation, but when she accepted, he was rapt.

After all, it was the Age of Aquarius. Aster Bee was a hippy chick. George was smitten from the first second he saw her. The next morning, George woke with a Cheshire grin, feeling on an incredible high. Alice woke extremely hung-over and feeling a tiny tinge of guilt from last night's memory. When they discussed Alice's thoughts about her linking up for a part of the trip around the north-west coast, George leapt at the opportunity. He would have taken her anywhere after their first night together. He started moving his goods and chattels around inside the bus to make room for his new friend and travel companion.

CHAPTER 15

The pair spent two days in Darwin, exploring. George bought tickets to a crocodile farm, which he thought might please the American's touristic pursuits, but she didn't display as much enthusiasm as he had predicted. He had intended to go out to Kakadu and camp for a few days, but Alice had presumed he was heading west. So he did, to please her.

They didn't have to, but they stuck mostly to major roads until the map suggested an interesting detour to the coast. The all-terrain machine forded rivers and drove across axle-deep streams and terrifyingly rocky tracks. Being amphibious, the vehicle took them along creeks and out into the sea, enabling them to bypass cliffs and thick jungle.

On occasions, George unloaded the motorbike and disappeared along trails to check out the terrain and search for rare insects. Most times, he'd come back very excited to tell Alice about an array of *uncatalogued* bugs he'd discovered. He would carefully place the samples in jars or press them into paper and click away on the typewriter, filling pages of report notes. He would carefully explain the different characteristics of the specimens, but she didn't get it. Politely, she feigned enthusiasm with some pretty bad acting.

Alice wrote too. Most days, she used the late-afternoon sun to update her journal. Her entries of the places she went and the wonderful sites she witnessed humbled her. She couldn't believe the opportunity George had allowed her. This was the trip of a lifetime. She wrote over five pages just on the spectacular vehicle they were travelling in, which she affectionately nicknamed the Blue Duck.

George told her that he had designed and built it himself from the ground up. The design, he said, was loosely based on a military vehicle, with modifications far exceeding the proficiency of army models. He told her that he initially intended to sell his patent to the Australian Armed Forces but wanted to trial it first to sort out any unforeseen problems.

It was constructed mostly of bimetals, most of which were of his own invention. The strong outer skin was similar to aluminium, with strategic carbon fibre bracings. He also designed and constructed large rubberised fuel and water tanks that made it lighter than its military counterpart. Its unique design was a key factor in giving it capabilities to drive on land for 600 miles and cruise on water up to 200.

George, she wrote, was a remarkable man, the cleverest man she had ever met, adept at creating amazing inventions like the bus, with its unique electrical systems and a davit to hoist heavy objects on to the roof. His orienteering skills and hunting ability, gleaned only from textbooks, came to him naturally even without practical experience. It gave her confidence in trusting him to get her back hale and healthy from the remote region in which they'd immersed themselves. Plus, he consoled her fears about survival with such facts as having enough food and water to keep them going for forty days if they needed to.

They were enjoying the sheer adventure of 'going where no man had gone before'. All of the bays, beaches, streams, and forests were stunning, but it wasn't until they had been on the road and the waterways for eight days that they discovered their version of Shangri-La.

The Blue Duck bumped and rattled along a rough track before descending a steep incline. The vehicle groaned over the potholed and rocky slope, and the brakes hissed and wheezed until they reached the flat. A trail twisted through a tropical forest of tall trees and thick undergrowth. Alice was amazed at the beautiful displays of flowers, birds, and animals. She thought this part of Australia was supposed to be mainly desert, but this terrain was a tropical paradise.

When they got back to the ocean again, Alice literally ran out of the bus, stripping off her clothes. She bolted across the white sandy beach and splashed into the crystal-clear water, completely nude. George was a lot more cautious, checking for crocodiles or other imminent dangers. He even locked the front doors of the Blue Duck before heading down to the sand to survey the water around Aster Bee Nightingale.

Several days went by before the pair settled comfortably into their newfound paradise. They set up a cosy campsite near a freshwater stream tumbling past them just thirty yards away. George strung up a hammock between two trees by the bus doors. A bountiful supply of fish, prawns, and crabs almost jumping out of the sea into their pan added another dimension to the tranquil setting. It truly was a wonderful spot on the map.

George proved to be a genius at finding and preparing bush tucker. Residing at Club Shangri-La was the first time Aster had eaten wild goose, and she found it to be delicious. The scientist showed his skill at snaring fish with a homemade trap that impressed Alice enough to write a page and a half on just how he did it.

The day before they found Shangri-La, they left the Blue Duck in the bush and rode the motorbike forty miles to a general store in the middle of nowhere. It was not the era of good wine in Australia, so they purchased cans of beer and topped up essentials such as soap, sugar, tea, and canned food. Alice loaded most things into the saddlebags and stuffed some into her backpack.

The American liked George a lot, but he was a little eccentric and far too set in his ways for her to form a long-term intimacy with, and she guessed she would be moving on some day in the not-too-distant future. George, on the other hand, was smitten to the core by this girl. She was smart, charming, self-reliant, energetic, and a good conversationalist with a gorgeous smile that melted his heart. Their time together was fantastic.

The adventure of sharing walks through the rainforest, swimming in the cool and clear ocean, and hiking to the top of their favourite rocky ridge with a view for miles in all directions was a marvellous experience. From the ridge, they could look down over their little patch of paradise, where the spaced-out-looking big blue vehicle sat shining up at them. To Aster, she felt the experience was straight out of a storybook.

It was closing on the last month or so of monsoon season, and the weather had switched to wet over the last two days. This was a wet like Alice had never before experienced. Rain fell in sheets and pounded the ground like large rubber mallets. The nearby stream raged and grumbled down its gully like a wild animal sending a muddy brown runway into the clear blue ocean. The broad-leafed trees bent under the weight of the torrential downpour in postures of submission. It kept pouring for ages until, almost as suddenly as it started, the rain stopped.

The two of them huddled inside the bus for the best part of a day and two nights until a bright clear morning drew them out into the cleansed air like a magnet. They were used to wandering around the campsite without shoes. The sunny day after the soaking, they ambled to the water's edge to paddle in the murky brine. Within a minute, George let out a painful scream and hopped to the shore. Alice grabbed his arm and assisted him out of the water and up on to the sand.

'What is it, George? What's wrong?'

George's face was contorted in an expression of absolute agony.

'I don't know, I trod on something. It stung me. I think it's maybe a stone fish or a cone snail.' His face was pale, and tears were filling his eyes as he twisted his hands around his ankle.

Alice helped him to stand and limp back from the beach to plonk heavily into a camp chair by the bus door. She retrieved a tourniquet from the medical kit and fastened it to George's leg above the knee.

The scientist was looking dazed and in extreme pain, and Alice's heart was pounding as she lifted his foot to look at the wound. There was a small incision consistent with the harpoon puncture of the infamous cone snail, but George expounded other possibilities.

'It could be a stonefish or irukandji or a sea snake or . . . Whatever it is, it hurts like hell,' he blustered.

Sweat droplets oozed from his forehead; he was rapidly going into shock. His breathing became shallow, his face drained as pale as a sheet, and he grimaced when Alice gently touched the bottom of his foot.

'We've got to get you to a hospital!' cried Alice.

'You're joking,' whimpered George with a half-smile at her gorgeous, concerned face. 'Wash the wound thoroughly and bring me the med kit.' His voice came out in a whisper.

By this time, Alice was frantic. She had read all the material on Australian critters that could kill you in a heartbeat, and she was well aware that the cone snail was highly ranked on the scale of lethal creatures. There was no radio, and the nearest civilisation they knew about could be a hundred miles inland over rough ground. Unfortunately, they were simple storekeepers as isolated as themselves. He needed a hospital fast.

She looked down into his face with no clue how to help. George was ransacking the medical box until he retrieved a bottle of peroxide, a jar of black ointment, a tiny phial, and a hypodermic syringe.

'Here,' he cried. 'Put this on the wound. Let it bubble, then wipe it clean, and apply this.' He held up the black ointment and went on. 'Then wrap it with this bandage.'

He pushed the articles into Alice's hands. She grabbed the tourniquet and wrenched it tight around his leg. He loaded the needle and jabbed it roughly into his thigh. His breath came in short sharp bursts as if losing control of his lungs. He had stopped sweating, but his face remained pale, and his eyes glazed. Without warning, he fell unconscious, and Alice's chest rose in a swell of panic. She patted his cheek but couldn't rouse him. She draped a wet towel across his forehead and whispered a quiet prayer.

George's coma lasted two days, and Alice, to her credit, kept him as comfortable as she could. She had no alternative; they were so far from anywhere, and she was a stranger well out of depth in a foreign land. The professor had done all the navigating, and she had no clue where they were. To add to her dilemma, she had never driven a car, let alone a monster like the Blue Duck.

The young woman somehow managed to wrestle George's large frame into the cabin, using the hoist. It was a tough job getting him through the rear door and on to the bed. She stripped off his clothes and washed him down with fresh cool water from the bus tank. She tried forcing water into his mouth, but he could not swallow, so she kept refreshing the cool wet towel on his forehead and maintained a close vigil.

Around twilight on day 2, he rallied. His eyes opened slightly, and he peered into her beautiful face through slits. She forced a smile with a tear in her eye and saw the recognition in his face. She sighed with relief that he was coming around; he had beaten the poisonous barb, and it looked like they were going to be okay.

At that point in time, Aster had no idea of the life-changing events that would take place over the next couple of weeks. George's eyes gradually gained focus. His skin was becoming clear and healthy, but something in his demeanour seemed different to the girl.

He didn't talk much, and when he did, his speech came out slightly slurred, and he found it difficult to walk unassisted. He appeared confused and anxious. Although Aster helped him to the toilet, he missed his timing twice, and she had to clean up the mess. In a slight panic, Aster kept offering to attempt to drive out of Shangri-La and get him to a hospital, but he refused to leave.

'I'll be okay in a day or two, I promise. I'm sorry to have to rely on you like this, Aster, but you wait. I will be all right,' he drawled.

He seemed so positive, and although Alice didn't relish being a nursemaid, she proved herself more than adequate in the role. She could see George was trying hard to organise himself but wondered what had happened to his mind and body after being poisoned by an innocuous-looking seashell. The American felt a long way from home; she was way over her head in the wilderness, caring for a man she had not long known who looked at times like he might not survive this expedition.

CHAPTER 16

Mid morning on the fifth day after the shell attack, Aster decided on the spur of the moment to take a long walk. She hoped the outing would help her de-stress and think of a way she could convince George to seek medical assistance. She slipped on her hiking boots, blue hot pants, and a white cotton top. The weather was too hot for a bra, so she left that sitting on the top of her pack. Then while checking her reflection in the bus window, she tied a brightly coloured bandana around her head.

Next she packed a small shoulder bag with a light jacket, her pocket camera, some wafer biscuits, sultanas and nuts, and some insect repellent. Around her waist, she wore a belt with a water canister and a bum pouch with a penknife, matches, and some sheets of toilet paper.

She had made a light snack for George, but he didn't eat anything. She left him some biscuits, water, and dried fruit next to his bed and told him she'd be back around dusk. It was a beautiful afternoon when she set out along a well-beaten animal track that ran horizontal to the beach. Not far along, the path rose over the headland, where the couple had previously spent many hours looking out over a picture-postcard bay.

The view relaxed her, but she only stopped for a minute, distracted by two brightly coloured parrots arguing in the trees above her head. On the other side of the second headland, the terrain dropped down on to a low mudflat practically level with the sea. The ground was soggy and sandy, with reed grass and a few young saplings trying desperately to match the height of the forest trees about twenty yards away to the east.

George had forewarned her about low ground with access to the sea. 'Watch out for crocodiles in these areas. They blend in with the undergrowth and lie in wait.' His serious tone impacted the girl well as she walked on, fully alert for any type of bushwhacker.

Coming up to some rocky ground with overgrown jungle, Alice decided to head on to the sandy beach instead of going inland. Just off the shore, she could see fish making swirls on the surface of the mirror-like ocean and sea birds diving at them in a feeding frenzy. The sun floodlit the scene and made the water sparkle like a vision, contrasting against the verdant jungle.

Alice began to feel more relaxed. The beautiful backdrop of this place took her mind off the terrible event she was going through with George. Pretty soon she got so absorbed in her surroundings that she had covered a mile or more of sandy beaches and pristine forest without one stressful thought.

On previous treks together, apart from their scenic lookout on the south headland near their camp, the two adventurers had always ventured north. It seemed an unconscious decision to head south now, but she was glad she did. Animal tracks made the going easier over the headlands, which stood like sentinels at each end of the beaches with milk-white sand. The coastland curved around a huge bay, chewed out in its middle by a magical inlet. The terrain dipped slightly, and Alice followed a path about seventy-five feet above the waterline. The ocean was glassy and bright blue, but the inlet, mirror-like, was dark green. The sun had now entered the western sky and made the water in the lagoon appear as dark opal.

Alice focused on her footholds as she descended the precarious slope down to the water. She noticed that to the south of the inlet was a shroud of mangrove trees. Then out of the corner of her eye, she caught a glimpse of a shiny white object. It lay just outside the mouth of the lagoon. She stopped dead and strained her eyes to make out what it might be. Reeds obscured part of it, and as she inched her way forward, it fell out of view behind the grassy barrier of the waterway.

Even at a mere twenty yards away she still couldn't determine what it might be. She thought maybe it was the broken shell of a caravan or a boat. As she got closer, it became apparent that it was a large white panel with a piece of rope strapped across its girth. It gleamed in the sunlight, and she was now positive it belonged to a boat, possibly a yacht. Still very aware of the crocodile threat, Alice carefully approached the wall of reeds. Quietly, she parted them to find out exactly what this white thing could be. Not ten feet away, floating in shallow water, she was shocked to see what lay before her.

The American tourist stood agape, looking down at a broken section of a boat over thirty feet long and almost as broad as the blue bus. It humped and bumped against the water's edge with the gentle movement of the incoming tide. Lying across the panel was a body. The body's navy-blue shirt was torn across the back and hung down over the top of a pair of ragged denim shorts.

It was a man with golden-brown, shoulder-length hair and a beard, but Alice could only see a little bit of the side of his face. Through the holes in his shirt, she noted that his back was blistered and red from sunburn, and his hair was caked with dried salt. She could not see any movement from his breathing, and she hoped upon hope that he was not dead.

She broke off a branch from a driftwood tree on the shoreline and prodded the body gently. Her voice was only a whisper as she said, 'Hello, can you hear me?'

She expected no response and began to think about what she was going to do to ensure the body wouldn't become a crocodile's dinner. When the fingers twitched, Alice dropped the stick and jumped backwards three feet and let out a 'Whaaa!'

She checked the area for any sign of animal ambush and stepped into the water to pull the frame of the raft closer to the bank. It didn't budge an inch.

She touched the man's shoulder and asked again, 'Hello? Can you hear me? Wake up.'

He groaned weakly, acknowledging her question.

She kept on. 'We have to get away from the water's edge. It's dangerous here. Can you move?'

The man lifted his head slowly. He was a lot younger than Aster first thought. His dishevelled appearance from the back made him look like an old man. His face was contorted and burnt, but his eyes were clear and vital. His voice cut in on her thoughts.

'Water?' he whispered. 'Do you have any water?'

'Oh, yes. Sure.' She fumbled to unhook the canister from her belt, unscrewed the cap, and leaned over to tip some water into his upturned mouth. He tried to drink, but he had to turn his body to get a better mouthful. As he shifted his weight on the rickety piece of fibreglass, it rolled and the two of them slid off the side into two feet of water.

Alice's heart rate quickened, and she jumped to her feet in a flash. The stranger's arm draped across her chest, and she grabbed hold of it and pulled. His head came above the water as she desperately tried to get them both out of the crocodile pond.

At the bank, she tripped backwards and landed on her bum in the reeds. Sliding into the water had revived the man a little. He grabbed some reeds and pulled himself gamely on to drier ground. That was when Aster spotted a ripple in the water about thirty yards away. A log-like object, probably six feet long, was propelling itself towards them with a long wavering tail.

Alice shrieked. 'Crocodile! We gotta get out of here—now!'

'Can you help me stand please?' he said coolly.

She bent and grasped his forearm. He gripped hers and pushed off the ground with his left arm. He was heavy and weak, and it was difficult for the girl to find a solid footing on the loose-sand ground. But with a little effort, she managed to get him to his feet. The stout branch she had poked him with he used as a crutch. He turned around to see where the croc was.

The curious animal had swam to within ten yards of the raft and seemed more than a little interested in them as a prospective dinner. What surprised Alice next was the reaction from the exhausted young man.

He rested a hand on her shoulder for support, lifted his crutch above his head, and yelled loudly, 'Get out of here! Go on. Scat!'

The croc stopped swimming and sunk so that its eyes were the only thing visible.

The man turned back to his young rescuer. 'Can you help me up the bank before I collapse? I feel like shit.'

They moved away from the water's edge, about a hundred yards, before the man said he could go no further. He plonked down like a bag of chaff and asked Alice for a drink. She looked at him with despair.

'Oh my god. I dropped the bottle when we fell in the water, I'm so sorry.'

'Well, you'll just have to go get it, won't you?' he said rudely.

'That's not going to happen, not with that man-eater on the prowl,' she gasped.

'Aw! Don't worry about him. He's only a little one, and they're usually pretty timid. Here, take this stick, and if it comes near you, just whack it on the nose. *Please* . . . I need water. I haven't had a drink for three days, and I'm too weak to go myself.'

Alice looked at him incredulously; she could see he wasn't joking. Her memories of the crocodile farm and the way these prehistoric creatures ripped apart the flesh of dead chickens and pieces of sheep made her cringe.

'Water,' he repeated and closed his eyes before sinking back on to the grass.

Aster was aware that the stranger was in a very bad state; by the look of him, he could possibly die. She had to make a decision quickly. There was no alternative; her mind was racing. If there was a plan B, she would have thought of it, so . . .

As she stepped gingerly through the reeds, Alice couldn't believe she was heading back to where the crocodile was lying in wait. She tried to tread quietly and moved the reeds aside with the stick as she went until she saw the croc in the water. He was still in the same spot where they last saw it, and she was sure it was looking at her. A ripple emanated from his tail end, and a part of his backbone rose out of the water as it skewed its head to point at her.

Then she saw the flask; it was floating in the water only a foot from the bank. The tourist was standing about the same distance from the bottle as the croc. She calculated she would have to run ten yards, bend down, and reach into the water to retrieve the flask before the croc could swim to her, propel itself out of the water, snatch her by the head, and eat her.

Without a doubt, what Aster did next was the bravest thing she had ever done in her sweet short life. She mimicked what the half-drowned man did.

Waving the stick frantically above her head, she screamed at the monster, 'Go on! Get away! Scram! Get outta here!'

As she shrieked, she moved deftly to the water's edge, scooped up the flask, and ran back up the bank. Her heart had never beaten so fast or so loud. She moved to a safer distance, adrenalin rushing through her entire body, and she burst out laughing.

When she got back to him, she knelt beside the shipwrecked sailor. He was collapsed into a most uncomfortable position with his back bent awkwardly over a lump of tussock grass. She lifted his head and gently administered the water. He coughed and spluttered as the liquid hit his parched throat, and he grabbed at the flask, trying to tip more water.

She pulled it away and said tenderly, 'Just take small sips. There's plenty here. That's it. Slowly, slowly . . .'

The man rallied and attempted a smile. Aster saw that he was quite a handsome man, with high cheekbones, chiselled features, beautiful teeth, and sparkling blue eyes. As beaten down as he was, he looked strong and powerfully built. She comforted him by stroking his hair up out of his salt-encrusted face. He'd been under a hot sun so long the tanned skin on his forehead was beginning to peel. His body began to go limp, so Alice lifted his head and shoulders away from the tussock.

'We can't stay here. It's going to be dark in a little while, and it's a long way back to our camp. Can you make it?'

'Yeah! No worries,' he whispered gamely.

The sailor stood up with Alice's help and groggily leaned on his tree branch. It was going to be a slow walk. She kept thinking about her last few days playing nursemaid to George. Now here she was, doing it again for a hapless stranger.

The thought made her smile when she reflected on a saying she had heard years before: 'If you have to cry, do it while you're laughing.' She laughed.

The trek back to the Blue Duck was exhausting. They both struggled. She kept trying to keep the sailor upright as he battled against exhaustion and dehydration. Every step was agonisingly slow and painful. The flats below the second headland now turned eerily dark, and the incoming tide had drawn the seawater to within a few yards of the trail. Aster wanted so much to rest, but the haunting crocodile warnings George had fused into her brain made her push on until they got to the top of the next promontory.

The darkness closed around them, and he was too weak to go any further, so she stopped by a tumble of rocks and helped the man lie down on the ground. There was a quarter moon throwing a shimmer of light across his face, and he looked dreadful. The half-light darkened the underside of his eyes, making them look hollow, and the leafy shadows reflected on his face appeared like black blotches. Aster helped him take a few sips of water again. He sighed heavily, laid back, and passed out.

She decided they would be safe here, but the mosquitoes and sandflies were attacking them mercilessly. She applied insect repellent to their arms, legs, and faces, which stopped the biting, but the itching from earlier bites was almost as bad as the stings.

Concern showed on her young features as she watched the stranger sleep for about an hour. She was herself too tired to wake him and a little afraid she wouldn't be able to. The night air brought a chill, so she took her jacket from her pack and wrapped it over the man's torn shirt. Feeling the chill creeping into her as the hours ticked away, she gathered some sticks and made a small fire in the middle of the path. Pretty soon, she too fell into a deep sleep. Neither of them moved a muscle until the morning sunlight leaked out through the tree line.

The small fire had burned to grey ash well before midnight, and the residue was as cool as the rest of the sand on the trail. Aster woke to an unfamiliar sound with a start; maybe it was a bird shrieking or a branch falling in the forest. She sat upright, stiff as a board, bleary eyed, and a little dazed. She rubbed her face with both hands until she remembered why she was where she was. Turning to look at the young man she had just saved from a gruesome demise, she was surprised to see him leaning back against the rock, staring directly into her eyes and smiling.

'Morning!' he said. 'You looked so peaceful I didn't have the heart to wake you.'

'We have to get going. George will be beside himself with worry that I didn't get back last night.' Her voice quavered.

The stranger was recovering slowly from the condition she found him in, but she suspected he was putting a brave face on the state of his health. He looked exhausted and quite drawn in the face.

He must have been through quite a bit, she thought.

'Do you have any food?' he broke in on her thoughts.

Aster had totally forgotten about the snack food in her pack. She automatically reached out and handed him the whole bag. He politely took it and rummaged out the salt biscuits before impolitely stuffing them into his mouth.

'Have you any water left in there?' Munching, he pointed to the flask.

Alice passed the flask while reminding him to eat slowly, as he was still dehydrated. He nodded and gave her a soft smile while he crammed more biscuits into his face and washed them down with gulps of water.

Alice shrugged. 'We're about a mile from our camp. We need to go. Are you up to it yet?'

The survivor nodded, and they set off single file, walking slowly. He leaned heavily on his tree branch, his right hand resting gently on the back of his rescuer's shoulder. Neither of them said a word, but their minds were working overtime.

Aster had been subjected to so much drama, but she was more concerned about her friend George. He would be frantic, wondering what had happened to her and probably wondering if he would be able to get back to civilisation on his own in his weakened condition.

The sailor had a whole different set of things running through his mind. He was working on a convincing story to tell his rescuers without arousing suspicion. He was also feeling physically weak and wishing he could just lie down and sleep for a month.

'Is George your husband?'

'Heavens, no!' exclaimed the girl.

Then she suddenly felt abashed at how quickly she denied an intimate relationship with the scientist and quickly added, 'We are good friends, and he's had an accident. It's maybe a stroke of luck that you came along.'

She was about to explain about the Blue Duck and how they were stranded because it was impossible for her to drive. But just as she began to tell him, they arrived at the top of the headland overlooking their campsite.

'What the bloody hell is that thing!' the stranger interposed on her before she could get any words out.

'I call it the Blue Duck,' she responded with a touch of indignation at the stranger's acerbic reaction. 'Oh, look! George has spotted us.' She waved at the scientist as he peered through the bus window.

George had been scanning the forest for signs of his missing friend and was relieved to see her waving. He signalled a response for a few seconds until his head disappeared below the windowpane.

When Aster climbed into the bus, George was prostrate across the bed. He didn't look right.

And then he spoke. 'I fort somesing tereble had happened to you. I'm glad yerr back.'

She looked at him lying there and couldn't believe what she was hearing. 'George, are you drunk?' she exclaimed.

And then the sudden realisation of George's condition hit her like a baseball bat. The side of his face had dropped, and his mouth looked like it had melted into his neck. The left eye socket drooped like a cocker spaniel. He was dribbling and had messed his pants. It was a shocking sight to see a man still a few years away from turning forty look like a dying geriatric patient. Alice sat down on the bed with a thump. She reached for the water bottle on the cabinet, poured some into her hands, and smeared it across his face.

'What has happened to you, you poor dear man?' She was close to tears. She poured more water on to a flannel and wiped the drool from around his mouth.

'I don' weally know. I thin' I mighta had a stroke. Can't talk proply,' he managed. 'Looks like you foun' a frien'.'

'You poor dear man George,' she repeated. 'I'll tell you all about it, but first, let's get you cleaned up so you can meet him.'

Consumed with pity for her friend, she was disturbed about her trip of a lifetime belly-flopping into a nightmare.

Aster cleaned George's bedding and rolled the sheets and clothes into a ball. She descended the rear steps and threw the bundle into the camp washtub. The shipwrecked sailor had passed out in one of the folding chairs. She brought him a bottle of water, a can of baked beans, and some dry biscuits and put them on the camp table next to him without waking him. The stress of her predicament threatened to close in on her, but she knew she was stronger than that.

It was still early in the morning when Aster Bee Nightingale pulled herself together, determined to prepare the best meal she could cook with what was available. Neither man had moved for two hours. Obviously, George had had no sleep overnight, worrying about his lost friend. And the sailor, well, she could only wonder what hardships he had endured.

She wasn't a great cook, but she was a good one, and she enjoyed cooking. More importantly, her indulgence took her mind off the insanity of the events unfolding in her life. Not satisfied with a good meal, she laboured over the whole dining experience. Laying out the cutlery, condiments, and seashell decorations on a makeshift tablecloth, she artistically placed everything as if it were dinner at the Ritz.

She picked some wildflowers to adorn the setting, and she lit candles in the middle of the day. When everything was ready, she turned up the volume on the tape player with a recording she had brought from home, the psychedelic soothing melodies of Country Joe and the Fish, 'Electric Music for the Mind and Body'.

The sailor stirred, and Aster noticed his nose twitch at the aroma of the sautéed frozen vegetables and spicy grilled fish. George had a different reaction. He woke and looked about blearily, pushed himself up on his elbows, peered through the window, and dribbled down the left side of his face. Undeterred, Aster assisted him to the davit, fixed the harness, and lowered him to the ground. With a bit of a struggle, she half carried him to the table, where he plonked down into a chair.

'Who is dis?' he laboured.

Aster was visibly taken aback. She had no idea of the man's name, and when he hesitated to answer, she responded to George's question.

'He's a shipwrecked sailor I found. He was almost dead, but he is starting to come around. You know, we never did exchange names. This is George, and I am Aster Bee Nightingale. Alice emphasised her full made-up hippy name, tilted her head, and eyeballed the dishevelled survivor with a 'Your turn, mister' look.

The stranger paused for what seemed a bit too long before finally taking his turn.

'I'm sorry to impose on you good people like this,' he stuttered, stalling for an alias to pop into his head. 'My name is Je-Jerry.' It was the best he could come up with. For the time being, that name would have to suffice. It was a cross between Jesus and Geronimo, but for the life of him, he couldn't invent a surname on the spot. He always was a terrible liar and found it hard to start now, especially with someone who had just saved his life. Then from somewhere not too deep in his imagination, a name fell out of his mouth, like someone else had thought of it.

'Ship . . . er . . . Shipley,' he stammered before joining the two words together. 'Shipley.'

The -*ley* was a quick afterthought, which he felt might be more convincing than the shipwrecked sailor being named Ship. He was a smuggler and in danger of being murdered by his nefarious employers or gaoled by Australian police or Interpol. His lie was not solely for his own protection either. Knowing his real identity may well endanger these good people's lives too. He was surprised at how easily it was to fool them, but he was not entirely comfortable doing it.

'Well then, Mr Shipley, it is a pleasure to make your acquaintance, and we're pleased that you can join us for lunch.' As formal as she tried to sound, the young American had tears behind her smile as she raised her glass of beer for a toast. 'Here's to getting home safely.'

The sailor ignored the beer and raised his mug of water, tapping it against Aster's glass and reaching across to her friend.

George groped for his drink, half raised it with difficulty and garbled, 'I'll drin' to tha', an' make it soon!'

The group protracted the luncheon into the late afternoon. Canned peaches and tinned rice cream followed for dessert, and more beer kept them at their forest restaurant as the day eased past. All the same, it proved to be an uncomfortable dining experience. George was flagrantly showing signs of jealousy. It seemed he didn't want to have to share their paradise and his new friend with a complete stranger. Alice didn't compute that fact; she just thought it was part of his reaction to the stroke he had suffered. But his behaviour didn't get past the young seaman.

All Jerry wanted to do was lie down and sleep. He held out as long as he could until finally he had had enough of George's antics. The irritation prompted him to suggest he would go for a walk and let the couple relax a bit. He stood shakily at first, hesitated, before walking slowly towards the beach. He got about thirty yards and staggered, reached out, and grabbed for a tree to support him. He had only wanted to drink water while the others were drinking beer, but he felt drunk and unstable. His head swam in a blur, and he lurched forward and vomited everything he had eaten of Alice's lovely meal. The next thing he remembered was Alice guiding him towards a camp chair. She wiped his face with a wet towel and pressed a mug of water into his hands.

'Thank you, Aster, I'm . . . I'm sorry. I don't know what came over me. I think I need to lie down.'

Without a word, Alice helped to lift him to his feet and guide him to the rear of the bus. She coupled him into the harness and raised him to the rooftop of the Blue Duck. There was a rolled tarpaulin there, and she persuaded him to lie down and get some rest. When she climbed back, she sprayed him with insect repellent, threw a light sheet over him, and left him a fresh-filled flask of water. He went straight to sleep.

The candles on the table had burned away, and the dishes were left where they lay, attracting insects. After Alice got George back to his bed, she went outside to lie in the hammock, where she sobbed herself to sleep.

George felt foolish. When he witnessed Jerry reeling and spewing, he realised the man was sicker than he first thought and under a great deal of strain. He had no right to behave the way he did at lunch, and he regretted his actions dearly. He was besotted by Aster, and watching her managing the disastrous events with diligence and dignity, he was even more in awe of her. He took a pen and pad from the bedside table and began to write.

His last will and testament took up less than a page. His scholarly endeavours, including specimens and documents from this tour, he would donate to the Museum of Natural History in Victoria. His worldly goods and chattels were to go to his parents. On the last few lines, he bequeathed his amphibious vehicle, complete with patents and all attachments and gear, including the motorbike, to 'my dearest friend, Aster Bee Nightingale'.

After folding the paper as carefully as he could with shaking hands, he poked it in a drawer by the bed. George lay back on the mattress and looked up at the sky beginning to grow dark. The first stars were switching on and brightening as the sunlight buried itself over the horizon. Though his face was distorted and wrenched to one side, he felt himself smiling. He was so happy to have met Aster, even it had only been a few short blissful weeks. Sleep came easy to him that night.

*   *   *

At the Blue Duck campsite before his accident, George had given Aster lessons on how to shoot a rifle. The amphibious truck's arsenal consisted of a .22-calibre rifle and a five-shot bolt-action 12-gauge shotgun and several boxes of ammo. George brought them along in case he needed to hunt for food.

The scientist left the big gun in its sheath and carried the .22 rifle to the sand near the water, where he set up a target log. He stepped out a reasonable distance for a practice range, and they fired from the camp table near the bus. The .22 was a single shot, and George instructed his friend how to load and aim. Turned out Aster was a pretty good shot; she had a good eye and a steady hand and hit the target twelve out of a dozen times. They left the rifle handy for Aster to practise any time she felt like it.

'Good shootin', Miss Oakley!' George jested in a poor attempt to speak in a Texan accent. 'You ain't ne'er missed yer mark in a dozen pulls, ma'am,' he went on.

Alice was daydreaming about their earlier times and reflecting on her first hunt as she continued packing up the camp. The young woman remembered the time she couldn't bring herself to shoot a wild goose. She told George she didn't have a clear shot, but he wasn't fooled by her story; he just admired her all the more for her compassion.

Earlier that morning, Jerry climbed off the Duck and refilled his water bottle after drinking another a large draft. The insects had cleaned the plates, but they were hovering around, waiting for the next course. As quietly as he could, Jerry took the dirty dishes, pots, frying pan, and the rest of the cutlery to the stream a little way away from the camp. He found detergent and a bucket and began washing up.

He felt a zillion times better now and was planning how to salvage the cargo on the *Crumpet* when Aster touched his shoulder. He had not heard her approach.

'It's okay. You don't have to do that,' she said gently.

She was surprised to see how well he had recovered when he looked up at her, and she told him so. Then she offered to make them coffee.

George woke as the smell of the coffee wafted around the camp. Jerry took a mug up to him; George signalled for him to place it on the cabinet next to the bed before he spoke. 'Um, sorry abou' ma aditude yesday. I had no cause to trea' you tha way I did. I want to say you ar' more than welcome to share wiv us. I would like us to be frens, at leas' until we get outta dis wilaness. I need ta show you how to operate the Blue Duck. Than' you fa tha coffee.' He reached out a shaky right hand, and Jerry shook it with a look of pity in his eyes.

PART IV

DEADMAN'S COVE

CHAPTER 17

Antonio awoke from his stupor; the pressure from his canvas cocoon was claustrophobic. He pushed out against the piece of sail, but it was wound tight, so he wriggled his body until he loosed an arm. He felt around for the rope holding him captive, loosened it, and crawled out into the hot afternoon sunlight.

The Aussie bastard was asleep on their makeshift raft not ten feet away from him. Bella Boy scowled and hissed a curse through his teeth. As far as he was concerned, the Australian was nothing more than a mutineer and a pirate. When it was all said and done, he, Antonio Belario, was the skipper of the *Crumpet*. The two deckhands had no right to do what they did. He despised them, conveniently forgetting that he was siding with Ernie Igmas, the would-be murderer who brought on the whole disastrous cock-up. His throat was dry, and his lips and tongue burned with thirst.

Next to him lay a jar of olives and a plastic half-gallon bottle of tomato sauce. They were secured in a bag made of sailcloth. He scrambled to it and gulped the sauce, almost retching as the sickly sweet tomato concoction went down. Unscrewing the lid from the olives, he ate greedily as the lid floated off the raft into the sea.

Then he sat back and surveyed his situation. His mind was a blank sheet. For a few seconds, he had no idea how he got here. All he knew was that he wanted to get off this cursed raft and away from the man next to him, the man he hated more than anyone.

Land was over a mile away, and Bella Boy was not a very good swimmer, certainly not able to swim that far. When he turned his body to look out to the reef, he bumped the open olive jar and it followed its lid overboard. Cursing, he stuffed the bottle of sauce back into the bag. It looked like their makeshift raft was drifting to the east, and Bella Boy reckoned they were making less than a half a knot. As long as the drift continued, they might be able to reach land before dark. But that was not going to happen.

A slight onshore breeze helped their plight, but as the tide turned, it began pushing them west-south-west. There was no apparent way the skipper could manipulate the broken craft, and he was beginning to panic. Lying beside him was a bit of bunk board. An idea came to him.

He could use the wood as a paddle. He picked it up and lamely tried to change their course to go east. In his weakened condition, having no food and water, and his energy sapped by the sun, his attempt to row the wreck proved futile. In a fit of temper, he paddled as hard as he could for two minutes with no effect.

When he realised it was hopeless, he cried out and threw the paddle into the sea. It woke the deckhand, who looked up just in time to see what the skipper had done. He jumped to his feet, ran at Bella Boy, threw him on his back, and bashed his head on to the fibreglass with a resounding crack.

'You are an absolute dick brain!' he screamed. 'Now go and get that paddle back before I—I dunno—fucking drown you, you great galoot!'

Antonio stared up at the decky with a look of complete incomprehension. He hesitated too long, and the Aussie threw him overboard, yelling, 'Go! Get the fucking paddle, you dumb shit!'

The cool water stirred Bella Boy to action, and he swam over to the piece of wood, which had drifted a fair way off. Pushing it in front of him, he tried to swim back, but the tide was strong and kept them apart. Pretty soon, as he tired from the effort, the decky could see he wasn't going to make it back on to the raft. He gathered up the longest piece of rope he could find, tied it to his waist, and dived in.

'Keep swimming towards me,' he called. 'That's it. Yeah! Almost there . . . Gotcha!'

He held the skipper by the scruff of his shirt and pulled them both back one-handed to the craft with the line around his waist. They were within six feet of what was left of the *Crumpet*, and Bella Boy saw something in the water.

'Shark!' he yelled and grabbed at the decky, trying to climb over the top of him on to the safety of the raft.

Thirty feet out were two fins, side by side, skimming fast through the water straight towards them. The Aussie pushed the Italian away with his hand hard across Belario's face. Once out of his clutches, he reefed the startled skipper towards the wreck and shoved him up on to safety.

Scrambling on board after him, he looked back to see an eight-foot wide manta ray swimming up to them. The tips of its gigantic wings slicing through the top of the water looked a lot like shark fins. Bella Boy's broken nose started to bleed again as he cowered at the feet of his aggressive lifesaver.

They had been on the flotsam raft for two nights and the best part of two days. The first day, the decky had eaten some olives from the jar and drank some of its juice, which proved too salty. He sipped some tomato sauce for sustenance, but it was nowhere near enough. He was starving and very, very thirsty. The first and second days were scorchers, and when they awoke on the third day, the same yellow swords of the sun started early, hacking at their exposed skin with yet another blistering performance.

The decky was monitoring the movement of the tides and figured that it was pushing them slowly towards land. He reasoned that the outgoing tide carried them out again but more to the south, where an opposing current kept them flailing in a holding pattern until the incoming tide caught them again. Thanks to the skipper, the olives were gone, and it looked like they could be floating helplessly out here for another two days. A plastic bottle of tomato sauce was not going to keep them from dehydration and death.

When a southwesterly breeze came up over their deck, the Australian put up his makeshift sail. This time, instead of asking Bella Boy, he grabbed him and pushed him into position, forcing his hands to hold the mast and a corner of sailcloth. Antonio was visibly surprised to see that the sail countered the effect of the tide and they meandered ever so slowly towards solid ground. The effect seemed to spur him on, and he manipulated the cloth to catch every wisp of breeze.

There was a problem with the way the wrecked boat travelled through the water. The skipper noticed that the craft was spinning instead of tracking. This way, he thought, they lost forward momentum, so he came up with a brilliant idea. He used a section of Ernie's bunk board for a rudder, placing it into a crevice at the bulkiest end of their wreck. This action brought the sharper end around to the front.

They were still heading more west than towards the land, so he tilted the board to the side. His plan worked. It skewed the raft around to track and run them sideways across the current. With a tilt of the rudder, he could control direction and steer a large section of fibreglass rubbish to go where he wanted it. When the younger man saw what was happening, he slapped Antonio on the back like he was a long-lost friend.

'You little bewdy Bella Boy, you're a bloody genius.' He smiled as he looked at the progress they made with the rudder.

Bella Boy was excited by his own ingenuity and happy to be moving towards the land, but he growled at the deckhand. 'Keep your a handsa off me. I don'ta wanna you touch me.' His accent thickened, making his words seem put on, and although he spoke in a guttural tone, his shipmate sensed that he was proud of his inventiveness.

The land loomed larger, and the heat of the day got hotter and stickier. By late afternoon, the tide had swung again in their favour, closing on the land to the point where they could make out shapes of trees and rocks.

The deckhand was trying to convince himself to dive overboard and swim a mile to the shore, leaving the crazy ding on his own. Bella Boy was hoping for a chance to get the drop on his shipmate, kill him, deliver the drugs to his boss, and be the hero. It was more of a daydream because he knew how dangerous his deckhand was.

Belario knew that winning a fight against an armed mafia soldier like Ernie Igmas was no mean feat. The kid was fast and hit hard too. He touched his broken nose on reflection. Nevertheless, he knew he had to be loyal to the boss, or much worse things would happen to him and his family. So he continued working on a plot to fulfil his daydream.

* * *

It was Christmas Day in Australia, boiling hot with beautiful bright sunshine. At the pool party, everyone was in full celebration mode, having a ball.

The deckhand was standing next to the buffet table, stuffing his face and looking at scantily clad girls water-bombing their friends with floppy balloons. Across the pool, Robert Plant and Jimi Page from the band Led Zeppelin looked over at him and waved. He smiled and waved back.

'Glad you guys could make it!' he hollered.

He grabbed a can of beer from the icebox and flipped the ring pull, but when he went to drink, he felt bloated and put the can down on the table. Just then a ruckus started up at the other end of the garden. Four men in dark suits walked around the corner. They were carrying pistols with silencers attached to the barrels.

The deckhand recognised one of them. It was Roberto, the guy who drove him to the river, the same man who drove them by speedboat to the *Crumpet*. He was one of Cuda's workers.

Jesus stepped forward to go and greet the men but paused when he saw his friend Dwayne suddenly run out of the house.

He appeared upset as he rushed towards the uninvited guests, shouting angrily, 'You guys are not welcome here! Get out! Leave now!' He was obviously very angry with them.

Without warning, the driver raised his gun and fired two shots, one into Dwayne's head and one into his heart. Jesus's friend fell backwards into the pool with a loud splash. Blood billowed out of his wounds, and the people in the pool ran or swam, stampeding in a panic to get away from the murderer.

The decky was shocked, and the shock woke him up.

He raised his face off the wrecked *Crumpet*, but he couldn't open his eyes; the sun was blinding. He could still hear someone swimming away from the body in the pool. It didn't make sense until he realised the whole scene was a dream.

When he could at last squint into the daylight, the first thing he saw was Bella Boy splashing loudly about fifty yards away as he swam towards the shore. Their raft was over a thousand yards out. The decky laid his face down again, too weak to do anything and too exhausted to care. The gentle rocking of the raft lulled him back to sleep.

CHAPTER 18

Aster, George, and Shipley began packing up the camping equipment and stowing it into the Blue Duck at camp Shangri-La. Just two days before, Bella Boy had dived off the hull of the *Crumpet* and made his way to a strip of beach three miles south.

On the first day, he tried instinctively to head south, but the forest and the rocky outcrops were impenetrable. After days and nights of making little progress, he decided that heading north might be an easier option. He ate birds' eggs and raw crabs drank from muddy potholes and slept rough. But he survived, albeit angrier and edgier than his time on the raft.

Following animal tracks and keeping the ocean in sight, he came across the wrecked piece of their yacht washed into the shallows near a small cove. No sign of the Aussie.

Good riddance, he thought. *I hope the bastard is dead.*

He used rope from the wreck to anchor it to the shore, took his bearings, and memorised the landmarks in the hope he could find it again. Coming upon a ridge on another headland, he noticed the remains of a campfire. Further along the trail, he heard people's voices emanating from a camp in the vale below him.

He crouched low and moved forward, careful to make sure he would not be seen. From behind some rocks, he reconnoitred the situation before making his move.

The past weeks had taken a heavy toll on Belario. He was about to collapse mentally and physically exhausted. Now as pangs of hunger cramped his stomach, he was at a stage of wild desperation. His plan was simple. The thought didn't occur to him to wait until dark; he had to go immediately. He would sneak on board the funny-looking blue bus, lock them out, and drive off.

He circled wide around the camp as noiselessly as he could and crept up to the driver's door. However, when the skipper climbed up into the compartment, he was surprised to see a person in the back, shuffling papers. There was a rifle lying on the step next to him, so he engaged plan B.

Jerry was helping to pack up the camp. He took down a tarpaulin used as an annex on the bus and was busy folding it to stow in the Duck's hold. George was trying hard to make himself useful, sitting on the bed and tidying up, when the driver's door creaked open behind him. Although he heard the door, he didn't pay any attention, but if he'd thought much about it, the driver's door was seldom, if ever, used.

'Don't move a muscle, and don't a make a sound.' The strange whisper prompted George to do exactly the opposite. He turned around.

The barrel of his own rifle was pointed directly at his face. A stranger—heavily tanned with long black hair, a bulbous nose, dark eyes, a thick and bushy black beard, and a murderous look—crouched near the driver's compartment. The man was snarling like some kind of animal, and the violence reflected in his eyes was too much for George. He raised his hand instinctively to cover his face from the muzzle pointing at him.

'Who ar' ya and wha' do ya wan'?' he shouted indignantly.

His words were garbled. The stranger stepped forward and hit George in the face with the butt of the rifle. The hapless scientist fell on to the bed and screamed in pain. Jerry took a quick look up at the window, but he couldn't see inside from that angle. He ran to the rear of the Duck and climbed the ladder into the cabin.

The first thing he saw was Bella Boy preparing to shoot at him. Instantly, he dodged right as a bullet flew past his head. He didn't realise it was a single-shot rifle, so he ran to Aster, grabbed her by the arm, and pulled her into the cover of the tree line.

'You'se better getta back here, or I kill your friend!' threatened the skipper.

His theatrically thickened accent sounded mental. Without hesitation, Jerry pushed Aster to the ground and stepped out of their hide. The girl began to protest, but Jerry shushed her and ordered her to stay where she was. Slowly he walked back to the bus while Aster watched a swarthy man with a rifle come out to meet him.

The girl could not hear what they were talking about, but it was plain to see that the tattered stranger was a fellow survivor of the man she rescued. She looked on as Jerry made a move to check on George. It horrified the young woman to see the stranger rip the rifle butt into Jerry's stomach. Jerry went down on one knee, and the rifleman raised the gun to smash down on his head. She jumped up and ran towards them.

'No! Stop!' she cried.

It was enough to stay the blow. Instead, Bella Boy whipped the barrel of the rifle around and pointed it straight into Jerry's face.

'Okay, the two of you get over there!' He signalled them to the side of the Duck.

Aster came forward to assist Jerry to his feet, and they did as the maniac ordered.

'What is your plan, Antonio?' Shipley hissed at the skipper.

'It's simple,' he retorted. 'You people are a gonna help a me to load the cargo on a this a truck. Then I'm gonna leave you here and drive off. Nobody gets hurt unless you try and fuck with me, okay?'

'What cargo are you talking about?' asked Alice, who was talking to the gunman but looking straight at Shipley.

Jerry noted the mistrust in her eyes and was a little surprised to sense disappointment in the way she looked at him. He had a sense of a comfortable bond forming between them. The manner she asked her question was a sign his feelings had been on the mark.

For her sake, he decided there and then to tell these people a version of the truth. The young man explained how they had ferried illegal drugs aboard their yacht and how the *Crumpet* ran into a reef and broke up.

'That piece of flotsam you found me on is loaded with contraband. It belongs to our boss, and bugger lugs here wants to take it back to him. Don't be fooled though. He's not going to let us go. We are going to have to—'

'Shut up your mouth!' the skipper yelled at Jerry furiously. 'I shoot you like a dog if you don't shut up!'

He raised the rifle and aimed it at Jerry. Aster cut in, pleading, 'We'll help you, but let us check on George. He is really sick.'

Bella Boy appeared tentative, as if trying to make a decision. After a few seconds, he came up with the idea for Aster to tie Jerry up. She obeyed, using rope she took off the hammock. Pretending to be a helpless female, she wasted time fumbling three attempts to tie Jerry's hands behind his back. The feigned unsuccessful attempts prompted the gunman to threaten her to do it again and again. When at last he was satisfied, he lashed the deckhand to a bracket on the side of the vehicle. Only then did he give the go-ahead for Aster to check on her friend.

George looked terrible; he was almost unconscious, lying across his bed. The side of his face was swollen and red, and he had lost a tooth. His blood was splashed over the sheets and splattered on a window. He had used his hands to shield his face from the blow, resulting in a broken finger. He looked up from the bed at Aster and attempted a smile.

'I heard everything,' he whispered. Then he added, 'Sounds like we've got work to do.'

As he spoke, he indicated with a twist of his head to a spot down the aisle behind the driver's seat. Aster didn't understand at first until she noticed the carved wooden butt of the shotgun poking out of its sheath. She spun around and literally ordered the skipper to get her some water.

Surprisingly, without hesitation, he fetched a jug from the table. This gave Aster the chance to unsheathe the gun and push it under the bed sheets. She grabbed a box of shells and quickly stuffed them into the bedside drawer. By the time Bella Boy came in with the water, Aster was tearing up a towel to wash George's wounds. She gave a curt thanks as she snatched the jug from him.

Bella Boy had not realised that the vehicle was amphibious until he started climbing down to check Jerry's bonds. When he got to the bottom of the ladder, he stalled to study the propellers and rudder.

'Holy mother of God!' he exclaimed. 'This thing is a boat. Okay! Okay! Okay! We must go now. Presto. You!' He frantically untied Jerry's hands, keeping the rifle aimed menacingly close to the sailor's face. 'You drive! Any nonsense, and I shoot you! Got it?' He was excitedly pushing Jerry into action as he spoke.

Shipley went to enter the bus by the front door, but Antonio pulled him back and ushered him to the back entrance. The sailor climbed up the ladder and looked darkly at George's broken face then at Aster. Bella Boy squawked at him to move on in as he followed up the ladder, never taking the barrel point off his prisoner. He stood on the back landing, barking out new orders in an agitated tone.

Jerry moved down the aisle, past his two new friends, and took his place in the driver's seat. Aster was standing in front of George, blocking Bella Boy's view. Suddenly, she stepped to one side, and there was a deafening explosion.

George fired the shotgun straight into the skipper's chest. The force of the shot blew him out the back of the bus, and he fell six feet to the ground, dead as a doormat.

'My god!' wailed Jerry. 'What happened? Oh no!' He ran to the rear of the duck and looked down at the mess on the ground.

Forgetting the ladder, he jumped to the ground and bent over the skipper. Feeling for a pulse on his neck and getting nothing, he looked up at Aster and shook his head.

She turned to George and said, 'You saved our lives, George. Thank you.' And she bent over, kissed his forehead, and hugged him.

The trio spent most of the afternoon in relative silence. Shipley carried the body well away from the campsite near the top of the second ridge, and they buried Bella Boy off the track in the bush. Shipley marked the site by stacking five soccer ball–sized rocks ten feet away, on the west side of the track. George was helped up to the top of the headland to attend the burial. It was clear that he was sorely affected by the horrendous act he had been forced to carry out.

Looking south gave a glimpse of the cove where Alice had discovered the wreck of the *Crumpet*. Aster explained to George that the inlet was where she had found Jerry.

'So that's where the smuggled cargo is?' he asked.

'Yes,' answered Aster. 'That's the spot. That's Smugglers Cove, and now there's a dead man's grave overlooking it. The whole scene is bizarre. It's like a novel or a movie.'

'Yes,' Shipley chimed in with a grim look on his face. 'We ought to call it Deadman's Cove.' He spoke sarcastically through clenched teeth.

Turning, he looked down to where the remnants of the *Crumpet* lay just out of sight. He let out a long sigh and rubbed his face briskly with both hands before he picked George up bodily and carried him back to the bus.

Back at camp, they unpacked some of the cookware, and Aster and Jerry shared in making a meal. They took their dinner up into the bus and dined with George by the bed. It was surreal. A day that started out with an aim to get back to some semblance of civilisation had changed all their lives forever.

CHAPTER 19

As their first priority, the group planned to drive out of the valley at dawn and get George to a hospital. After sleeping on it, the scientist came up with other ideas. He proposed they float down to Deadman's Cove and retrieve the drugs. He reasoned that they could drive right up to the wreck and lift them on to the roof, using the sling on the davit.

Surprisingly, Jerry was the main objector; he didn't want them involved. Aster, in an excited voice, suggested it would be pretty special to see a large cache of drugs. She responded to Jerry's protests by adding that they could say they simply found them when they explored the wreck. If Jerry wanted to, they could hand them in to the authorities.

The next step was for George to instruct Jerry on how to drive his machine. Turns out it was relatively simple; when entering the ocean, a flick of a switch sent it seamlessly into boat mode. Before heading south, Jerry was forced to drive out to sea around the headland because of a line of rocks jutting out over two hundred yards.

They reached the wreck as the sun topped the trees. The driver reversed the bus to within three feet of the raft. George stayed on his bed, looking out the window, watching Aster and Jerry attack the fibreglass with hammer and saw. Within two hours, they had recovered dozens of oilskin packages and laid them out on the sand.

George struggled up on to his elbows to get a better look and called through the window, 'Well, come on then. Open one up, and let's have a look at what we've got.'

It was uncanny how the three of them now got along so well together. Rallying to the job at hand, the sailor smiled and pulled his trusty ten-inch blade to cut through the outer skin. Up until now, he had not sighted the drugs at all, not during the transfer, during the visual checking, or while stowing them into the airtight chambers. He had been at the helm, holding the *Crumpet* steady the whole time.

For the first time, Jerry saw that the bags were different; aside from the size and shape, three of them were tagged with white patches, and sixteen had black leather patches sewn on to them. The others bore the standard, plain oilskin wrapping. He was in for the biggest shock of all when he reached into a black marked bag and pulled out what looked like a slate roofing tile.

It was a two-pound block of black hashish. Good-quality hash was highly profitable and a very popular drug. An ounce of the stuff sold for the same price as a pound of marijuana heads on the black market.

The trio's curiosity prompted Jerry to open a white-tagged bag. What they found was even more startling. It was loaded with packets of white powder. Jerry suggested it was probably heroin. He suspected the plain brown bags would be ganja but checked one anyway. He was right; it was the culprit that caused the pungent odour, and when he opened the bag, the smell was almost overpowering.

Shipley juggled some calculations in his head and was overawed by the astronomic figures these bags would be worth on the street. It was all starting to get too much to work out without an abacus or a pencil and paper. By his reckoning, the brown bags could be worth hundreds of thousands. The hashish usually had a higher value than the ganja, but there were less of them. When he began to think about the heroin, his only idea of its street value was gossip. The figures he had heard bandied around put the value at one to $200 a gram. He couldn't put a price on that. He did a quick count of the bags laid them out on the sand. There were forty packages in all.

He called out the contents and his estimations to George, and the scientist instantly called back a conservative estimate of the total value.

'Wow! That's well over $7 million. Mate, you certainly don't do things by halves,' he quipped with a chortle.

Aster stood silent, holding a slate of hashish. Jerry sat down on the hulk of fibreglass with a gasp. He stood agape, wiping his forehead. When he looked up at George, he saw him grinning down on them through the window.

After a couple of moments, still smiling, he spoke in a matter-of-fact manner, as if he might be asking them to do the dishes or shell some peas. 'Well, let's get it on the roof.'

Opening the airtight containers and pulling the drugs out on to the beach was relatively easy. Getting them stowed safely on to the roof of the Duck presented a host of different problems. The cargo had to be packed flat so as not to raise the height of the bus too much. A lot of necessary equipment had to share the space; that meant they would have to knit the bags in with the other equipment, nice and snug.

George was on the ball with weight-to-ratio calculations. He suggested they jettison everything they could do without to allow for the extra half ton or more the Duck would have to carry. Then there was also the problem of the smell. Although it was not as overpowering as when it came off the *Narwhal*, it still emitted an alarming odour.

Jerry wrapped the goods in tarpaulin and literally buried it under camping equipment on top of the roof. Aster asked about keeping some out to smoke, but Jerry advised against it. He argued that it would draw unwanted attention when they got back to civilisation. He also reminded Aster that they might have to use her story that they found it and were in the process of handing it in to the authorities. She reluctantly went along when George admitted that their new friend was right. It would give them an out if they were challenged.

The afternoon was quickly turning to dusk by the time they had packed the roof, so they decided to head back to Shangri-La and spend the night. Aster rustled up some canned stew and fresh-baked damper before the night closed in on them. They ate dinner inside the Blue Duck so George wouldn't have to climb down the ladder. They drank the remainder of the beer and talked well into the night. Jerry stayed tight-lipped about his employers and the attempts made on his life.

Although it appeared difficult for George to talk, he was the most dominant throughout the whole conversation. He told Jerry the story of how they got to be there in the north-western wilderness, some of his amazing discoveries, how happy he was to have met Aster, and what a wonderful woman she was.

Then he got on the subject of practical information about his invention. He explained in detail the refuelling process, checking oil levels, and the watertight seals around the axles. As an experienced teacher, his instructions were simply stated and careful to make sure Jerry understood.

Listening in, Aster became concerned about his tone. He seemed to be alluding to the probability that Jerry and Aster would be travelling alone.

At last she interjected. 'Whoa there, good buddy! You know you *will* be coming with us. You know that, don't you? I am not about to leave you behind after all you've done for me, George. We will get you some medical attention and be on the road in no time. And if we have to wait for you to get better, we will.'

For the first time that night, Jerry saw what Aster had noticed in George's countenance. He was quitting; the instruction he was expounding sounded like a subtle farewell. The younger two looked at each other in stunned silence.

Then Aster asked George a serious question, phrased in a light-hearted manner. 'What's your plan, man?' She smiled as she spoke, but her eyes were intensely scanning George for signs of his real intentions.

George looked shattered; the left side of his face had melted even further into his neck. His eye, cheek, and jaw were swollen, and the missing tooth made him look like the worst end of a car accident. He was hunched over, sitting on the side of the bed and looking forlorn.

Lifting his eyes directly to Aster, he smiled his bent smile and jokingly said, 'Don' worry 'bout me, girl. You no' going to ge' rid of me tha' quick.' He ended with a half-hearted laugh, but it was very theatrical, and George was not good at acting.

Jerry could not sleep on the roof because of the rearrangement. The hammock was packed away, so he made a nest of clothes and towels and settled by the ladder on the rear deck of the bus. It was cramped and uncomfortable, but he didn't complain. When Aster threw him a cushion, he smiled a 'Thank you' at her and went to sleep.

Next day, it was raining, and George, dressed only in a pair of shorts, pulled on a mackintosh to go to the toilet. He stood near the passenger door and called for assistance. Jerry helped him down the front steps and watched him disappear into the forest. Aster and the sailor were occupied with preparing breakfast with a minimum of utensils. It was going to be spaghetti with canned tomatoes and some leftover damper. It was nothing exciting unless one was hungry, and Jerry was.

Everything was ready to eat, and Aster and the sailor drank cups of black tea while waiting for George. A while later, she called out to George and asked the sailor which way he went. Shipley pointed, and the girl walked off, informing the young man behind her that George might need help. Not long after she was swallowed by the undergrowth she called again, but George didn't answer. The young man joined her, and they searched together. Aster began to get panicky. Shipley was unsuccessfully trying to convince her everything was okay while trying to contain a lump of his own dread.

The pair searched for an hour, trying to find the scientist. They split up and followed two potential tracks which might have been George's. In the late afternoon, Aster returned to the Blue Duck. She fetched a bottle of water from the refrigerator and drank thirstily. She was about to take Jerry some water when she noticed the letter on the bedside table.

She read it aloud and started to cry. Stepping out of the bus, she noticed for the first time that the rifle was missing. When Shipley returned to the Blue Duck, he asked what had happened and she showed him the note.

The handwriting was scrawled across the page in a hand befitting a drunken preschooler in the middle of a fit. It was barely legible, but the message screamed 'suicide note'.

Shipley's brow furrowed with concern as his eyes processed the scrawl. When he finished, he looked at Alice. His lips were tight, and his jaw scrunched into a set of helplessness.

The note read:

Dear Aster

I have lived a wonderful life, a dream run so to speak. So many good things have I seen and experienced. Everything, and I mean everything, and everyone pale into insignificance to the last few weeks I have spent with you. I did look forward to more time exploring this beautiful country, but I didn't count on finding you. You completed my life.

I thank you from the bottom of my heart.

Aster said, 'Then I found this.'

She showed Jerry the letter George had written, outlining his last will and testament. Jerry started to read but was interrupted by the sound of a gunshot. He shoved the papers into Aster's hands and ran towards the sound. The American followed quickly behind him.

A hundred yards into the forest, Jerry stopped to listen for any clue as to where the shot had come from. Another shot cracked the peaceful air of the valley, but this time, it came from behind a thicket quite near them. The sailor ran through a small gap in the bushes and saw George.

'Bloody hell, it took ya long enuff ta fin' me.'

The scientist was standing in a clearing, using the barrel of his rifle as a walking stick. He told them that he got disoriented and went the wrong way. He could hear them calling for him, but he couldn't yell loud enough. It was a story that Aster and Jerry didn't swallow, given the notes he left, but they let it slide, knowing how fragile George was after all that had happened to him.

Aster was the first to speak. 'Thank God we found you, George. We were really worried about you. Come on, let's get you back to camp.'

'I'll carry the gun,' said Jerry as he took the crutch away from George, held his arm, and provided his shoulder for support. 'We better get you to a hospital, mate. Hope you're up to a long drive.'

George was a man who was always full of surprises, but the young pair couldn't believe his next suggestion. He struggled with his words as he explained what he had in mind, reiterating Shipley's tale of shipwreck and how he had drifted into Deadman's Cove. It was obvious he had given his plan a lot of thought. All the details of the sailor's explanation George recited verbatim: how far out they were when they struck the submerged ship, the story of how long they had drifted, and the last sighting of the other half of their boat. He had also calculated an approximate position for the wreckage.

But his proposal was outrageous. He wanted to find the rest of the *Crumpet* and retrieve the remaining cargo.

'Adding it to the current haul could well and truly double what we have on the roof now. It's literally millions of dollars more!' he declared.

It was even more preposterous that Aster went along with the whole shebang. Was she just humouring him, or was she serious? Jerry couldn't believe his ears. He used every negative reason he could think of to not go along with such a crazy plan. Every argument he came up with was countered by George's brilliant mind.

Even though George should be seeking immediate medical attention, Jerry had to agree that the scientist's plan was a solid one, so he reluctantly consented to go with it. They would set out early in the morning.

So it was that they followed George's suggestions, sailing south in the Blue Duck. Aster and Shipley were mainly concentrating on rocky outcrops and scanning the shoreline.

After travelling about five miles, George suddenly cried out, 'Wreck ahoy!

He'd been behaving like an excited schoolboy all morning, and as they closed in on the wreck, he was shaking with anticipation.

The starboard section of the *Crumpet* lay three quarters of a mile offshore. With their eyes focused landward, Jerry and Aster would have sailed right past it. It appeared that the sunken mast had snagged on the bottom and held the wreck fast on a submerged reef in about ten feet of water. The sailor suggested they drop anchor while he dived down and checked out what she was snagged on. But George had a better idea.

He asked the sailor to unhook the sling on the hoist and replace it with the grappling hook stowed in the hold.

With a slight tug on the line, what was left of the *Crumpet* trailed easily behind the Blue Duck. As they headed to shore, the mast came free of the reef and dragged across the sandy bottom until finally catching on another snag. With a burst on the throttle, the mast snapped off, and the raft of drugs came away easily. Aster spotted a strip of beach that they all agreed would make a suitable landing.

Before nine o'clock in the morning, they had hauled the sealed section of the *Crumpet* on to a beach, ready to gut it. It took the rest of the day to reorganise the roof again and unpack the cache and hoist it into position. Thirty were brown bags. Ten were marked with the black patches, but there were no white ones.

Before Jerry rolled the tarp over the load, George asked him to come down. He handed the younger man a bottle from his mobile lab. It was full of pickled insects.

He instructed Jerry to drain off the liquid, crush the beetles, and smear them over the packed cargo to cover the odour. The smell of the bugs was overpowering, but the sailor persisted, and for an hour, he could not get rid of the stink from his nose. But the application worked. From the ground at least, you couldn't smell anything of the drugs, and magically, the smell of the bugs infused with clean air until it too was hardly noticeable.

The group headed south and entered a wide river mouth, motoring east-south-east for the rest of the day. Aster shuddered as she took photos of a crocodile eating some unidentifiable part of an animal on the riverbank. They anchored the boat in the middle of the river that night and slept restlessly. The next day, they saw that the river bent southwards, and they journeyed another four hours before Aster, on lookout, saw a white line heading over the hills up ahead. It ran up from a muddy bank at a bend in the river.

'There's a road! There! It comes right down to the water,' she called out excitedly.

The driver spotted it and began manoeuvring the duck directly towards the narrow gravel path. The weird boat ran up the muddy strip and magically turned back into an all-terrain vehicle again. They stopped well away from the river under the trees and out of the heat, boiled the billy on the gas stove, and enjoyed a well-earned mug of tea before setting off for civilisation.

CHAPTER 20

Many days had passed since Aster and George had seen other human beings, but for Jerry, it had been almost three months. After a day and a night on a rough track, they finally reached a main road with a bitumen strip in the middle of wide gravel edges. Jerry turned south and drove for eighty miles before they saw any other vehicles. A Land Rover with a tin shed on its back came at them from the south. The blue bus moved its nearside wheels on to the gravel, and the oncoming vehicle did the same in order to pass safely. Everyone waved at one another with huge smiles on their faces.

Not long after the sighting of the other vehicle, a roadside diner loomed up in the distance like an oasis. No one had to ask to drive in and buy something to eat; they were all keen as mustard for a change in their diet. The sailor wrangled the Blue Duck over the crushed-gravel driveway, avoiding the awning covering the petrol pumps. He parked fifty feet away from the diner, under the shady part of a spindly tree.

The trio bought burgers and a giant bag of french fries. They washed these down with several bottles of Coke. The food wasn't very good, and it was the most expensive meal Alice had ever heard of, but she enjoyed every morsel. George insisted on paying. Jerry went along with his offer happily because he had no money on him.

All his earnings from the last fishing season were on loan to a bank in his account. At this stage of the journey, he had no identification with him, which made him a pauper. Fortunately, he'd washed his shorts, thrown away his torn shirt, and borrowed one of George's slightly-too-small T-shirts to make himself half respectable.

The shop girl and the man cooking in the kitchen didn't bat an eye at the dishevelled travellers. It was a lonely road miles from anywhere, and Aster guessed they had seen plenty of weirdoes before their lot walked in.

As full as cattle ticks, they got back into the blue bus and set off again down the narrow highway, with the setting sun blasting through the driver's window. Around six thirty, they pulled into a road stop to stay the night. Shipley kept well away from a road train parked at the other end of the stop. The night was uneventful except for the arrival of another three road trains. They set out again at sunrise. At noon, the bus passed a sign announcing a town twenty-five miles further down the highway.

Before they reached the town, about four miles out, the driver spied a large dusty blue sign hiding amongst twenty trucks, some of them dragging multiple trailers behind. Jerry struggled to get the Blue Duck between the gigantic rigs and pull alongside the bowsers, keeping the left side to the pump, as directed by the inventor.

He watched his sick friend in the rear-view mirror. George pulled up a hatch from the bus flooring and exhumed a steel box with a combination lock. Upon opening the safe, he handed Jerry a wad of notes.

'You'll need this to pay for tha' fuel,' he drawled. 'And you and As'er can decide wha'ever food you wan'. Oh yeah, you'll need two gallons of mul'igrade oil.'

Jerry was amazed at the amount of money he was given for fuel, but after twenty minutes of pumping petrol into the hungry beast, he started to think he might need more cash. In outback regions, the price of fuel almost doubled that in urban service stations, and the pump under the big blue sign was no exception.

Shipley eyed the attendant suspiciously as he handed over the money and mumbled under his breath, 'Could'a bought a car for that price.'

From the fuel stop, they ate while driving until they came upon a motel on the outskirts of the next town. Everyone agreed that it was a perfect place to spend the night. George went to the office to handle the booking. He prepaid for a family room quite near the manager's single-window workplace. The hotel room had a double bed, a single bed, a double bunk, a radio, a Bible, and a phone.

For the first hour, the bathroom was the most popular room in the seedy motel. Aster was first to emerge from the shower. She looked more beautiful than ever. Her hair shone like jewellery, and all the dust and dirt from the road were washed away, leaving her skin looking as pure as polished alabaster.

The men had their turn, and neither of them was impressed. The bore water didn't allow the soap to lather, and it stung their eyes. The showerhead dribbled instead of spraying, and the hot water ran out after thirty seconds. Shipley's shorts had all but fallen apart, so he borrowed ill-fitting clothes from George. This prompted him to speak privately with the scientist.

George sat in a chair on the veranda just outside the motel room, casually draining a can of beer. Out there, he explained, he could keep an eye on the Blue Duck, as it couldn't be locked up. Jerry asked him in an embarrassed tone if he could borrow some money to buy clothes. As collateral, he offered to gift him the entire cargo of smuggled contraband. He told George he would have gladly left it in the yacht because he didn't want anything to do with it.

'Sure, there's fifty grand in the safe. Take what you need, mate!' George responded pleasantly. '*But*', he added with a touch of acerbity, 'I don't want the drugs either; I just wanted to know what it feels like to be a smuggler, you know, now that I'm a murderer.'

Up until that point, Jerry assumed George had recovered well from the nightmare of Bella Boy's attack. It was a certainty that the episode caused George to consider suicide until he snapped out of the ghastly thought. Yet when he and Aster found him in the scrub after he had wandered off, his demeanour was bright and cheerful.

Jerry had been hatching a plan for the drugs he didn't want, but he never brought it up before because he thought George and Aster wanted them to sell. When he explained his plan to George, the scientist pushed back his pain and laughed long and loud.

Aster came out to see what the fuss was about, but the two men didn't tell her the plan right away. Instead, George lifted himself out of the chair and hobbled off to the front office. He ordered takeout Chinese, Australian food, and more beer, and for an extra fee, the manager sent a young woman off in a car to fetch it. The group dined over the double bed and drank long into the night before traipsing off to their respective sleeping arrangements.

Jerry awoke to the sound of voices. The sun was up—just. He ambled to the peephole and peered through. A police officer was talking to George and pointing to the Blue Duck. He shook Aster awake and hushed her with a signal, a finger across his mouth.

'There's a cop outside, talking to George. Get dressed and ready to move quickly,' he whispered.

He went into the bathroom and wound the window out to its full extent. Aster and he would never be able to fit through the small gap, so he broke the winder off, allowing the window to be pushed wide open. When he went back to tell Aster, he was surprised to find that she'd gone outside and was talking to the policeman with George.

Shipley crouched inside the motel room door and tried to hear what was being said. The voices were muffled, as the people had moved away to the front of the bus. He went back into the bathroom, closed the door, took a seat on the lid of the loo, and prepared for the worst.

Very soon, Aster returned to the room and called out, 'It's all right, Jerry. He just wanted to look at the unusual vehicle. He didn't even ask for registration. I think George overawed him with a sense of mechanical wonderment. He went away very impressed with George's invention.'

The sailor shook off his wariness and urged his travelling companions to get going. They arrived in the town a few minutes from the motel, and he and Aster went shopping. She proved a brilliant aid in getting him outfitted. Her design skills and colour coordination enabled Jerry to look like a million bucks even with the limited stock available in the outback village.

During their time in the shops, Shipley hinted about his plan to get rid of the drugs and sensed in Alice's response that she would be okay with it.

The shopping spree produced for Jerry a pair of sandshoes, two sets of clothes, and three pairs of socks and undies.

The young sailor protested that he preferred 'free balling'. 'Undies are a waste of money,' he squeaked.

But Alice bought them anyway. She also selected a cheap pair of sunglasses, a jacket, a towel, and a small backpack. With his new garb and feeling a little more human, they ate lunch in the Busy Bee Cafe in the centre of town. After devouring a mixed grill, Jerry chatted while his friend picked at the remaining pieces of a huge seafood platter. They finished their meal with milkshakes made from boxed UHT milk, which they both agreed tasted revolting.

Before returning to the bus, they sat under a tree in the park and chattered as their meal digested. The bond between them was growing in strength. Alice was very attracted to the young man. He was handsome, very fit, always polite and considerate with other people, and especially kind to George. The sailor thought of Aster as a woman he could only dream about being in an intimate relationship with. He knew she was with George, so he would have to keep on dreaming.

They were sitting with their backs against the trunk of a large tree with bushes adding to the shade. A well-worn dirt path ran along the highway on the other side of the tree. Just then a car pulled over, and they listened in on a conversation that they were not supposed to hear. A man walking the path was stopped by two men in a dusty sedan.

'Macca, where's our fucking money, man?' yelled the driver, obviously unaware of the couple behind the tree.

'Yeah, mate, no whuckin furries. I got it here. I'se just comin' over to give it to ya's an' get some more shit.' Macca's high-pitched voice sounded like a metal spike scraping on a tin can.

'The dope went like hotcakes, mate. I couldn't believe it, you know, being crap quality and that.' The man with the squeaky voice winced as he realised he needn't have added the last comment.

The passenger took the money and told Macca there was no more, and the car sped off. Before the pedestrian got ten paces down the track, Aster was up and speaking to him. Jerry joined them.

'What's the dope scene like here, man?' she enquired.

For a good five minutes, he protested that he wasn't into that sort of thing. Then he relented and told them that the town was dry and there was no one to score from. After a few more minutes, he relaxed enough to tell them that the miners were begging for it, but there was a chronic shortage.

They had heaps of money and would pay anything for the shit. Aster was full of surprises, as she produced a chunk of hash wrapped in foil, broke off a small piece, and handed it to the stranger. Macca snatched it and pushed it up to his nostril.

'Man, this stuff smells unreal! How much of it have you got?'

'How much do you want?'

'Do you have ounces?'

'Sure, for two hundred bucks.' Aster didn't waste a second to answer.

'Fuck!' gasped Macca. 'I'll take an ounce right now.' He dug in his pocket and fished out a bunch of mangled, well-handled notes and began sorting them out to make up the $200.

Aster turned to her friend and asked him to fetch her bag from the 'van'. A short, mild tiff later, Jerry jogged back to the bus and returned on the motorbike without explanation to George.

The dealer's eyes bulged as he watched Aster pull out a sizable slab of hash from her beach bag. She had obviously slighted it away for a special occasion. When she made no attempt to conceal it from Macca, his greedy eyes widened as he mooned at the black tile of powerful dope.

'Geez, thanks a lot,' he almost sang. 'Do youse want ta get ripped? I got some papers and some spin. Let's get ripped!' He let go a stupid laugh as if he were descending the arc of a roller coaster.

'No, thank you,' replied Aster politely. 'We have to get going. Bye, I know you'll enjoy it.'

It was a dangerous game she was playing, selling dope to a loud-mouthed simpleton she'd never met. Jerry called for her to jump on the back seat, and they motored off to the rear of the shops, where the Blue Duck was parked. She put her arms around Jerry's waist and stuffed the money into his shorts pocket. She revealed she had overheard their conversation about borrowing money and decided to help Jerry out whenever the opportunity arose. It seemed the opportunity came along quicker than she predicted.

Jerry wasted no time hauling the bike on to the roof and making sure it was well out of sight.

They didn't say much to George as they hurried out of town. Shipley confided in Aster to lay low on their drive out. Overcautious, he wore his new sunglasses and wore his hat low on his forehead. He didn't want anyone to identify them in their very obvious vehicle. He drove a good sixty miles before he started to relax.

Just as he removed his hat and the tension rod between his shoulders and settled into the driver's seat, George moved up and sat behind him.

'I need help, Jerry,' he admitted. 'The motel manager said there is a hospital in Roebourne. Will you drop me there please?'

He was quite calm about it, but looking at him, Shipley thought he had left it too long to volunteer for medical attention. While he admired the scientist's strength of will, he could not wait to tell him how relieved he was to take George to the hospital.

'We're about four hours out, mate. Can you hang on?'

George didn't answer. He staggered back to lie on the bed, and they motored on in silence.

Late in the afternoon, they arrived at a spread of small stone buildings, each with its own little wooden veranda. The Blue Duck pulled up outside the administration building. The hospital was well kept, even though it looked as if it was built in the nineteenth century.

The three of them went in together to be met by a matron who was in the process of arguing with a woman sitting at a typewriter. She expertly dismissed the secretary and walked over to assist George to a bench seat by the door.

'How long has he been in this condition?' she commanded and, before they could answer, cried, 'Dorothy! Call nurse Avril please. Tell her it's urgent. I will meet her in room 3.'

With that, she assisted the scientist down the corridor, firing off questions at his two compadres. Aster informed her of the incident with the cone snail and George's slide into his current state. When they got to room 3, the matron confiscated George, sent them back to admissions, and disappeared through the door.

They waited there for what seemed like an hour before a younger nurse in her late thirties came out to them.

'He's had a massive stroke, causing paralysis in his neck, left shoulder, and part of his thigh. Also he has trauma to his face and hands. Was there an accident?' Her pause wasn't long enough for them to give an answer. 'We don't know yet how serious it has affected his internals, but he's going to have to stay here until we find out.' Her voice raised a level to the point she was scolding them for not bringing him in sooner.

'I'm sorry, ma'am, but we have been in the wilderness hundreds of miles from here. George fell out of the vehicle after he had the stroke. It's been an epic journey and a miracle we got here at all,' Alice responded quietly but firmly, which quelled the nurse's tirade. She clearly understood the obstacles the Top End could throw at them.

'Yes, of course.' Her voice turned to a whisper. 'Well, he's here now. We'll do our best for him.' Then she raised her voice again. 'It's just that if he had received treatment quickly, he could have a better chance of full recovery. We've got him on an IV, and he's been given aspirin for the moment. Matron is very good at her job, but unfortunately, there is no doctor available to prescribe anything else.' She went back to scolding mode. 'You see, we are in the process of transferring the hospital to Karatha. There is only a skeleton staff and minimal equipment.' After apologising flippantly, she hurried back into room 3 and closed the door.

The young couple stood for a moment then asked the receptionist if it would be possible to see their friend. She phoned the room before informing the couple that the matron would let them know.

The sun was setting as they wandered outside in the hospital grounds. A cool breeze blew in from the nearby Harding River as they discussed what they would do while their friend was laid up. As they were speaking, a woman appeared on the veranda of the admissions building and waved them over with an update.

'I'm sorry to inform you,' said the woman in an extremely professional tone, 'but your friend is to be transferred to Karatha in the morning. He will be taken by ambulance, and looks like he may be there for at least a week. Matron advised me that you may visit him now.'

Aster and Shipley raced into room 3 and were met by a lopsided grin on their friend's face. He was happier than they would have thought, but he explained that they should carry out their plan and come back and pick him up.

The matron, standing beside the bed, interjected. 'You would be well advised to ring the hospital at Karatha before you come back,' she stated with her custom-made annoying and overbearing tone.

Ignoring her, Shipley asked, 'Is there anything you need from the bus, George?'

They arranged to transfer some of George's personal items, including a textbook and his writing file. Shipley drove into town and bought him a lolly box and some glossy magazines from a service station. They put together a small package that could be carried in the ambulance and said their goodbyes.

George had written a shaky letter advising whomever it concerned that he had given them permission to use the bus as they saw fit. He placed the letter and a note in Shipley's hand and told him where to find the registration papers. The sailor opened the note a slit and, without fully reading it, nodded assent that he understood what it was about. Aster ran back to his bedside and gave George an extra hug and a kiss.

They walked out of the hospital for the last time. It was a very emotional time as the Blue Duck pulled on to the southern road minus its greatest asset.

PART V

THE STASH

CHAPTER 21

The Blue Duck was as reliable as sunset; she was as tough as mallee root, but her top speed was only forty miles an hour. It wasn't too noticeable on the skinny tarred roads or the dirt tracks of the outback, but once they got on the dual highway, it felt slow. It took ages to reach a mark on the horizon. And as they closed on larger towns, there was more traffic, and most of it passed them like they were standing still.

Retarding their progress even more was the danger of driving at dusk or dawn or through the night when the nocturnals came out to play. Hundreds of kangaroos and wallabies, dozens of emu, and the odd wombat and echidna presented major hazards to the unwary driver. Crows, bush rats, and ants were the only benefactors.

The evidence of unwary drivers was displayed as zillions of carcasses lining the edges of the highway. Jerry had no desire to be labelled a UD, so he made a habit of pulling over when the day turned to dusk and wouldn't set out again until the earth turned far enough to see the sun again.

After two full days of driving, they were getting close to their destination. Jerry Shipley was invaded by daily pangs of guilt. He tried to work out how he was going to explain his other life, including his real name, to Aster. He pushed back the thoughts and concentrated back on their new mission.

'Okay, Aster,' he blurted, 'here's how the plan is going to go down.' His tone was a little too peremptory. 'I'll park in an inconspicuous spot, and you will stay with the Duck. I don't want anyone to connect me to this contraption. It will be dangerous for you and George.' Alice agreed, and Jerry continued, 'When I come back, we'll leave tomorrow morning, so don't worry if I'm late tonight, although I hope I won't be.'

Half an hour later, he pulled off the highway, rattled along a gravel track, and parked under a grove of tamarisk trees. To the west was a walking trail over small dunes, lending itself to the sea. Time was slipping them into the afternoon, and Jerry had to leave quickly. He had been to this place before and told Aster about a safe swimming spot at the beach. He mentioned the need for keeping a low profile, having no campfires, and keeping a distance from anyone who came by. He hooked his pack over his shoulders and jogged up the trail to the highway.

In less than fifteen minutes walking down the highway, a woman with blue hair driving a car to match her toner picked him up. She was going through to Perth and seemed a little disappointed when Jerry asked her to drop him off just ten miles down the road. There was hardly any traffic on the side road, so Jerry jogged and walked the couple of miles to town. When he got there, he saw a familiar sight outside the pub and patted his panel van like a cowboy patted his horse as he walked into the hotel.

'Hey, look what the cat dragged in!' An excited call came from his friend Don.

Don was carrying three schooners across from the bar to a table where Taffy and Lee sat with three other people Jerry didn't recognise. His friends were elated to see him and eager to learn about his job with Geldo the pirate. Don pushed the three beers over to his friend and told him that he had to drink them fast to catch up with the rest of the group. Of course, Jerry refused, but he was grateful to drink at least one of them.

Questions began flying at the itinerant fisherman, questions that made him squirm. He didn't want to lie to his mates, but he knew he could never tell them the truth about the last eleven and a half weeks of his life. It would put them all in danger just knowing the smuggler who robbed from the mob.

'Sorry to tell you, boys, but I've got to pick up my car and leave town right away.'

'Shit, that's fine. It's your car, but you can't leave now. You just bloody got here,' blurted Don. 'Besides, we want to welcome you back. We've got to have a celebration. Here's to you, Badger!' He raised his glass, and everyone at the table clashed them together.

'The Badger!' they shouted in unison.

Jerry had not heard his nickname in some time, and it was surreal to hear it now from his mates and total strangers. He pondered over his real name, reflecting on his ding names, Jesus and Geronimo, and his assumed alias, Jerry Shipley.

'Fuck, my life is un-fucking believable at the moment. I'm sorry, I do have to leave today,' he cried out, a little miserably. Then composed himself and added, 'But, yes, seeing as you asked, I will have another beer.'

He chugged his second beer like pouring water into a bucket of sawdust and banged it down on the table.

'I've really got to go, guys. Is there any petrol in the van?'

He saw the disappointment in their eyes and regretted having to lie to them. There was nothing he could do about it except apologise and tell them he would see them again soon.

Lee told him he had filled the tank that morning and sidled over. He gave Badger the keys and a hug to say goodbye. Don and Taffy hugged him too, and so did the strangers, which Shipley thought was kind of funny. Jerry assumed he was leaving without giving too much away.

Then Don shouted, 'Who you working for now, Badge?'

He turned with a blank page in his head, but before he thought of anything, Lee asked, 'Which way you headed?'

Still nothing formulated in his mind except a tiny twinge of guilt that the question could catch him out. He smiled and pointed a pretend gun at them. 'Can't tell you, boys, or I'll have to shoot you.' He swallowed hard and walked out.

One of the new friends called out, 'What's her name, you lucky son of a gun!' It was as if a penny dropped on the group, and they all laughed.

'Yeah, Badger, what's her name? Must be a hot chick if it's so important that you have to leave right away!'

As difficult as it was to leave, he felt good to be back in his own car again. He revved the engine and spun it backwards out of its bay like a rodeo bull coming out of the chute. The torque on the V8 was ten times that of the Duck, and he spun the wheels and smoked out of the parking lot.

Reaching under the seat, he pulled out the towel containing his wallet, including his driving licence. Up to now, he had been nervous whenever police were around, but now he was as legal as he was gonna get again, and it felt good.

The beautiful Aster had just come back from an ocean dip. She wore a skimpy bikini, and her hair draped wet across her tanned shoulders. She continued drying her dark tresses, staring hard at the strange white van coming towards her down the gravel track. She smiled a big hearty smile of relief, pleased to see it was Jerry.

The driver's window was down, and he smiled back at her. The look in their eyes was definitely attraction, and they both realised it at the same moment. She leaned in and kissed him. It was a kiss that neither of them wanted to end. In a fit of passion, Jerry pulled the girl through the car window while their lips never parted.

It was midnight. They had been in the white van since before the sun went down. It was more than passion. It was as if they had waited for each other since the time they were born. Both lived a world apart. Both grew up in different cultures. Both had been anguishing over falling in love with someone who didn't know their real name. She would have to leave the country soon, so Alice's confession bubbled closer to the surface than her friend's. Jerry diffused the angst when he began organising the next phase of their plan but got a surprise at her response. He'd never considered for one moment that Aster had never driven a car.

'But you come from America!' he yelled incredulously. 'America is the land of the cars. Everything we do from here depends on you being able to drive a car. I thought you didn't drive because the Duck is kind of . . . er . . . like . . . er . . . a truck or something.' He inserted a sigh to calm himself. 'I don't know what I thought,' he stammered. 'I'm sorry, Aster. I just assumed.'

'I'm a fast learner,' she offered, opening her palms to the space between them.

By sunup, her lessons began in earnest. She drove the panel van at least fifty times around the parking area near the grove of trees. They were laughing and hugging each other as the instructor covered the basics: reversing, braking, accelerating, signalling, and the whole shebang. She was right. She was a fast learner.

Although the van was more difficult to reverse than a sedan, she did well, even perfecting the reverse park, using the rear-view mirrors and mastering the three-point turn. It took most of the morning to complete the driving lessons, as they were interrupted with several passion stops. Eventually, they got back on their road trip, this time in separate vehicles.

The risk was if she got pulled over without a licence; they'd be in big trouble. It was too much to ask for her to drive the Duck, and the plan had been to smuggle the cargo in the van so the duck could remain anonymous. This would change everything. Jerry prepared for plan B, and they took off to the south. Aster drove the van behind the bus, with Shipley keeping a wary eye on his friend via the rear-view mirrors.

A small fishing town, complete with a crayfish-processing factory, loomed up in front of them. They were several miles off the main highway, closing in on a massive bay. Jerry led the two-vehicle cortège. He pulled to the side of the road and wedged the Blue Duck alongside some bushes between two hillocks. He considered anyone driving at speed would probably not notice the Duck in this position. He jostled Aster across to the passenger seat and drove the van a short distance into town.

They parked in the Bay Hotel car park amid forty or fifty other vehicles. Aster wanted to use the loo, but Jerry advised against it.

'Sorry, my dear. We can't risk exposing ourselves around this district.' He chuckled at his pun. 'You'll have to tie a knot in it until we get to a bush.'

She was a smart girl; she understood.

They trudged back to the Duck, cranked the engine, and took off. A short distance later, they took a turn down a sand track tracing the coastline, retracing the same trail where he and Abelio had collected a truckload of crayfish.

'God, it seems a lifetime ago when I came up this track.' Jerry spoke with a touch of anguish. His face was a carved block of concentration when they passed the micro shed that marked Geldo's gate.

He kept driving for a mile or so until they reached a disused fisherman's hut, where he swung a right down a sandy pathway. It was the place where he had found the oar and was a perfect place to park. The hut hid the bus from the sand track. On the seaward side, they were tucked in behind the dunes. The couple walked up over the sand hill and looked out.

In the distance, Shipley spied the *Tulip* anchored in the same spot he had left it many weeks before. What pleased him more was, he spotted the *Black Queen* anchored alongside it.

That is Geldo's brother's boat, he thought. *Great! They teamed up.*

All the smugglers had to do now was wait. Aster cooked dinner on the gas stove. They settled in with something folks back in the day referred to as champagne: a bottle of Barossa Pearl. A poor substitute, it tasted like wine and was full of bubbles. Although it was good to be alone together, they remained apprehensive, thinking of what would happen tomorrow.

Jerry heard it first. It was the muffled sound of an outboard motor. He jumped out of the bus and ran up over the sand dunes. It was easy to make out the familiar shape of Geldo's dinghy running out to his freezer boat. Aster joined him in time to see Geldo's brother puttering out to the *Black Queen*.

'Good!' exclaimed Jerry. 'They're leaving together.'

The pair crouched and waited until the two fishing boats were well out of sight. He signalled Aster to get back in the Duck, and to her surprise, he gunned it flat out to get over the soft sand, where it splashed into the sea. Hooking a ninety-degree turn, he sailed straight up to where the squatters' houses sat close to the water. An old jinker lay between the houses, and on the jinker was a dilapidated fishing vessel, a total non-floater and a perfect place for them to stash the drugs.

Jerry cruised the Duck up on to the beach and drove it alongside the wreck on the jinker. They took about half an hour to transfer the bags on board the wreck. Another hour later, they secreted it to a dry place in the hold and set the trap. Jerry was assiduous in moving two large barrels into the hold alongside the drugs.

He took a scrap of paper from his shirt pocket and followed the instructions with the tools and equipment he had on hand. It proved difficult to cover their tracks on the land until they got some help from the rising tide. The high water erased the distinctive tread marks of the Blue Duck. The trap was set. Now it was up to fate to see if it would work.

They sailed back to the deserted hut, hit the beach, and followed their wheel marks on to the sand track and back to the van. Three hours later, the two vehicles were travelling north, miles away from the scene of the crime.

Coming into a moderately large municipality, Jerry pulled up underneath some trees and parked in the shade. Aster manipulated the van to park in behind him. There was a public phone box on the street and a drinking fountain outside a toilet block in the park nearby. By this time, it was late afternoon, so Shipley asked Aster to wait at the bus, and he strode off in the direction of the main street. He wasn't gone all that long. He returned with several shopping bags laden with mysterious items.

'More food?' inquired Aster.

'Buzzzz! Wrong!' Shipley smiled.

He climbed up into the Duck and emptied the contents of the bags on the bed.

'How's your painting skills, Aster?' he beamed.

There were three rolls of masking tape and at least thirty spray cans of paint: greens, browns, blacks, greys, and white. She laughed.

'What the heck! What is all this for?' She was very curious.

'We are going to paint the Duck! This machine is like a neon sign because of its awesomeness, but on top of all that, it's bright bloody blue. It's like saying, "Hi, everybody, we're here!" We were in the top end and then we went south and now we are here. "Oh, that's funny, strangers sold drugs to a madman, and the blue bus was spotted. Oh yes, and drugs were found in a wreck, and guess what, yeah, there was the Blue Duck there too".' He waxed theatrical as he spoke, gesticulating and posturing like he was acting out a TV soap opera.

'You're so crazy, right, you lovable rogue you.' Aster laughed, reflecting the same zany antics.

The two-vehicle convoy drove out of town after dark without seeing any road kill. Any stray wildlife had been thinned out by unwary drivers as the town expanded. Jerry found a suitable place to pull off the highway and settle for the night. They threw themselves together in the bed on the Blue Duck and woke in the morning feeling fantastic. After a scout around the camp, Jerry reckoned that he found a good place to do the job.

He drove further off the road and stopped in a clearing sheltered by sandhills and scant hardy trees. The two of them went to work until the bus resembled a camouflaged army vehicle with pike. Aster thought the paint job did the bus justice, and in a funny sort of way, the new paint did give the effect of making it look less conspicuous.

Jerry simply commented, 'It will do!'

CHAPTER 22

They spent the rest of the day exploring the sand tracks while the paint dried and, the next morning, headed out early. Driving back to town, they stopped at the same spot by the park and made several calls out of the smelly phone box. One of the phone calls was to find out how George was doing at the hospital.

They were formally and a little caustically informed that his parents had organised a private plane to collect him and relocate him to his home in Victoria. The woman's voice also relayed a message that George would send a parcel to Perth City Post Office in the name of Aster B. Nightingale. Jerry was annoyed that they had spent money and time on painting the bus. Not having to pick up George meant that they could now leave it somewhere in storage.

They also made a call to the Cuda, and Aster gave the story they had concocted to the mafia boss and quickly hung up. With George's departure, they needed to change their plans and get rid of the Duck. So they searched the phone book for storage facilities capable of securing the vehicle. The first option wasn't even a consideration when they drove out there. It was a wrecking yard, and the slovenly owner wanted a small fortune to leave the Duck in an open paddock. Option two was much better. The fellow on the phone promised that the storage shed was kept locked most of the time because it housed valuable aircraft parts. So they wasted no time driving out there.

Arriving at the airfield nearly five miles out of town, Jerry parked the Duck behind his van by the side of a hangar and signalled to Alice to wait while he went to check things out. He proceeded towards the door under a brilliant white-painted sign with black writing shouting, 'Office'. He turned a knob and pushed the door just below another sign that quietly stated, 'Open'. Three steps into the little room, he breasted a tall, counter top hiding a desk and peered down on a typewriter, telephone, and a woman busily sorting through a pile of receipts. His inquiries induced her to summon the manager, Mr Baladene.

Mr Baladene came out of a side office and, with a handshake and a smile in his voice, turned himself into Bob. His familiarity unsettled Jerry, who wracked his brain trying to put a finger on where, when, and if ever they had met. Bob Baladene by look, name, or nature didn't flick any switches in Jerry's recall box. In fact, he was quite certain they had never met, but it was weird how the guy smirked like he wanted Jerry to wake up and recognise him.

Maybe Bob's style of friendliness is nothing more than a simple flaw in his personality, thought Shipley.

Alice remained in the van with the radio on ABC talkback when the manager enticed Jerry into the hangar, where they just happened to pass by his newly acquired airplane.

'Shipped from the United States. Just arrived last week,' Bob proudly confided. 'Only flown her twice. Been too busy. Haven't had time to scratch my arse lately.' The manager kept on talking to Jerry like he was his long-lost buddy.

The pair walked around the propeller end of the plane and stopped by the far wall. Bob leaned against a metal box containing a compressor motor, a row of switches, and a gaggle of hoses. Jerry stood behind the big blue box, waiting for a break in the conversation so he could ask about garaging the Blue Duck.

Bob, however, was more interested in bragging about his new acquisition. He began in an imposing manner, introducing the plane as his new Cessna 172K. For whatever reason, Bob started giving Shipley a rundown on the specifications of a big boy's toy Jerry really had not the least amount of interest in.

Shipley began getting edgy. It seemed like this Baladene guy was stalling, trying to distract him. Suddenly, he felt himself seized around his chest by a pair of strong arms. His own arms were locked to his side, and he could feel a man's breath close to the back of his neck. His brother's training kick started his reflexes. Instantly, he lifted his right leg and pushed off the heavy metal box. The force sent them both hurtling backwards into the wall behind. In the same movement, Jerry dropped his body to the floor, slipping through the attacker's grasp.

He rolled on his back and, without losing momentum, swept a kick across the man's shins. The sweep took the man's legs out from under him, causing him to topple heavily on to the hard concrete floor. Jerry didn't stop the counter-attack; in a blur, he was on top of the man with his fist raised. He was about to deliver a shower of punches on the would-be attacker's face, but he stopped short.

'Marin? For crying out loud, what the hell are you doing?' Jerry yelled, a look of bewilderment clouding his features.

Marin held his hands in front of his face, ready to defend the blows. 'Well, Badger, I was trying to surprise you, but I won't fuckin' do that anymore. You're a fucking nightmare, man. You almost fucking killed me! In fact, I think my arm's fucking broke. Help me up, fuck yah.'

Baladene was laughing his box off, watching the practical joke backfire. He came forward, and together he and Jerry assisted Marin to his feet. Bob explained how Marin had recognised the van burbling up the driveway to the hangar and asked him to set up a little surprise welcome.

'A prank to give you a bit of a friendly welcome.' He described it.

Bob Baladene, whom Marin referred to as BB, had remained firm buddies with Marin after fighting together in Vietnam. They were part of an attachment of navy troops flying helicopters from Vung Tau, Nui Dat, and Long Tan. They were a couple of larrikins trying to live with a lot of fucked-up realities from their past. Jerry knew enough about Marin to know that he didn't always think things through before he acted, and it seemed his mate had the same shortcomings. He apologised to Marin and offered to look at his arm. But the veteran shrugged it off with a laugh.

During the reunion, Shipley felt hunted. He let the war buddies ramble on while he tried to process an alibi for turning up with Alice in the Blue Duck. Alice didn't yet know his real name. How could he explain to her and Marin that he was living a dangerous lie, a lie that could get them all killed.

And Marin! Shipley's mind was racing. Marin and he had tripped and surfed together and got inside each other's head deeper than an old couple on their golden wedding anniversary. He might have some mental issues, but he was no fool and could spot bullshit a mile away. Shipley decided there and then that he would have to trust him. Although their friendship was not like the brotherhood of war buddies, he knew Marin loved him like a brother and that his loyalty was uncompromising.

Apart from saving Marin's life, Badger was the first civilian who had sincerely tried to understand where he'd been and what he'd gone through in the war. He was the first one to accept his fucked-up mental moods without making a leper out of him. Shipley was the first person to welcome Marin as a friend and stand by him when others wanted him gone.

Most people tolerated him because he always carried dope to smoke with them, but Jerry never worried about that. He understood that Marin trusted him as a loyal friend. As far as Marin was concerned, it was because of Shipley's simple acts that he reckoned he owed fealty to him. He made some kind of screwed-up pact with himself to be his friend for life, and he told him so often.

The day was dragging itself towards lunchtime, and apart from hunger pangs, Alice was getting hot and restless sitting in the van. She got out and stretched her arms over her head and shook her hair away from the perspiration at the back of her neck. As she wandered casually around the rear side of the hangar on the opposite end of the office, she saw the tail of a small plane poking out of a pair of gigantic open doors. She strolled over to check it out.

On hearing people talking, she faltered and strained to hear if Jerry's voice was one of them. A man was telling a story about how he came to be working for a man called BB. They had been flying helicopters together in Vietnam, and this guy asked him to come and work for him. She couldn't hear Jerry's voice, so she turned around and wandered back towards the office. At precisely the moment she rounded the hangar wall, out of earshot, Jerry interrupted the buddies.

'Listen, guys!' he projected. 'There's something I got to tell you, Marin.' He looked directly into Marin's eyes, and straight away, Marin caught the gist.

'Sure, mate. We'll just be a minute, Bob.' He dismissed his war buddy.

Shipley and Marin walked out of the big shed on to the tarmac and stood together in the hot midday sun. The man with many names began his story with a military flair.

'This is top secret, Marin. I need your trust on what I'm about to tell you. Have I got it?'

As insouciant as ever, Marin parried, 'Badger, you know I'd give you me arse and shit through me ribs. Brothers for life, mate. Of course, you can trust me.'

If anyone else but this guy responded in such a flippant manner, no one in their right mind would believe they could trust them. But Shipley knew Marin better than that. So without giving too much detail of the amount of drugs involved, he gave Marin a rundown on how he met Alice and why he changed his name. Describing the mafia threat along with the potential danger of the Kraggasti brothers, he finished off with their need to hide the Blue Duck. Marin's response made Jerry laugh.

'I gotta be honest with you Badger, but you coulda told me any fucking name you want. I only know you as Badger.'

Jerry divulged his secret. 'Well, it's Shipley, Marin. Jerry Shipley, and while we're at it, what's your last name?'

'Dougherty, that's how I got the Doc tag,' Marin answered, sounding dejected.

'The . . . *Doc tag*?' Shipley tilted his head.

'Yeah, the Yanks branded me with it in Nam. We flew with 'em for a while, and they translated my initials from MD to Doc. It stuck too, so all my mates call me that now—everyone that got back alive, that is.' His voice trailed off as he began to tip into depression.

Jerry stepped forward and gave his friend a hug. 'Glad to see you again, Doc!'

'You too, Jerry.' Marin smiled as he warmed to his friend's gesture, at the same time making a big deal out of rubbing his swollen elbow.

It turned out to be a very good day for Shipley. Although most people considered Doc a loose cannon, Jerry was pleased to reunite with him. Doc's mate BB owned 50 percent of the airfield he managed and was happy to give Jerry 'mate's rates' for harbouring the weird-looking vehicle. George had left them plenty of money for expenses, so Shipley phoned through a telegram to George, letting him know where he could retrieve the newly painted Duck. What was more, Marin and BB owned and piloted a plane and a helicopter between them, and they offered their services any time Jerry needed them.

Sheila, the receptionist, made coffee for herself and Aster. The girls came out with a stack of sandwiches, and they all sat round a table with a perfect view of the new Cessna 172K and ate lunch. Jerry refused a barrage of insistence from the host, Mr Baladene, to have a third beer.

'No, really, BB, we have to get on the road. If I have any more, I'll be here till breakfast.'

'That's the fucking idea, *Jerry Shipley*. We love you, man. Why can't you fucking stay?' Doc over emphasised the name so dramatically it could have sounded threatening except Jerry knew Marin better than that. It was just his odd sense of humour.

They said their goodbyes in that familiar manner of embracing one and all with loudly spoken farewells. Even Sheila got in on the act, and she'd only just met Aster and Jerry.

The V8 engine burbled slowly along the concrete driveway as they left the airfield. Then heading south again, Jerry and Aster reminisced about their time with George and his amazing invention. Going down the highway, seeing no other traffic, Aster sat in silence, feeling a touch of guilt over having been with George and her blossoming romance with Shipley. Jerry's mind was occupied with the confession of his real name, but he had no idea how he was going to breach it with his amazing new girlfriend.

PART VI

GELDO'S HELL

CHAPTER 23

Cuda put his phone down and sat staring at the ceiling for a good minute. He then made a dozen calls to organise a meet with the other executives. Only two were contactable, but three made a quorum, so they got right to it. A call rang out to his driver, Roberto, and another to Wheezer, the foreman. The boss organised them to gather for breakfast at his Villa Napoli Restaurant.

Roberto and Wheezer sat at a table just inside the front door, while Cuda squeezed himself into a booth further back near the kitchen opposite the bar.

Twenty minutes later, two gentlemen turned up dressed in expensive suits with open shirts and no ties. Both were unshaven and looked as if they had rushed to get to work on time. They hunkered down in the booth with Cuda and got into a serious discussion. The wait staff didn't bat an eyelid when the three men near the kitchen erupted in curses and loud diatribe.

Wheezer looked back a couple of times to check they were not killing each other. Satisfied, he went back to sipping his coffee. Before his cup was empty, however, Cuda beckoned him to their table. He whispered for a long minute into the big man's ear, and Wheezer left the restaurant. Roberto sat nursing his coffee cup by himself while the little boss man got back to his conversation.

'I got a crazy call this morning, but there was too much inside information to ignore it.' Cuda mixed his languages in a perfect blend of coded ding speech. 'Some bitch and her husband who would not leave their names found Belario running scared along a beach.' The two men nodded for him to continue.

'Yeah! Belario! She said the skipper asked for the couple's help to escape from someone trying to kill him.'

The gentlemen sat back out of their huddle with astonished looks.

'Belario!' one of them gasped. 'We expected him weeks ago!'

'Don't fucking worry about it. It gets fucking worse.' He swore in English then reverted back to ding. 'The sheila said Belario gave her my number and told her the Rook's got the goods.'

The three discussed minute details of the phone call. They each agreed it sounded suspicious, but it smacked of authenticity in that the skipper would be the only one to know about the shipment and pass on Cuda's home number. There was a lot that didn't add up, but like Cuda said before, the important facts might mean that millions of cash would 'go down the gurgler'. There was just too much at stake to ignore it. Between the three of them, they agreed to organise a team to reconnoitre Geldo's lair while they waited to contact the rest of the investors and bring them up to speed.

It took no time at all for Cuda and his cohorts to arrange enough soldiers and get them a four-wheel drive to check out Geldo's desert hideaway. Then as an extra security, they had three men take a long-range speedboat and go into the camp from the ocean side. All seven men were going in heavy. All owned pistols, but they were also armed with shotguns, rifles, and machine guns. There was enough ammunition in the vehicle and the boat to win back a small country.

Roberto drove the boat, and Tony Alma and Chicken Man Prino rode along with him. Vito drove the car, with Wheezer riding shotgun. The two men travelling with them in the rear seat were shadowy figures, conscripted by the foreman for this mission at short notice. They hadn't been solidly tested, but Wheezer was going to make sure today was going to change that.

The new recruits were firm buddies. One was tall and light-skinned, borderline albino, while his friend was swarthy, short, and stocky. Within the ranks of mob soldiers, they were called Salt and Pepper because they looked like shakers. Their stature and nicknames made them appear comical, but in truth, they were a couple of seriously bad men. Myth and legend had it that they had police records so long they had to be lugged around in a pickup truck. Salt and Pepper sat in the back seat like an odd pair of tombstones, listening to Wheezer's instructions.

Their vehicle turned on to a sand track and proceeded slowly south, stalling for time to allow the speedboat to get into position. None of the group in the car was familiar with the area, so the slower pace became a benefit for the driver to get used to driving on sand. They made a stop at a small roadside shed, parked their vehicle in the centre of the driveway, and walked on to the property.

A man in his early forties was chopping wood near the corner of his house. It was a ramshackle fisherman's hut thrown together with odd building materials and an amateurishly patched roof. The axe man looked up, eyeing the foursome suspiciously.

'Can I help you, blokes?' He spoke loudly with more than a touch of aggression.

He kept the axe across the front of his body, grasping it with white knuckled hands.

'Yeah! We're looking for the Kraggasti brothers. Are they home?' Wheezer was the spokesman.

'The Kraggastis? That makes sense. Hope you catch 'em,' said the man knowingly. 'Those cunts don't live here though. They're about three miles down that way.' He pointed the head of the axe to the south.

Wheezer asked him what type of cars the brothers drove. His answer seemed satisfactory to the foreman, but before they went, he asked, 'We are going to need to look around, mate. You don't mind, do yer!' His voice held a threatening tone.

The axe man nodded faintly with a look of concern. Then he added, 'There's nothing here, mate. All of my pots have been burned by some crazy person. I'm out for the season, so I got fuck all. So sure, go yer hardest. Have a look!'

That was enough for Wheezer. He clearly understood what the man was up against with neighbours like the Kraggasti brothers. He gave the signal to his cohorts to head back to their vehicle, and they drove away. From the car, Wheezer caught glimpses of the ocean between the dunes.

At last he sighted what he was looking for: two boats anchored in the distance. The *Tulip* was familiar to him, and he assumed the other one was the *Black Queen*, so he ordered Vito to slow down.

'We should be getting close. Keep your eyes peeled for a white Ford truck and a black Holden ute. Before he had finished speaking, Vito pointed at a roadside mini shed.

'That'll be it!' the driver exclaimed.

'Yeah, reckon yer right. Just drive straight in and pull up close to the house.' Wheezer sounded confident.

Vito swung the Toyota around the little shed and gunned it up to the house, stopping just ten feet from the door. The four men exploded from the vehicle like a pack of front-row forwards. Wheezer called out Geldo's name as he stepped to the side of the door, drawing his pistol. There was no answer. He called again, this time louder. Still nothing. He nodded at Pepper, who immediately smashed his shoulder into the door. The force busted the flimsy catch, and the door flew open. Pepper and his taller counterpart raced into the house with their guns aimed from chest height.

A few seconds later, Salt and Pepper emerged from inside the house with the empty news for the foreman. Wheezer responded by getting the binoculars out of the glove box and surveying the boats anchored on the horizon. Further away, he spied familiar white sprays coming off an approaching boat moving at speed. Then Salt nudged his boss's elbow, and without a word, he pointed to the house on the other side of the jinker.

There was smoke rising from an outdoor fireplace. Around the smoky area was a gathering of twelve people enjoying the sunny afternoon with a keg of beer and a pig on a spit. They had seen the Toyota race in and watched dumbfounded as the four men conducted their raid.

When Geldo saw his house broken into, a volcano of rage bubbled up from his gut. He was about to run at the strangers and bust their heads, but when he saw they were carrying guns, he faltered. He yelled at his brother, and they sped inside and came out with a bunch of shotguns and rifles. They dealt them out to the revellers like a pack of cards.

Wheezer counted six weapons and mentally checked their effectiveness against what he and his team were carrying. It took him no time at all to make a decision. There were half a dozen armed fishermen against four hardcore gangsters, and Wheezer figured his boys could easily take them out.

To avoid a bloodbath, he called out to Geldo in a confident and surprisingly relaxed tone, 'Put your guns down! There won't be any need for all of *you* to die today! We need to talk to you, Geldo. Just you. So drop your weapon and walk over here by yourself.'

Geldo was not a man who could control his temper easily. As far as he was concerned, these men had broken into his house and ruined his party for no reason. There was no way he was going to do what they asked.

He bawled back at Wheezer, 'You fuckin', come over here by yourself if you want to talk to me, and after I finish ramming this shotgun up your arse, I'll bury yer fucking cronies in Davy Jones's funeral parlour.'

Geldo's response put Wheezer in a bit of a predicament because his orders were to reconnoitre the pirate's lair and report back. It didn't take much to see that several members of the group were unarmed bystanders. He would not have concerns about killing the Kraggastis and their henchmen, but a dozen murders posed a bit too much of a problem. His bluff hadn't worked, so he needed to settle the situation down, bring in some calm, and try a different tack.

Salt and Pepper had no such thoughts. They walked straight at the party people, shooting anyone carrying a gun. It all happened so quickly nobody at the scene had time to do anything about the black and white maniacs. Geldo got hit first and then his brother. Next to them were the three guys with rifles, and they fell like ten pins. The pirate and his brother were only winged because they were moving when they saw Salt and Pepper go insane.

There were people running in all directions. The party guests were screaming. A woman fainted, and her friend tried to pick her up amid the flying bullets. Panic overran her, and she left the wounded female on the ground and fled around the back of the house, ducking and weaving to avoid a hail of incoming lead. One or two shots came back at the foursome, but the two killers had loosed both magazines with deadly accuracy. The shootout was deafening. No one could hear Wheezer screaming at everybody to stop firing until the first reload. By then it was too late; there were five dead on the ground and three injured.

To make matters worse, Geldo's rage hit fever pitch, and he began firing his shotgun wildly. He had taken a bullet through his chest, affecting his aim, but his pellets ricocheted off a wall and sprayed across Vito's face. Vito dived down behind a pile of wood five feet from the house. He couldn't see out of his left eye, so he stayed low and picked at the metal balls stuck in his cheek.

The older Kraggasti, Lannis, had a slug next to his heart; it was only instinct and reflex that got his massive body into the house. He lay in a pool of blood on his kitchen floor. Geldo sat in a chair by the back door, wielding his shotgun. He was badly shot and had difficulty reloading. He called the skinny kid over and told him to bring more shells and load for him. Astonishingly, the kid was more interested in killing the four shooters. He squeaked his protests at Geldo, who looked back at him like a proud father.

'Just do what yer fucking told. Load this one and that one.' He pointed to the rifle next to his dead brother. 'Then get over to the window and see who we're gonna kill first.'

With a bullet lodged in his chest, it was difficult, but he managed to swivel his head to check where his allies were. Mighty Mouse was cringing against the wall on the other side of the room. He had soiled his pants.

Geldo raised his eyebrows and snarled at him. 'You! Get as many bullets as you can find and bring them to me. There's a pistol in that drawer. Give it to me now!' He pointed the barrel of the shotgun towards the bureau.

When Mighty Mouse didn't budge, Geldo aimed the gun at him.

'I'm talking to you, Stinky. Move! Now! Go before I shoot you myself,' he wailed.

A long, long time ago, when Robbie Burns ploughed over a mouse nest, he coined the famous line 'The best laid plans of mice and men can go awry'. So what chance would the hurried, emotional plans of the wounded Kraggasti have to avoid disaster? It didn't look good for the pirate.

Outside, Wheezer was detonating a verbal atomic bomb on the Shakers. He called them back to Geldo's house and commanded them to get Vito out of the firing line. The foreman's anger got the attention of Salt and Pepper, but only in a matter-of-fact way. Wheezer might as well have been talking to his knees; their reactions were blatantly dismissive. They stood playing with their pistols and shuffling like they wanted to get back to their killing spree.

The roar of a speedboat resounded from the beach, and they heard the calls of Roberto and Chicken Man. Wheezer dismissed the maniacs with a grunt and strode down the side of the house to meet his more disciplined crew. He yelled across the water between him and the boat.

'They've got two wounded and one, two, possibly three other shooters. There're at least five down on their side, and Vito's copped a shot. See if you can cover the rear of that house.' He pointed to Lannis's place. 'But stay in the boat, and for crying out loud, try not to leave too many bullet holes like those two idiots did.' He flicked a ripple of sweat off his brow and went back to Vito and the maniacs. The boat gurgled along calm water just off the strip of beach and headed towards Lannis Kraggasti's squat.

Inside the death house, Skinny loaded two guns and left them on a chair next to the Rook. He snatched the pistol out of Mighty Mouse's hand and drooled over it as he carried it like a minion to his master. Then he picked up a semi-automatic .22 repeater and went to check the rear window. An open boat motored past his window not fifty yards away. He sighted down the barrel and pulled the trigger. Tony Alma was hit between the eyes with a perfect sniper shot. The boat roared to life and sped up to get out of range. The bow rose out of the water as the props dug in, sending a spray twenty feet into the air.

Chicken Man gave Roberto the bad news, confirming that Tony was dead. The driver turned the boat back to shore a hundred yards north of Lannis's house. He jumped ashore with a pistol in his belt, carrying a machine gun and a determined look on his face. He ran over the beach and took cover behind a hump of sand. Prino jumped out of the boat with an anchor on a rope and whacked it into the sand high up on the beach. He joined the driver with his two weapons.

Roberto waved hand signals for his partner to take a high track and come at the house from the eastern side. Twenty yards away, between him and the house, was a stack of oil drums and a couple of old craypots. Roberto shielded himself behind the drums and peeked out. There were three windows and a door on his side of the squatters' home. No sign of life showed through, so the driver ran directly up to the wall. He stooped low to pass under a window and stayed bent over as he headed for shelter behind some crates. It was then he noticed a woman's legs poking out from behind the boxes.

There was a trail of blood leading to her hide. When he crept up, he saw that she was still alive but had lost so much blood she would not survive. Her breathing was so faint he thought at first she was already dead. Then she opened her eyes and looked into his face. After a brief moment, she lapsed back into unconsciousness.

Roberto spat a bad taste out from the corner of his mouth and moved over to the door. The entryway appeared eerily ajar, so he got on his knees and peeped into the shaded room. The space was built over a concrete floor occupied by a laundry sink and washing machine. The internal door on the other side of the room was shut. He went in and listened for noises inside the house but could not hear anything.

Roberto flinched when he heard a gunshot. It came from behind him, outside to the east of a pile of drums. He checked for a response inside the house and then moved across to look outside. Above the grassy ridge, he saw Prino's thin frame jump down into a sandy crater, and a second later, his head appeared again as he waved at Roberto. He signalled to the driver that he had shot someone and gave an all-clear hand gesture.

Just then the knob on the inside door started turning; someone was coming out. Roberto turned and fired off four pistol shots through the flimsy door. He heard a faint call followed by a thud as a body fell to the floor. Quickly hurling himself forward, he kicked the door open and let loose with the machine gun.

Mighty Mouse was dead in front of him, and Skinny was running up the hallway on his way to Geldo in the kitchen. The bullets were ripping the guts out of the squatter's beach shack.

He heard Skinny yell, 'Ah! I'm hit!'

Meanwhile, Wheezer wrestled with his own set of problems. He was ropeable at the Shakers. He would not ordinarily make a call like this, but he had to bring this bullshit to an end.

He pointed at Salt and Pepper. 'You guys take out the shotgun! I'll go around the other side and block the exit.'

The Shakers smiled, rechecked their handguns, and ran to Lannis's house. When they got to within ten yards, they started firing through the half-open door. When no shots came back at them, Pepper took a snapshot look through the doorway. With a hand slide across his throat, he conveyed to Salt that Geldo was dead in the chair.

Salt and Pepper both entered the death house, single file. Geldo's left side was covered in blood, and he was slumped at an awkward angle in a chair by the door. His chin lay on his chest, and his right hand dangled lightly, holding a pistol with its barrel touching the floor. There was a shotgun across his lap and a rifle on a chair next to him.

Pepper picked up the shotgun and bent to grab the pistol. Suddenly, Geldo's hand came up firing. Pepper copped one at point-blank range. Then as he fell back, the pistol cracked five more times, and Salt joined his friend wherever seriously bad guys go when they check out.

Wheezer watched the scenario unfold from the west end of the building. He had run across open ground and sidled along to the kitchen window. Geldo appeared to have expired after taking out the Shakers, but Wheezer made sure of it with a bullet to the pirate's head.

When he fired the shot, he heard a muffled cry from the back of the room. The skinny punk had been watching reverently when Geldo killed Salt and Pepper, but when his mentor got shot in the face, he recoiled in horror and tried to suppress a scream too late.

Wheezer spotted the kid and let him have it before Skinny could raise his rifle. The foreman was a big man with stony features and glassy slits for eyes. After this fiasco, he was at breaking point; killing a kid almost tipped him over the edge. He walked into the kitchen and kicked Pepper's corpse.

'You fuckin' mental bastards!' he fumed and spat at Salt's bloody head. 'Look what you fucking done, ya crazy arses.'

Vito came in and laid a knowing hand on the foreman's shoulder. 'We gotta clean this up, boss,' he whispered. 'I'll get the boys, and we'll fix it, mate.'

'No!' said Wheezer. 'You wait a second. I'll take care of it. This is my mess, Vito. It was me that brought these fuckwits along. It's my fault. I'll get it sorted.' His tone was melancholic.

He walked outside and flapped his arm at the sandy ridge. Prino stood and started loping across the loose sand towards Lannis's shack. He gestured to the laundry door, where Roberto came out of his hide and walked warily up to his boss. Experience was a good teacher, but today's scenario was far from ordinary. It was a gruesome scene approaching that of a war zone. The foreman was an old soldier; he had seen death in many forms. He didn't flinch at taking out other soldiers or gangsters, but shooting the kid affected him more than he thought it would.

Still the ultimate professional, he already had a plan to clean up the bodies. He ordered Prino and Roberto to start collecting the corpses and drag them to the dinghies on the beach. Five were near the outside fireplace, one in the dune, and one behind the crates. Inside were Mighty Mouse, Geldo and his brother, and the kid. Their team had lost the Shakers and Tony, and Wheezer wanted their bodies placed separately.

When he checked the count on the beach, he looked about charily. 'I counted twelve. There's one missing. Come on, men, let's start combing the area. We can't afford witnesses on this little outing.'

Searching took twenty minutes out of their clean-up time. Then Prino noticed some footprints in the soft sand leading away from Lannis's barbecue area. They disappeared eastwards over the top of a low dune. When he followed them up, he saw that they led into a thicket, where he spied a patch of blue material glinting through the weeds.

'Okay! Come out, or I'll shoot,' he threatened.

He got a surprise when he saw a person slowly stand and walk sheepishly towards him. She was a girl about fifteen or sixteen years old. She had bruises on the side of her face and a black eye. Prino noted what looked like signs of rope burns around her wrists, and her dress was torn at the shoulder.

As she came to Prino, she held out her arms, and the gunman braced himself for an attack. Then he realised she wanted to embrace him.

'You killed them! You killed them! You got those horrible people! You saved me! Thank you so much!' Her voice was hoarse from either crying or screaming or both.

Prino held up his gun, but the girl ignored the gesture, moved closer, and wrapped her arms around his waist. She cuddled into him like a daughter finding her long-lost father. He pushed her back and held her at arms' length while he looked at her relieved features.

His mind raced; this was a serious situation. She was a witness to a mass murder, but it seemed that she was also a victim of the pirate's clan. Prino couldn't deal with killing her until he consulted his superior. He took the girl's hand and led her gingerly down the slope to the foreman.

Wheezer was a man used to making spontaneous decisions, especially under extreme conditions. He picked up on the scenario as his man brought the hostage to him. It didn't take much imagination to determine what the girl had been through as a prisoner of Geldo and Lannis Kraggasti. The difficult decision rested on whether to keep her alive to testify against his crew at a later date or set her free after being in the clutches of evil. There was no contest.

He reached out for the girl to come into his embrace for safety, the look on his face reflected sanctuary. The girl followed the foreman's signal and sidled close to him. He hugged her to his chest and, with the skill of a soldier and the movement of a striking cobra, snapped her neck so that she died instantly.

His team could see the effect the murder had on their foreman's face. He looked instantly older, until he shook himself like an animal fanning water off its fur. The shudder lasted three or four seconds before Wheezer started barking out a new set of orders.

'That makes twelve. Let's get 'em in the dinghies and out to the *Tulip*. Vito, are you well enough to keep watch on the gate?'

Vito nodded.

'Then make sure to stop anybody that tries to come on to the property. Can you do that?'

He nodded again and Wheezer turned around.

'Roberto! Put the Shakers in the speedboat with Tony and covered them up. I'll help you.' The wheeze in his voice was exacerbated to sound like grating iron. 'Chicken man! While we're gone, I want you to pick up all the weapons and ammunition and stow them in the Toyota. Then scour the area and try to find as many shell casings as you can and be prepared to help Vito stop anyone coming through the gate if he needs you.'

The dinghy motored towards the two boats on the horizon. They hefted the bodies on to the deck, and the two professionals started working on a *Tulip* bomb. Both men had plenty of experience rigging car bombs during their tours in Europe, and it wasn't too different getting this thing to explode, but Wheezer wanted to add an extra twist.

He wanted to weigh anchor and send the boat out into the deep ocean before it caught fire and cremated the bodies on board. The difficulty, he explained to Roberto, was making sure the wooden hulk burnt to a crisp before she sank. This way, there would be less evidence to search through. However, he reasoned that the fire might attract assistance before the *Tulip* disappeared forever, so the whole thing had to burn quickly.

Roberto had it covered. He convinced his foreman that he could make the thing explode using stuff he could find on board plus some explosives from the speedboat. Wheezer left him to it while he dragged the corpses and placed the gruesome cargo strategically around the forecastle. Kraggasti's dinghy was tethered to a mooring line. Before

Roberto climbed back into the speedboat, he sent the *Tulip* on its way due west at roughly six knots. On autopilot, it chugged and bumped against a head swell and a rising south wind.

Back on shore, Prino and the wounded Vito had hurriedly cleared up most of the death site to a reasonable degree. They began following their plans to search for the stolen cargo. They split up, except for Vito, who went back to sentry duty near the gate, nursing his swollen, still-bleeding face. The three others conducted a thorough search on both of the houses and the drums and crates spread over the two properties. Carefully, they checked for fresh-dug earth until at last they met back at Lannis's barbecue and shrugged at their futile efforts. Prino poured some beers from the keg and took a tall glass up to Vito at the gate.

All the men were tired. They'd been going full bore since early morning. Meeting with the bosses and organising the extra men and the vehicles were the easy part. The drive up the coast was mostly taken up with instructions from the foreman. Salt and Pepper might as well have been wearing earplugs. They didn't obey his orders, and that worried Wheezer more than all the other chaos. He had chosen the Tombstones for this job, so he would have to answer to the big bosses for the fuck-up.

Now as the three men stood wondering blankly where the drugs could be, Wheezer suddenly hit himself on the forehead with the heel of his palm. 'Did any of you search that rotting hulk on the jinker?'

Prino looked at Roberto and shrugged. Roberto shook his head and was about to voice an excuse, but Wheezer interrupted him.

'It's okay. It's so fucking obvious we all forgot about it. Let's have a look-see, shall we?'

Prino was the youngest and fittest. He leapt up on to the tyres and hoisted his thin frame over the bulwarks, landing with a hollow thud on the deck. His teammates jumped on to the deck, four seconds after him.

'What a piece of junk!' mouthed Roberto.

'Matches the rest of this shithole,' said Wheezer.

Chicken Man had gone below deck, but when he looked up, he could see Roberto through a massive hole where the engine hatch might once have been.

'I think we got something here, boys!' yelled the younger gangster.

He strode over to where a bundle of odd-looking packages were stowed in a dark corner near the stern. Wheezer got on his knees and bent over to look through the engine hatch to see what Prino was pointing at. He noticed the drums lying alongside a pile of leather bags. There was a strip of metal winding down the side and under a plate just in front of his man.

'Stop!' was the last sound that emanated from between Wheezer's lips.

Prino triggered the ingenious ignition designed by a master engineer. The explosion ripped Chicken Man to pieces. Roberto was blown through the air and landed ten yards away on the sand. Shrapnel from the blast caught Wheezer in the face, and he fell forward and down into the hold, where the fire was already burning with such ferocity that Roberto couldn't get anywhere near him. All the driver could do was abandon the hulk and stand back and watch the inferno devour everything.

It wasn't such a relatively loud blast but more an enormous thud, followed by a hiss as the flames blew out of the confined space and into the bright-blue sunshine. For such a large explosion, there was very little smoke, with everything being consumed by intense heat. Vito came running to help Roberto, who was reeling from the shock of seeing two more of his work buddies die.

'That fucking Geldo!' he fumed. 'He's taken us all out even from his place in hell!'

'Well, almost,' said Vito. 'At least we're still here.'

Roberto turned on Vito angrily. He grabbed him by the front of his shirt and shook him. 'You think we are going to survive this after we tell the boss what happened?' He paused, snarling, 'Then you must be living in Disneyland!' His eyes were watery, and the look on his face brought Vito back to reality.

PART VII

SMUGGLERS INC.

CHAPTER 24

Raindrops the size of locusts smashed against the windscreen, leaving broken little crystal bodies of water fluttering until the wipers batted them away. Brooding black clouds backlit by white sheets of lightning loomed around the plane like phantoms.

BB grappled the controls, desperate to hold the seaplane on course. It didn't seem all that long before the storm broke that he had taken off from a mowed-grass airstrip a hundred miles out of Koepang in Timor. BB pulled back the stick and watched through the blur of the prop as the little aircraft soared into clear blue sky. Within an hour and a half, a different kind of sky was trying hard to evict him.

Bob Baladene's battle to keep his plane in the air lasted another hour until at last the black clouds bowed a retreat behind the Cessna's tail. The welcome sun blinded the west window with ultra-white light and painted the sea below with a carpet of sparklers. Eventually, when the pilot spied land through a haze in the distance, he dropped the plane so close to the water he could almost put his feet in it. Several miles offshore, he let the floats touch down, and idled the plane to within ten yards of a cruiser anchored well outside a wide bay.

From the top of his peak, Marin watched through binoculars as the little plane set down beside the gleaming white pleasure craft. Quickly making his way to a helicopter, he strapped himself in and took off, heading towards the cruiser. As he hovered above, the walkie-talkie on the seat beside him blared.

'Okay, man, let her rip,' the crackle screeched.

Marin let down the cable and, in no time at all, hauled a bulging satchel on board. He landed back on the hill, unhitched the electric winch, delivered it and the bag to a woman in a waiting car, and then watched her as she drove away. The seaplane was nowhere to be seen since it had departed minutes after landing. The transfer was over in less than half an hour. On the surface, it seemed like a simple and unnecessary operation, but the military-style skill and timing involved was second to none. The profits from the escapade would be astronomical, while the exchange cut the risk of interception in quarters.

Marin checked his instruments against one last look at the car speeding along a dirt road far below him. He smiled as he addressed the microphone attached to the Top End helicopter flight company.

'This is Tango Echo Foxtrot. Come in, TEHC base. Over.'

A woman's voice from the base responded with radio etiquette.

'Sorry, guys, had to put her down for a bit. The old girl was losing oil pressure. Turned out to be a faulty seal on the oil filter. It's all right now though. I stopped the leak with a piece of my shoe,' he spoke casually. 'I repeat—all good now! ETA will be forty-five minutes overdue. Over.'

'Okay, what are your coordinates? Over,' said the voice with a touch of angst.

Marin read out his approximate location, using poetic licence to throw the base off the scent, and signed off. 'Over and out.'

BB and Marin were old hands at this game; they'd set up many similar runs since returning from the Vietnam conflict. Mostly, they brought in marijuana and sometimes heroin with the help of a bunch of veterans who were always on hand to link the chain. The major difference this time was that they were not smuggling drugs.

The station wagon pulled up at the rendezvous point at the same time the helicopter set down. Jenny jumped out, locked the car, and strapped herself in next to Marin, who operated the magic stick to return the whirlybird to the TEHC base. The convoluted action plan produced a maze of tactics designed to throw off any ideas of where the contraband could be found. It would require a large team of trackers to be at the crucial exchange points in order to witness the relay of the smuggled goods.

'What went wrong?' The flight centre manager was impatiently waiting out on the tarmac before Marin Dougherty landed the Bell 47J Ranger.

'It was a failed oil filter seal. Had to fix it with a piece of my shoe. You owe me a new pair of desert boots.' Doc laughed, diffusing the interrogation.

It was a simple matter to unscrew the filter, slip in a piece of pre-cut tongue from his old shoe, and screw the vital piece back on. Part of the plan required him to wear the evidence of mutilated footwear.

The manager relaxed visibly before he performed a quick check on the offending part and walked off to organise a mechanic.

When the season demanded it, Marin and Bob both worked for TEHC, flying tourists around and giving them the opportunity to marvel at the Top End extravaganza of Australia from a bird's eye perspective. It also allowed them access to the Timor Sea and a legal excuse to be where they could channel illegal goods on to the continent.

They changed their modus operandi regularly to reduce pattern play. This was the first time Jenifer had been involved in their game. Marin convinced Bob she would be a good ally after their relationship blossomed from the seeds sown at the Noosa Heads experience.

Jenifer drove the Mini Moke from the airfield to the station wagon, where she dropped Marin. He wasted no time hitting the hundred-mile trail to Darwin. After returning the Moke to the rental company, Jenny jumped aboard her waiting tourist bus and arrived in the Northern Territory capital two days after her boyfriend. They linked up again at the Victoria Hotel in the heart of the city, to all intents and purposes posing as nothing more than a local pilot and a tourist in a chance meeting at a pub.

CHAPTER 25

It had been over a year since I left the fishing industry well and truly behind me and swore off drugs forever! Twelve months full of business deals and long journeys for me. Then finally, after an in-and-out trip to Burma, I returned to Australia. It was difficult to get more than a seven-day visa to Burma in the early seventies. I didn't need a lot of time though. It was easy to get from Rangoon to Mandalay on train and bus.

A day and a half was enough time in that city, and then it was back to the capital on a slow boat down the Irrawaddy River. Arriving in Rangoon for a very short stay, I soon settled down in a Third World business-class seat on a flight to Bangkok before my Burmese visa expired. From the Thai capital, I got lucky and caught a standby flight to Darwin via Singapore.

Safely back in Oz, I walked into Room 23 at the Orel Eagle Hotel to see Marin and Jenifer in Kama Sutra position number 106. It wasn't my fault I caught them like that. I had the key for the room, because it was booked in my name.

They didn't stop even when I dropped my backpack heavily on the floor and turned my back to the room, calling out in a loud husbandly voice, 'Honey, I'm home!'

I walked back outside in the sunshine and sat on a flimsy chrome camp chair near the car park. Marin came out about fifteen minutes later with a masterful look on his face and a fake apology for my inconvenience.

'I thought Jenifer would be back in Queensland by now,' I said, not able to hide the inflected irritation in my voice.

'Yeah, er, her flight got delayed, and she'd already checked out, so I invited her here. Sorry, mate.'

It was really no big deal. Besides, I'd seen most of the Kama Sutra positions before in Bangkok. If the truth were known, I was crankier from jet lag because of rapid-fire flights in and out of four different countries than I was for my friends.

'What the heck, it's cool, man. I brought a heavy six-pack with me. Let's drink to safe journeys for all of us.' My 2.25-litre Darwin stubby clinked against Jenny's and Marin's bottles.

We were good friends, and I was actually very pleased to catch up with them both again, albeit if it was just for one night.

As Mr J. Shipley, I hired a car to drive down the centre track to South Australia. Jennifer left early for the airport, and Marin stuck around, talking non-stop while I transferred the satchel into the boot of the rental. Down the road, I snapped a short stopover in Cooper Pedy to transact some business and let my hair down at Theo's Acropolis Restaurant.

Theo's legendary restaurant in the interior of Australia was going off! It held over 300 patrons and had 2 stages with live bands playing back to back. The place was like Mardi Gras that night because a prospector had struck it rich and shouted that the entire room would have free drinks of anything they wanted. He was throwing $20 bills around like confetti and stuffing them into barmaids' cleavages with joyous abandon. Over a hundred tipsy revellers threaded through the tables in a giant conga line. It felt great to be back in Oz.

The Stuart Highway is a long, lonely road, so I decided to make a holiday out of a business trip and take my time, four days all up. Eventually, I arrived in the South Aussie capital, relieved to get the opportunity to soak in a hot bath and wash away the outback dust at the Barton Hotel.

It was the first time I had been able to afford the rates of the Barton, handily situated smack dab in the centre of town. Winter was supposed to have set in already, but Adelaide City hadn't noticed yet. The sun was shining out of a clear blue sky high above Rundle Mall. A young busker kept twenty or thirty people engrossed in the magic of his street talent. After an alfresco breakfast, I was trying to enjoy a mug of cappuccino while reading the newspapers, but the headlines sent a shiver up my spine and left a nasty taste in my mouth.

Both the *Sun Herald* and the *Australian* ran articles about the rise of 'a new scourge' they termed the Australian mafia. The *Herald* rehashed an old story about a drug-smuggling incident gone wrong in a fisherman's squat on a deserted beach twelve months before.

'The men in question mysteriously disappeared, but authorities discovered evidence that a large amount of narcotics might have been hidden on the premises. Two houses and a boat were burnt to the ground, and police found bullet casings and slugs and were treating the case as a major drug import gone horribly wrong.'

Their story was a response to the breaking news outlined in the *Australian*. It seemed that recently a fisherman had pulled up his craypot in seventy-five fathoms of water with a piece of wreckage snagged on it. Forensic tests concluded that it was a piece of the missing fishing boat that belonged to Geldo Kraggasti, a known criminal.

The reporter reiterated that Geldo and his brother had mysteriously disappeared months before. 'Police *are* mounting a search in the area.'

I winced as I read the dramatic tale, knowing that I had more than a bit to do with whatever had transpired. Just then a man approached and tapped me lightly on the shoulder. He wore jodhpurs—yeah, jodhpurs—poked into high tan leather boots. His brilliant white shirt sat snug around his neck, fastened with a brown knitted tie. A tan waistcoat shrouded his broad shoulders. On his head, he had what looked like a policeman's cap with a golden insignia of a bird on the front.

The garb was so far out I thought it must be a fancy dress prank until he spoke.

'Excuse me, sir, are you Mr Shipley? Er, Mr Jerry Shipley?'

I nodded assent.

'Then, sir, I have been asked by Mr Ramsay to collect you and take you to him—that is, if you have no objection.'

I kind of twigged who Mr Ramsay was but wondered how the hell he knew I was here. The only person who knew I was in Adelaide was Alice Bergstrom, but she was in New York. She was back in her home city, running a hugely successful jewellery enterprise. She and I were now on a real-name basis—well, almost. She confessed to me that Aster Nightingale was a hippy name she made up, but I never did get around to telling her my secret—at least not yet.

It was paranoia plain and simple. I wouldn't take the risk that the mob could discover the connection between us. At great expense, I procured a false identity through a well-respected forgery gang operating out of Bombay, India. Quite a few people knew me now as Jerry Shipley, so I kept the alias with the JS initials. It was a comprehensive changeover, twenty grand worth, complete with birth certificate, driver's licence, and passport.

My alias proved to be an essential tool for success in my new career. I was living every surfer's dream. Jet-setting around the world was now part of the job. As my own boss, I got to choose whether to take a surfboard and stay a little longer if there were good waves nearby.

As an agent for a genuinely fictitious import–export company, I had an expense account to go to exotic places I never dreamed I would get to. It was my choice whether I wanted to cross a border for business or pleasure or both. Sometimes the box you ticked made the difference; it was a constant learning curve, but I was finding a rhythm and adapting fast.

Alice and I kept contact by letters and phone and met up once in California and once in Hawaii. The distance between us had not jaded our romantic feelings for each other one little bit.

From Adelaide, I had spoken to her over the phone on that very morning. She was about to leave her office at the end of her working day, but we maintained an expensive chat for over two hours. We talked about George, but I never heard his last name mentioned. She told me she was going to contact him, and I put two and two together and figured George's name must be Ramsay.

'Sure,' I said to the chauffeur. 'Is it far?'

'Oh yes, sir,' he replied. 'I'm afraid it is rather a long way. Would you like me to help you pack?'

This was getting weirder by the minute. This bloke looked as if he just stepped out of a movie set. But as strange as it was, I rolled along with it. I laid back into the spirit of it all and watched it get more bizarre.

Firstly, I'd never ridden in a Rolls-Royce, and frankly, I was suitably impressed. Lance, the chauffeur, encouraged me to enjoy the minibar in the Silver Cloud, and I did have fun looking through it but settled on Perrier water with ice, chortling over the fact that I was pouring it from a bar in the back seat of a limo while rolling along the highway.

The chauffeur would not allow me to do anything for myself. It was like having my very own magic genie. Apart from throwing my scant belongings into a backpack and brushing my teeth, I did little else. He carried everything but me to the limousine. My rental car was in the car park. After I wrested the valuable satchel and my personal items from it, my genie organised for it to be returned. After an idiot check to make sure I had not forgotten anything I would need, we set off on a very comfortable drive to Victoria. A lunch stop and eight hours later, we pulled into one of Melbourne's ritziest suburbs and headed for the Ramsay Hut.

The lights in the house were burning brightly when the Rolls pulled up the crushed-marble drive. A butler appeared from the double oak doors to take my things from Lance and welcome me to sir's place. I suppressed a schoolboy giggle. The whole experience was surreal. I had only seen such opulence in the movies, and when I stepped inside, a bubble of disbelieving snigger escaped. If the butler had said his name was Jeeves, I would have pissed my pants laughing. Fortunately, he told me it was Roger.

I thanked him and said, 'Pleased to meet you, Rog. Call me Jerry.'

He manufactured a fake smile. 'It's Roger!' he emphasised.

I thought his manner was rude, so I threw him a 'Whatever, Rog' and left it at that.

George was in a wheelchair, drinking tea in one of the mansion's six kitchens. He was visibly pleased to see me and made me feel like I was visiting my very best friend. I bent to embrace him as such and looked him up and down. He looked good. The melting face thing had largely been rectified, and his speech impediment was hardly noticeable.

The wheelchair, he assured me, was purely cosmetic, but looking at the awkward slant of his body from his shoulder to his left leg, I guessed he was lying. He told me he had retired from the university. Apart from consultancy work, most of his days were now spent at home in his thirty-million-dollar shack. I detected a lonely streak in his voice.

Apart from the chauffer, butler, maids, gardeners, personal chef with kitchen staff, bankers, lawyers, accountants, and the telephone, there were no familiar voices of family or friends in the house. After Rog showed me my room and gave me a quick rundown of where some of the eleven bathrooms were, I took a more formal tour.

This time, the scientist was my guide as I pushed him around in his chair. We talked nostalgically about our extreme adventures and swapped the details of what happened after we left the western state. I brought cuttings from the papers with me, but he had already read them and understood that the story was probably related to us. Later on, after a wonderful dinner, we got down to a more serious topic regarding the main reason for him summoning me from Adelaide.

Alice and I had been doing business together for the last six months. She maintained contact with George, and he had graciously offered to pay for a holiday for him and her on the express condition that she brought me along. I spent another night at George's before trundling off to tie up a few loose ends. We met again a week later at Tullamarine airport and boarded a private jet, along with a government envoy and two members of the Asia Pacific Agency for Nuclear Energy (APANE) and four security officers.

Two security officers took their stations at each end of the cabin. George went along in his capacity as APANE consultant. I was his carer/minder, and because of his disability, we had our own area and were able to sit together in first-class luxury for the entire journey to New York.

Alice was very excited to meet us there. Standing next to her driver, she flashed her beautiful smile as I wheeled George through the outlet.

She looked a little tired, and I was glad to know our time together was going to be spent on a holiday instead of working. The two of us used half a day sorting out business and two days enjoying each other's company and making up for lost time.

While we were flitting about, having a wonderful tour of the capital of the world, George attended his meetings. He hired a private nurse and a driver to ferry him around the Big Apple and take care of his needs.

When the three of us eventually met up again, our host told us what he had in store for us. We were grinning like Cheshire cats as his plan unfolded. The APANE consultant had chartered a plane to fly us to San Juan in Puerto Rico, where we were to enjoy a relaxing seven days.

We stayed across the bridge in a guest house with easy access to the lagoon and the beach in the Condado District. Over the course of the week, we packed in day tours around the island and regular trips to all the tourist hotspots we could find. On a hired yacht, George sipped martinis while Alice and I dived the reefs. We explored the massive fortifications of Castillo San Felipe del Morro and San Cristobal before linking back up with our host and partying long into the nights.

We spent many hours tasting Puerto Rico's myriads of rum concoctions in lively bars and a memorable little, go back to hotel on Calle de Cristo. It was the first time I had ever tasted a conch lunch in a simple little Haitian al fresco eatery set on a cobblestone street. Next to the bistro was a street stall that served coffee to die for.

The three of us were letting off steam, acknowledging the fact that we were now officially a company of smugglers. With my recent trips to South East Asia and the help of Marin and BB, who made up our company's newly formed wing division, I procured gold and precious jewels for our business: rubies from Mandalay, opals from central Australia and—oh yeah, did I mention that the gold from the jungles of Irian Jaya has a unique deep-yellow lustre which makes it a brilliant setting for rubies?

On the trip to New York, we transported contraband on a chartered jet with diplomatic immunity. The new stock created quite an impact on Nightingale Ltd's finances, jacking them up by a fabulous $260,000. Once worked into Alice's patented designs, she expected her already-famous Songbird Collection to fetch as much as $1.5 million in retail sales.

True, it's nowhere near as lucrative as smuggling drugs. True, the gaol time for getting caught is relatively the same as drug smuggling, but I have to say, jewellery makes people feel happy in a much different way than drugs do.

CHAPTER 26

Once upon a time, I thought jewel smuggling was a lot less dangerous than running drugs until the time I took a trip to Mauritius. By sheer coincidence, I ran into a Dutchman who knew my Durban connections. Because the islands of Mauritius hosted some excellent surf spots, I went there on holiday solely to go surfing. I was getting barrelled on the left-handers at Tamarin Bay when I met another surfer who told me he had links to an organisation that relayed certain materials from the Skeleton Coast in West Africa.

Diamonds were brought across the continent to be smuggled out to a host of islands and selected countries. The prices were absurdly low considering the quality of the stones, and Mauritius happened to be on the list for the jewel stops. I surfed with the Dutchman for two weeks, getting to know him before I brought up a proposal. I aimed to see if we could do some business together. He told me he could obtain certificated gemstones, including diamonds, and have them delivered to Mauritius or India and parts of Indonesia for a pittance.

The buying price for stones coming by boat from mainland Africa was dirt cheap. Aalt Van Tol, my new surfing buddy, became a valuable connection for our company. It was all panning out splendidly until my third trip to the beautiful islands when I was held up and robbed at gunpoint by three local hoons. Luckily, I didn't have any diamonds with me, but they took all my money and my personal documents. I was not physically hurt, but the mugging left me in a precarious situation, and in order to get out of the country, I had to report the incident to the police.

As I was rendering my statement to the authorities, I noticed a shadowy figure in a back office of the police station. He ducked out of sight when he saw me looking his way, but the glimpse I got was enough to identify him as one of the heavies who robbed me. A shudder ran through me when I realised he was a policeman. The penny dropped. I seriously believed it was a set-up that the police were out to trap me, so I demanded to see a lawyer.

The cops frigged around, suddenly pretending they didn't speak English. It was a pantomime to check my story and validate what I was doing in their country. If they had kept me away from my one free phone call for another half hour, I would have been a goner. As I picked up the receiver, I sweated that Aalt was at his hotel. When the concierge phoned his room, he picked up.

Twenty minutes later, Bede Mathy from a law firm in Port Louis walked into the station at the same time I was blowing my top at the officer who was harassing me. I jumped out of the chair, pushed the officer aside, and literally ran into the back office. There were five other policemen chasing me across the room when I pointed to the figure huddled on the floor behind a desk.

'This is one of the men who robbed me!' I shouted to make sure everyone in the neighbourhood got my drift.

Two cops hurtled towards the crazy tourist to tackle me but faltered after a 'Stop!' shout and accompanying gesture from the leading officer. The cop who had been directing my interrogation magically started speaking English, but only after the lawyer politely touched his shoulder and spoke in a firm and officious voice.

'As this man's legal representative, I would like you to tell me immediately of all charges, if any, that you may have on him.' His tone didn't waver. Mr Mathy was obviously no stranger to the police, and almost as one, their mood changed.

The tension in the room was about to relax when I happened to glance down at the skulker behind the desk. He was stuffing something under a mat. When I saw the small blue cover of a passport, I literally dived on it. Of course, it was mine; I held it up as I swivelled away from the dirty cop's grasp.

'This is mine—*mine*!' blared out of my mouth as I pointed a finger at my chest. 'Now hand over my wallet, you thieving bastard!' I added with as much volume as I could muster. Even people on the street outside the station got notified. I was going ape shit.

Suddenly, the room was abuzz as everyone inside the station reverted to speaking French or Creole, even my lawyer. I tried to get close to the thief in an attempt to rifle through his pockets, but he kept hitting my hand away like a kid trying to protect his bag of marbles.

'Enough!' shouted the senior gendarme with a glare and a voice loud and final. The foreign language switched back on and continued between the locals for another five minutes. The pause created just enough time to let the veins in my neck shrink back to normal.

Without Bede Mathy in that room, I was pretty certain I'd still be in gaol somewhere. Sometimes naivety could be a good thing. Like in this case, if I had thought the situation through a bit more, I probably would not have raced over to the cop in the corner or dived on my passport. But I was bloody glad I didn't always overthink before acting. Whether or not all the cops were in on the scam, I would never know. I left Mauritius on the first plane out with nothing but a bad experience and a few bucks from Aalt. My exit was so fast I sold everything I could for next to nothing. My Dutch surfing mate was now the owner of two of my boards, spring suit, and a bag of clothes.

Alice and I had been working our system for a few months before our Puerto Rico holiday. We had been buying from contacts from friends of friends. One such contact led us to discover places to buy precious metals and gems for absurdly low prices. We never asked where they came from or whether or not they were procured from legal sources. In fact, I was pretty certain the deals had not always been legal, but as a little Italian fisherman once told me, 'Sometimes in business, it's not the legalities. It's the challenge.'

Sure, it was hard work but it was exciting, and allowed me more surf time than any other job possibly could. I often thought about Garret sending his goons to give me a beating as being a lucky break. It was the catalyst to send me into another life. Without that change, I might never have met Alice and George. When I was catching waves in some exotic land, I reflected on the fight that changed everything. It was a freedom laden with opportunities. With a constant hope, the highs continued to outweigh the lows.

What was jokingly called Smugglers Incorporated ran along nicely. We had set up an established line of long-term contacts, thieves, transporters, and dealers. The two of us explored different ways to circumvent customs and immigration checks and obtain certificates to legitimise the stock. It was working fine, but I must admit we were running low on ideas until, as luck would have it, along came George to swell the ranks of the company.

With his brilliant mind, he didn't join for the sake of the money; he already had tons of it. No, George just loved the adrenalin rush of 'working with soap shoes on the slippery tiles of destiny', as he called it. Turned out he was pretty good at coming up with ideas too. He brought so much to the table in working out the details of the trade to make it safer and more efficient. But like they said about the life of every good dog, that special day came along all too fast.

On the other side of the world, after a big night out, I was sitting alone at a table on the street, enjoying one of Puerto Rico's famous sweet and creamy rum coquitos. Beside the street bar was a fashionable hotel with a stream of expectant touts waiting to organise a tour guide or a taxi ride or bus service for the cashed-up visitors. A tall burly chap with a ring of frizzy black hair, garnishing a bald pate, had succumbed to the hypnotic voice of a spruiker. Pushing American dollars into the hand of the tout, he ushered his family out of the hotel to load them into a waiting cab.

All of a sudden, the father stopped to look at me. His face burned fifty feet of air in my direction, gazing long and hard, until I saw a spark of recognition light a flare in his dark brown eyes. Bugger me if it wasn't Big Guzzy Gerome!

Every nerve ending in my body was screaming at me to run, but I didn't. My long golden curls of last year's hairstyle were now cut short, and the beard was traded for a skinny goatee. I figured I could hide in plain sight. My hippy sunnies were transformed to mercury mirror wraparounds. The embroidered black-and-white cowboy shirt and black jeans with Cuban heeled boots were very non-hippy. And I watched Gerome trying hard to fit my new image into his memory banks.

He started walking towards me when as if on cue, all hell broke loose behind him. Police cars converged on a building not fifty yards behind Guzzy on the opposite side of the street. Three men ran out of a giant pair of glass doors, and one of them fired two shots from a pistol. Like a scene from a Wild West show, the police returned countless shots. The gunman fell back against a parked car before rolling on to the road.

People began running in all directions, and Gerome raced back to shield his family into the waiting taxi. I joined up with the stampeding throng and bolted away from stray bullets. Slowing my pace as I got to the first intersection, I glanced back.

The Guzzy gang in the cab wove through the fleeing traffic straight past me, with Gerome hanging out of the rear window with a super 8 movie camera. I turned my back to the street but not before the whirring lens drilled into the mirror of my sunglasses. Deep in my soul, I knew his identikit memory had done a good job, and now he had my new image on film.

Whether the mob bosses believed him or not, they now had an opportunity to study the image. If they were to decide to start a new project on how to find Jesus or Geronimo, they would certainly have the resources to do a good job. Although Puerto Rico was a one-off visit and my girlfriend lived in New York, my home was Australia. I couldn't think of any other place I would rather live my life.

The slim chance that my new look might have thrown them might also have given them a new image to look for. It's no good pretending I wasn't scared; the mafia is a scary organisation and way too big to hide from. Up to this point, they probably believed I was dead, but Guzzy's film might have provided enough evidence to change their minds.

Even before I got back to our apartment, I hatched a plan to get that camera away from 'Big Guzzy' Gerome.

But that's another story I'll have to come back to tell another time.

———

ABOUT THE AUTHOR

Charles Anchor resides in the beautiful Illawarra region of NSW Australia, where the Great Dividing Range touches the Pacific Ocean. From a farm in New England his experience includes; professional musician, construction worker, professional fisherman, juvenile justice officer and manager. He completed studies at the University of Technology Sydney (UTS) and attended creative writing courses and workshops.

After years of creative writing for leisure Charles has made the leap into the publishing world. With a diverse range of employment skills, study, talents and experiences, he is able to cultivate a unique quality and style of writing. His stories are energetic and action packed, humorous, passionate, illuminating and always intriguing.

Printed in the United States
By Bookmasters